COMMON

COMMON PEOPLE

MARTIN KNIGHT

[signature]

MAINSTREAM
PUBLISHING

EDINBURGH AND LONDON

First published in Great Britain in 2000 by
MAINSTREAM PUBLISHING COMPANY (EDINBURGH) LTD
7 Albany Street
Edinburgh EH1 3UG

ISBN 1 84018 332 2

Reprinted, 2004

A catalogue record for this book is available
from the British Library

Typeset in 11 on 15pt Adobe Garamond
Printed and bound in Great Britain by Antony Rowe,
Chippenham, Wiltshire

'If you didn't have a wasted youth,
you wasted your youth'

Man in pub, circa 1987

Acknowledgements

Thanks to Val, my wife, and the children, Michelle, Billy, Zoe, Daisy and Joe.

Thanks to my mum and dad and Sally, Laurence, Liz, Vivian, Stephen and Fiona, my brothers and sisters. We had a marvellous time growing up together.

Contents

CHAPTER ONE

Our House

Life on Watermead in those early sunny days was idyllic. At least it was for a small boy feeling his way into the world. The sun always shone and the smell of freshly cut grass hung in the air. The bare-chested and sweating council workmen were forever pushing their lawnmowers up and down the grass verges and greens. House sparrows hopped on and off knee-high garden walls and older boys lay flat on their stomachs in the road, retrieving plastic footballs from underneath parked cars. That's how I remember it.

Watermead was a small council estate of about a hundred and fifty houses built in the 1950s to cope with the burgeoning suburban population of outer London. The development was a simple crescent called Common Crescent with a small circle of houses on the inner side, named Common Way. We lived at number 11, Common Way. Some well-meaning planner had named the area Watermead, probably to conjure up images of meadows and rivers to make the new inhabitants feel good about living on a fresh estate constructed on a festering old sewage farm. But in those early days we were the only people who called it Watermead. Outsiders referred to it as 'the Common estate' and us as 'Common people'. A council estate was a novelty in this area of mainly owner-occupiers which not so long ago had been a rural community.

What those others meant by 'Common people', I was never quite sure when I was a kid. Did they mean 'Common people' or common people – 'common' being a word that was often expelled from the lips with distaste. I'd heard adults use it when describing people they believed to be beneath them: 'She's very common, you know.' What did that mean? There are lots of her? No. It meant she was undesirable. Lacked a certain something.

The houses had been erected next to the railway line that stretched from the densely populated hub of Waterloo out as far as the hills and heaths of deepest Surrey, where older people still spoke with a country twang. We were somewhere in the middle. Unlike many other council estates, Watermead was quite small and isolated. On one side of it stood the local football club (founded in 1919 – foundering ever after) and on the other side was the remainder of the old sewage farm, now overgrown and teeming with wildlife.

Everyone was starting out, pleased as punch with their new solid and scrubbed houses. Young couples with young families, all of them. Glad to get away from lodging with their parents or out of the flimsy prefabs that still dotted the area. A few people owned cars and parked them proudly outside in the road, but most of the adults got around on foot or on bikes. Most of the dads worked in the local factories or in one of the many lunatic asylums (later we were taught to call them mental homes) that were built a hundred years before on the edge of town. Winhurst was a racing town also, close to many racecourses. A number of trainers based their stables in the area and this industry, too, was a big local employer. The children played together in groups in gardens or on the grass verges and the greens that were neatly laid on the corner plots.

My earliest memories are of those sunny days, sitting cross-legged and running Dinky cars through the mud and grass, every patch of green and brown a huge terrain and my legs acting as huge fleshy bridges. I set my heart on an Aston Martin model car that was in the window of the toyshop up on the main road. It was 9/11d and was known as 'the James Bond car', the chief attraction being the ejector seat that was pictured in glorious action on the box it sat proudly on top of. I somehow purchased it eventually and recall placing it grandly on the garden wall, in all its glory, and noticing how inferior my other toy cars now were.

Toni Bell arrives heralded by 'Greensleeves' playing through a tinny loudhailer that sends us kids scurrying indoors to pester our parents for money. Toni Bell is the ice-cream van, a pink-and-white vehicle with a dairy cow's head, smiling widely, protruding above the windscreen. A queue forms with the older sisters and brothers ordering for the whole family. A 99 (large cone with a Flake) for Mum, medium cones with nut shavings and raspberry sauce for the older boys and today Zoom lollies for us. I like the lollies: they last longer and they change colour too. You even get picture cards of pop stars free with some of them. I collect the cards. Adam Faith with a quiff and brown cardigan is on one, and The Tornadoes, suited and booted, on another. I glue them to the wall beside the bunk-bed I sleep in. The round-faced smiling Italian ice-cream man gives us broken wafers when Mum and Dad refuse to give us money. His generosity is appreciated by all. (I appreciate him so much that once I attached myself to the back of his vehicle and he drove off. Before anyone realised, I was disappearing out of Common Crescent, screaming and clinging on for dear life to the back of the van. I panicked and jumped off, injuring my head in the process. Mum had to take me up the hospital in a neighbour's car. Lots of attention. I was four.)

Those dreamy, hot days were punctuated by a steady stream of outsiders visiting the estate, like Bill Best, the greengrocer, who turned up a few times a week selling direct from his lorry and delivering ready-made orders to customers. He was a show-man, picking the kids up and launching them into space, producing an orange from his ear and slipping it into our eager palms. For the adults he would roll his leather trilby hat down his arm from his shoulder and catch it with a flourish in his hand. He'd chat to the ladies, sing and generally show off as his own kids darted around fulfilling orders. Bill Best the house-wife's pest, some of the dads called him.

The visitor us kids liked best, though, was the rag-and-bone man. He announced his arrival by a weary uninterested ring of a heavy old school-playground bell, shouting something un-intelligible and jolting his horse and cart forward a few paces. We would surround the old horse, stroking its mane and feeding it grass and perhaps some of Bill Best's dropped carrots. Occasionally a grown-up would approach the man and throw a bag of old clothes or maybe a bike frame on to his cart. I was always touched by this generosity from the adults on the estate and wondered what I could give the poor old man and his horse. He didn't really speak to us kids. He was old and grey with a stubbly chin and a red polka-dot handkerchief tied around his scrawny neck. Very Steptoe. I suppose I thought of him as a mounted tramp or beggar. How surprised I was when I found out, years later, that he had a house overlooking the golf course up at Winhurst Downs and was by all accounts a very wealthy individual. (Some ten years later I had cause to recall him when his oldest boy, Gary, was murdered just up the road. Gary worked in the bookie's, chalking up the prices. One Satur-day afternoon, as he and his boss were just finishing up for the day and the last of the punters were lamenting their bad fortune, an armed gang burst in. They shouted for everyone to lie on the floor and not look up. Gary looked up.)

Then there were the visitors who actually knocked on the door in the early evening. Doorbells hadn't been invented then, at least not on Watermead. The rent man: we all knew him. It was obvious he was not from the estate – he wore a shiny suit, had neatly groomed hair and carried a leather briefcase without a handle that he tucked under his arm. I don't think anyone resented him; he was just collecting the rent. No direct debits in those days. I doubt if anyone even had a bank account. But he was different and no one made more than polite conversation with him. He drove into Common Crescent in an old black Ford Poplar that probably wasn't old then. It had indicator arms that came out of the side of the car, above the door, and flashed orange.

The pools man: he was altogether more welcome. That was money well spent. He represented hope – a punt on a dream. How the adults on the estate wished they could spend their millions like good old Viv Nicholson whose downfall, chronicled gleefully in the Sunday tabloids, was eagerly lapped up. Tuesday night he knocked for the coupon and the money. He was from Crowley Lane, a few miles away, and worked the estate to top up his earnings. He stank of stale cigarettes, Woodbines, I think, and had yellow nicotine-stained fingers. I heard Mum and Dad talking once after he stopped coming – something about not forwarding the cash to Vernons. The ritual of checking the coupon against the football results on the telly on a Saturday afternoon was one we all enjoyed. 'Never mind, there's always next week,' Dad would say.

The TV man. He had a car too, a little mini-traveller with

'DER' on the side. All tellies were rented and all tellies went wrong and the TV repairman was almost as regular a caller as the rent man was. Different bloke each time, nearly, but a familiar figure nonetheless in the corner of our room fiddling away behind the TV as six children sat in front of him, cross-legged and wide-eyed, eagerly awaiting the resumption of normal service.

The Burlington lady. That sounded very grand and I sort of expected her to be wearing furs and carrying a Pekinese under her arm. But she was a neighbour simply collecting cash for goods bought from a mail-order catalogue. Everything was on the knock then. The new catalogue was always eagerly awaited. At my young age when a new one arrived it was straight to the back for the toy section, salivating over Johnny Seven guns and radio-controlled cars, toys that made only guest appearances on our estate. As I grew older, the ladies' underwear section held more attraction: see-through nighties, black bras and girdles galore. I'd carefully keep my thumb inserted in the toy section so that if anyone walked into the room I could flop the bulky book back open on to the toy page. Even now if I come across one of these catalogues I automatically and eagerly flick to the female lingerie section.

The house was pretty basic but it was functional: three bedrooms, a small kitchen, a small dining-room and a lounge. Small garden back and front. Heating was by electric fire or oil heaters. Dad used to take an empty can down to the shops to fill it from a paraffin machine that had the smiling Esso Blue man on the front. He was familiar from our tellies singing:

'*They asked me how I knew,*
It was Esso Blue,
I of course replied,
No smoke gets in your eyes . . .'

Some people still had coal fires and the coal lorry came weekly, although as the years went by the vehicle with the long flat back held fewer and fewer sacks as people moved on to other forms of heating. We had no fridge but there was a cold larder in the corner of the kitchen. It couldn't have been too hygienic in summer but we knew no different. No telephone. I didn't see one in the flesh until the day Dad gave me a crossbar into his work at one of the several local psychiatric hospitals and there was a big black shiny one on his desk. My little fingers could barely move the dial away from nought. Carpets weren't fitted and there were rugs everywhere. A big fireguard dominated the lounge keeping us kids away from the electric fire. One bar or two.

The *TV Times* and the *Radio Times* lay neatly on a little coffee-table next to Mum's armchair, as did the *Daily Mail* and *Woman's Own*. The dining-room had a drop-leaf table, which was set up and dismantled three times a day for meals. Bunk-beds stood in the bedrooms; my parents employed the same strategy as inner-city town planners at the time: pack them in by building upwards. In the garden were a couple of sheds. These were the only 'rooms' with keys and were therefore, with five brothers and sisters always around, the only place besides the attic I could guarantee myself privacy. I would often take the key and lock myself in. The feeling of freedom once the key turned was overwhelming. Of course, there was absolutely nothing to do in there. I would often while away this solitary time by reading comics or testing my pain threshold by seeing how far I could tighten Dad's carpentry vice on my thumb.

I only really read *The Dandy* and *The Beano*. My older brother Ian liked *Valiant*, *Victor* and *Hotspur* but, although I tried, I could not see the attraction in stories about the war. I read *The Dandy* and *The Beano* avidly: Korky the Cat, Desperate Dan, Greedy Pig, Winker Watson and Big Head and Thick Head were my favourite characters. Never did I laugh, though, and never did I see other kids laugh. They were called comics but they weren't actually funny. It was just escapism for kids. I especially identified with the rebels. You could stick your Billy the Cat and Q Bikes (kids fighting crime) up your arse. I revelled in Winker Watson, the crafty and naughty public schoolboy, Roger the Dodger and Dennis the Menace. Even at that young age it was the more dangerous characters that captivated me. I preferred John Lennon to Paul McCartney, The Rolling Stones over The Beatles and Sweep over Sooty.

Until I started school I didn't realise there was life other than estate life. We rarely ventured off the estate and assumed the rest of the world was the same. Once at school I learnt that many of the boys in my class lived in bigger houses, in tree-lined roads, that their mums and dads all had cars and generally they were that bit tidier and smarter than us. Walking home from school I could see that the spacious houses and the tree-lined roads were plentiful. It was our little estate that was unusual in this part of suburban outer London. This feeling of being different was reinforced when I heard, during play-time one day, a dinner-lady say to another about a misdemeanour committed by me and my pal Jacko – whatever it may have been – 'They're off the Common estate, you know,' with a knowing look and a nod of the head. But this was not a problem, just a realisation of who we were and what we were. There were enough of us and we were pretty self-contained. We made our own fun and only really mixed with each other.

We were a close family, Mum, Dad, my brothers and sisters and me. We did a lot as a family: holidays to Hastings and

Sheppey; walks in the country; trips to the pictures to see *Mary Poppins*, Norman Wisdom, *Bambi* and others; fishing for sticklebacks and redthroats down the river and much, much more. Christmas at Common Way was the best time of my childhood, though – so much so that however much I try, I can't help but get melancholy at Christmas now because they just don't match up.

It was the build-up that did it. Scrambling the decorations out of cardboard grocery boxes and putting them up around the house. Licking and linking the paper chains. Choosing and buying the tree. Checking through the Christmas *TV Times* and *Radio Times* to pick out the programmes to see and the films to watch. Travelling up the railway line to Clapham Junction to fetch Grandma. The endless speculation over what our presents would be. There was no problem in getting us to go to bed on Christmas Eve – we just wanted Christmas Day to arrive as fast as possible.

Christmas morning we'd be up by five, foraging through our stockings or pillowcases laid out on the end of the bed. In here were the trinkets and small gifts gathered together by Mum and Dad.

I'm thrilled this year because I've got 'I Want to Hold Your Hand' by The Beatles, all black and shiny in its green-and-white Parlophone sleeve, among other Beatles paraphernalia.

Christmas was just as much about The Beatles as anything else to us, then. The country had gone mad about them, and nothing like it has ever been seen since. Unlike the excitement around The Bay City Rollers, Take That, Bros or The Spice Girls, that surrounding The Beatles went much deeper and was far stronger. It was bigger than anything, and no one quite knew what was happening. They surged out of our radios and

TVs, from our record players, newspapers and magazines. A power had been unleashed. It was a power that was neither contrived nor planned, not the result of a carefully orchestrated PR campaign. I saw it again, briefly, when Princess Diana died, in those days immediately afterwards: the people took control. The country was carried along by a force and, just for a minute, the establishment shit themselves. The Beatles thing was a bit like that. When the Stones came along a couple of years later I worshipped them like a 'naughty' uncle, but the Beatles would stay with me forever.

When we had tired a little from our first batch of presents, we bounded into Mum and Dad's bedroom, tipping our gifts all over their bed, babbling with excitement and telling them what had turned up in the night – as if they didn't know. We knew by then there was no Father Christmas, but didn't want to upset Dad. He would get up and take us down to the lounge where our 'big present' awaited us. This would normally be the gift you'd been asking for all year.

This Christmas I've got a Hornby railway set and I hog the room by setting it up all over the floor. I can smell the oil now on the little engines and see the livery on the lovely Pullman coaches they pulled around the room.

We switch the telly on and Leslie Crowther is doing the rounds at the hospital, handing over presents to bedridden children. Making jokes. Making them smile. The smells of turkey, stuffing and gravy waft in from the kitchen.

Grandma eventually gets up from bed at this time and Dad helps her to a chair. 'What's this old rubbish?' she asks as the arm of the record player knocks 'I Want to Hold Your Hand' on to the turntable for the seventeenth time. 'Bleeding Beatles this, Bleeding Beatles that!' she moans.

We sit round the table for dinner and there are crackers by each plate and serviettes in little silver buckles. At Christmas we use a serviette to wipe our mouths though the rest of the year our sleeves will do. In the centre of the table are big bottles of Tizer, ginger beer and lemonade. Mum has the radio on as background music and 'Little Drummer Boy' is playing. We pull the crackers, read the jokes, throw the toys away and then tuck in. After the Christmas pud – Sandy had the threepenny bit in her portion – Dad rolls a cigarette from his brown tin, Mum lights up a Guards from the nice packet with the red soldier wearing a black bearskin hat on the front and Grandma sucks on a non-tipped Weights. All three of them tuck into some sherry. We kids excuse ourselves and get back to the lounge to catch Top of the Pops. *Kathy Kirby is singing 'Secret Love', the record Ian got in his stocking. The sherry must be kicking in because Grandma has started to sing a Marie Lloyd song from a lifetime ago.*

Grandma was from another lifetime. She was already out at work when Queen Victoria died. The last of her brothers and sisters had died in 1951. According to his death certificate, one brother, Dan, had died from malnutrition – that's starvation to you and me. Another brother was also a casualty of the Depression of the 1930s and had jumped off Battersea Bridge, fearing he and his family would be destitute. Dad remembers Uncle Dan coming around to his basement room on Sundays specifically to drink the green water Grandma had strained from the vegetables. Her sister died in the bombing during the Second World War and the last brother expired from a disease contracted when working in a Peruvian tin mine where he had gone when there was no work to be found in England. Grandma's husband, too, was long dead; even Dad hadn't met him, his own father. His last earthly deed, it seems, had been to impregnate Grandma when he returned, sick and shattered, from gruelling First World War service. Right up to the end of her life she stayed in Battersea where she was born. In the end she was surrounded by people who'd come from the other side of the world and, later, by yuppies. As a frail old lady in her nineties she would throw open the window of her ground-floor flat and hurl abuse at groups of West Indian teenagers sitting and chatting outside. She would stagger up Lavender Hill laden with shopping, buying goods from traders who were now pricing their products at people with a much higher disposable income than her pension. It terrified us.

Eventually the adults rejoin us and it's time to distribute the presents that are wrapped up and piled around the tree. The telly is switched off and the picture disappears to a white dot in the middle of the green screen. Dad picks a helper. It's my turn this year. 'For Sandy from Auntie Ethel,' he announces and I eagerly take it from Dad and deliver it to Sandy all of three feet away.

I rip the paper off my presents to see what I've got as soon as Dad passes them to me. Ian piles all his presents up neatly until the giving-out is complete and then slowly he unwraps them. I am jealous because he always has stuff left to open long after I've pillaged all of mine. But every year is the same: I never learn. And every year I am eyeing his presents when the first novelty of mine has worn off. Last year I was particularly taken with the Escalado horseracing game that my uncle and auntie bought him. That was as good as my big present! We set it up on the table and played happily all afternoon. It even appealed to Grandma's gambling instincts.

I've got plenty of good 'tree' presents, though. The Dandy Annual *with Korky the Cat on the front, a Letts diary with all the birthdays of pop stars marked, a water pistol and a Popeye glove puppet. These will keep me occupied through to the evening when all eyes will be on the telly for* The Morecambe and Wise Show. *I don't really understand the jokes but I know it makes the adults happy and I love it for that. The Beatles are on it this year and John Lennon delights us all by giving funny old Eric as good as he gets.*

Boxing Day, we'd venture back outside and meet up with our pals and play in the street. If it had been snowing we'd make sledges and pull each other around the paths or, if not, get our trolleys out and swerve around the bends and corners like budding Graham Hills. The trolleys were made from planks of wood with old pushchair or pram wheels attached to them. One kid would drive, steering the thing with his feet, and some poor sod would push from behind. At half past two, the dads would reappear on the estate, back from the pub, socialising more today than they had during the entire year, and our mums would stick their heads out the front doors and call us in for cold turkey and ham.

CHAPTER TWO

Common People

I started to notice the grown-up characters around me. Mrs Bird: she lived a few doors down. In the winter she wore fur and in the summer the tightest tigerskin slacks you could imagine. Her face was a different colour from just about all the other womenfolk of the estate. It was orange, almost. Make-up, my mum told me. *Look at her, done up to the nines,* was the usual comment from the other mums as she wiggled past them. Her boy, David, was my age. We played together although he was careful not to take me into his house. Most of the other houses were open, with kids running in and out all day. His old man was in prison – don't know what for, but it must have been a fairly serious offence because he didn't come back until we were much older and by which time David had a new dad on board.

Old Ma Johnson: she lived on the corner and her garden almost backed on to ours. She was barking mad. Her husband was a little man, prematurely old, who followed her to the shops like an obedient dog. He reminded us of the old bald-headed bloke in the Benny Hill sketches and, like Benny, she used to slap him around the head. She thought nothing of cursing and shouting at him in the middle of the street – *You fucking useless individual, you! Look at me when I'm talking to you! I'll knock the rest of your fucking teeth out in a minute!* The voice on her was unreal, so loud and gravelly, like Peggy Mount on steroids. Us kids were scared shitless of her.

One early evening, when children's television had finished and those tedious news programmes had begun, we were playing football on the green next to her house and she came flying out of her door, apron flapping in the wind. She leapt the wall and grabbed the ball. Out of her apron she pulled a bread-knife and stabbed the ball with fury. Her ample jowls trembled with anger and froth fell from her mouth as she did this – like a big old Saint Bernard but not so friendly. Not a word was said. We crapped ourselves and all ran home. Before long the story was embellished and eventually it became estate fact that a crazed Old Ma Johnson had chased us around the block threatening to maim us with a machete. The police gave her a tug, I know. Mum said we shouldn't wind her up: she was mental and she couldn't help it. Mum reckoned she could play the piano beautifully and was a highly intelligent woman.

They got her on drugs and she quietened right down. Jacko and I passed her garden one day. 'Excuse me, boys, are you going down the shops?' she said.

We were shocked. Normally we would be greeted by 'Go on, get away from here, you fucking hooligans!' and a look that little children are not used to receiving from adults. We told her we were and she asked if we could bring her back some potatoes. 'Come in and I'll give you some money for sweets and get you a bag out of the shed.'

We followed her up the garden path and she disappeared into the shed. The rusty old key was in the lock. Jacko looked at me and I looked at him. We both started to laugh as our unspoken idea crystallised in the space between us. We turned

23

the key. You could hear her still hollering half an hour later, half a mile away.

Her three sons were clever and attended the local grammar school, which was not the norm for estate boys. They didn't mix with the other teenagers at all, because of embarrassment over their mum, I expect. I used to notice the oldest one, resplendent in his blue school uniform and cap, popping into Mrs Bird's house at lunchtime. I thought nothing of it. Then things started to happen. The two eldest boys left home suddenly. They were sixteen and seventeen years old. Mrs Bird was pregnant and rumour had it that the sixteen-year-old was the father. This was the best scandal on the estate thus far. But Mrs Bird didn't give a monkey's. She held her head high and carried on in her own sweet way, and when the baby was born she pushed it around the estate in a big old pram with a hood and tassels. The milkman took the place of the schoolboy as her main gentleman caller and he eventually moved in and became David's new dad.

When Old Ma Johnson was put on some new drugs she really mellowed out. She became a shadow of her former self. Now that she was weak and we knew it, though, us kids became merciless in our persecution of her. Her boys were gone and her poor old husband had died soon afterwards. (If his tombstone had had 'Peace at Last' inscribed on it, never would there have been a truer epitaph.) She was alone and rendered defenceless by numbing tranquillisers, and we regularly charged through her garden and smashed her back windows. On the few occasions she appeared and tramped down to the shops, we openly abused and tormented her. The other adults did nothing to stop us. Eventually she stocked right up on the pills and topped herself. She was barely fifty yet to us she was ancient.

Right next door to us in Common Way was Mrs Lumsden and at times she made Old Ma Johnson seem like a demure Sunday-school teacher. When she was a young girl she'd had half her face blown off in the Blitz. Now she placed a beret on the side of her head and used lashings of whitish make-up to hide the damage. Bright red lipstick and her thin pencilled-in eyebrows made her look quite ghoulish. She reminded me of that French mime artist who'd pop up on our TVs every now and then. She couldn't stand noise or kids, which made life on the estate unbearable for her. She'd collect up dog and cat shit, and lob it over the fence into our garden. She swore to another neighbour that she would kill her cat and when the animal disappeared one day it was generally assumed that she had carried out her threat. She would shout at me sometimes, childlike, as I passed her house: 'John Hay, go away, come back another day'. Like Mrs Johnson, drugs regulated her moods and there were months when we would neither see nor hear anything from her. Then suddenly it would start up again and she'd be mad and ranting for days on end. We were playing on the green late one afternoon when she appeared in her front garden. Nervously we started to gather up the ball and our pullovers, which were used as goalposts, to run off to the safety of our houses.

'Who's your favourite team?' she asked.

We were dumbfounded, as she had never made conversation with any of us boys, ever.

'Spurs,' replied my older brother, who was always polite.

'My old dad supported West Ham,' she said as she sat down on the wall. 'Would anyone like a drink of squash?'

Was this a master plan to poison us and be rid of us once and for all? We didn't even answer, just scampered off to our various homes. Not very long after, as dawn broke, the milkman was leaning down to pick up her empties when he saw a note folded into the mouth of a bottle. 'Call an ambulance, I am dead,' it read. And she was.

Death was something we got acquainted with quickly on the estate. I remember the excitement when a house around the block went on fire. Black smoke billowed out from a bedroom window and the fire brigade had the ladders up and were squirting water in. We had all gathered outside on our bikes, leaning forward against the fashionable cowhorn and apehanger handlebars. We had cheered the engine when it arrived and had all started singing 'Call the fire brigade, call the fire brigade', which happened to be a song in the charts at the time, as the firemen unrolled their hoses. Suddenly the atmosphere changed. One of the firemen had made it known that there was someone in the bedroom. Up to that point everyone had believed that the house was empty. We were ushered away and Mr Jones's lifeless body, covered by a blanket, was eventually brought out to a waiting ambulance. Apparently he worked nights and had returned home in the morning, gone to bed and fallen asleep with his cigarette still smouldering. They said he had taken pills so he would be able to sleep during the noisy day, and that was why he didn't wake in time.

Then there was the geezer whose teeth my pal Vic and I found. We never knew his name – he wasn't on the estate long enough. He and his wife and teenage kids had moved in just across the road. He was working under his Ford Zephyr when the bricks with which he'd jacked the car up on toppled and the full weight of the car crushed his head. Vic and I watched the commotion and when the ambulance finally sped off we ambled over to the kerbside to inspect the pools of blood. That didn't really faze us at all, but finding some of his teeth, which must have shot out on impact, some distance across the road, brought home the violence of it.

As a youngster, it was the 'big boys' who fascinated me. 'Big' meant anyone over twelve years old, and there were plenty of teenagers on Watermead. I watched them firstly as mods and rockers and later as skinheads, greasers and hippies. They'd be skidding around the paths on their home-made bikes with playing cards pegged to the spokes for special noise effects; then, by the time I was on two wheels, they were smart in their washed-out Levi jeans and Fred Perry shirts, steering their scooters in and out the estate. Some of the really senior ones had cars: wonderful Fords, Cortinas and Corsairs, all polished up and with fur covering the steering-wheels. Summer afternoons they would be parked up, all four doors open, Mungo Jerry happily drifting from the radio and a couple of girls sitting on the kerb and chatting, winding strands of hair around their fingers, whilst the boys busied themselves with imaginary problems under the bonnet.

Occasionally, there would be trouble with boys from other parts of town. One night, as I lay half-awake on the top bunk, listening to a muffled Radio Luxembourg through my pillow, I heard the sounds of fighting and shouting outside. Pressing my nose up against the window, I could see a mass punch-up between thirty or forty youths right out there in the road. It beat *The Tony Prince Show* any day. I discovered later that lads from town had come down to 'give the Watermead a pasting', but Watermead, it seems, prevailed on that occasion.

Many of them 'got in trouble with the police', as my parents put it. Pale-blue-and-white panda cars had replaced the ice-cream men as the most regular vehicular visitors to the estate.

The house they called upon most frequently must have been number 99, Common Crescent, home of the Ducketts. There were fifteen kids in all – ten boys and five girls – although I don't think they could ever all have lived at home at the same time; they couldn't have, with just three bedrooms, and one tiny at that. Old man Duckett was a dustman and some of the older boys worked the dust with him. Him leading five or six of the younger lads, like a duck with its ducklings, up the Winhurst Road to the public baths to attend to their ablutions was a familiar sight. Daddy Duck and the Duckettes.

Most of the residents looked upon the Ducketts as a cross they had to bear: giving the estate a bad name – as if that were possible. But they were not a bad lot at all. Driven out of London to avoid the bombing during the war, they were genuine old-school Cockneys. The family just reflected the times, that was all. The '50s boys got in a bit of bother – scrumping and nicking, no more; the '60s lot were a bit more serious – robbing the milkman and doses of borstal; and the '70s and '80s Ducketts got caught up in fighting, drugs and scams and some ended up doing a bit of real bird. Some used to say, out of earshot, that old man and old lady Duckett encouraged the older boys to get into trouble so they'd get locked up and there would be more room at home for the new arrivals. The mum was a permed blonde with big blouses and too much make-up. She held the family together by working as a cleaner at the school to bring in the extra pennies. She made many trips to and from the police station to fetch her younger boys and visit the older ones when they were under lock and key. She had a sharp tongue and no one messed with her. She didn't care what people thought – she didn't have time to care.

Blokes like Steve Langton and Andrew Halliday were a bit

more complex. Mr and Mrs Langton didn't belong to the estate. They lived on it but they didn't *belong*. The old man was a court clerk of some description. One of his duties was collecting cash from the youths when they were paying instalments of their latest fines. He used to work in the local magistrates' court but was transferred soon after his son became a frequent visitor. She worked in a local solicitor's office as a personal assistant and was active in parent-teacher associations and other local groups. We never understood how they ended up on Watermead. I guess it was their start in life and they envisaged moving next year to the land of owner-occupiers. Always next year.

Steve rebelled against his parents' aspirations to join the middle classes. He had to go one better than the other boys to compensate for his parents' élitism. He nearly caused a train crash when he was about ten when he and one of the Ducketts carried a sofa on to the railway line and watched from the bushes as the 5.12 from Waterloo hurtled towards it. And it was common knowledge that it was Steve who burned down Watermead School after he was expelled. The thirteen-year-old got his first taste of fame when Shaw Taylor appealed to the British public to identify the arsonist one Sunday afternoon on *Police 5*.

'It was Stephen Langton that done it,' I muttered.

Mum and Dad sat upright in their armchairs and fixed their eyes on me. 'How do you know?'

'Everyone knows.' By now I was glued to the opening credits of *Randall & Hopkirk (Deceased)*.

'You shouldn't go round saying things like that unless you really know,' chided Dad and no more was said.

Other escapades involving Steve and Andrew became part of estate folklore: the robbing of graves in the old churchyard of finger rings and coffin handles; the burning down of the church and their subsequent involvement in fund-raising to replace the medieval organ; their sham collection for the starving children of Biafra which the good people of nearby wealthy Belstead contributed to in spades; and many, many others.

Andrew Halliday was the only son of two hard-working Scottish hospital auxiliaries. Steve was mad but Andy was bad. Us younger boys would nod at Steve when we saw him and he would nod back and pass the time of day, but we didn't dare catch Andy's eye. There was something about him even then. They were both good-looking – one slight, the other tall. They were well groomed and dressed immaculately in the latest skinhead fashions. But they didn't, once they'd found each other, run with the main estate gang. They made their own fun. Andy burned down a school, too, and before long they had tasted borstal together. This more or less set them apart from all the other lads.

Andrew in particular had a strange sense of fun. One time they sat in his house, smoking, playing cards and generally attempting to stave off their boredom. The cricket ebbed and flowed on the TV and they watched it vacantly.

'The old man's there,' remarked Andrew.

Steve smiled. Andrew smiled. Andy pushed himself out of the armchair and into the hallway where most people kept their telephones in those days. A few minutes later he returned to the lounge and slumped back in his chair, but not before turning up the volume knob on the TV.

'Important message. Ladies and gentlemen, attention please: will Mr Patrick Halliday of Winhurst, Surrey, please return home immediately. Repeat: will Mr Patrick Halliday of Winhurst, Surrey, please return home immediately.' This came through loud and clear on the TV.

'That's fucked his afternoon up,' chuckled Andrew. 'I told the bloke at the Oval that his wife had been seriously injured in a road accident.'

Although these two had set themselves apart from the estate hierarchy, even they knew there were certain people not to upset. Sid Smith was one. Gypsy-bred, he had ten years on me and a good five on the main rump of estate boys. He didn't follow fashion and he didn't really mix. He moved on to the estate later than most, having already married and had kids. But family life had not quietened him down and tales about his younger days were plentiful: bare-knuckle bouts, run-ins with the police and pub fights almost every weekend. He famously tied a dog to the bumper of a visiting police car, which caused much distress to us kids playing on the scene when we heard it squealing as the police drove off. As the new boys came through and started to use the pubs Sid made it his duty to assert his authority and give them a slap. He was a big man with no fear. His hands were covered with spider's-web tattoos, and a homemade Indian-ink swallow adorned his cheekbone. Most disliked him for the bully he was, but no one had the nerve to tell him.

I saw him once with his sleeves rolled up, his arm dangling out the open window on the passenger side of a battered old Buick. I was only about twelve but I knew even then not to catch his eye. I caught his forearm, though, and there, clearly tattooed, was the name 'Evlis' inside a crudely drawn scroll. It made me laugh when I was safely out of sight that he had misspelt the King of Rock 'n' Roll's name in such a permanent and obvious way and no one felt able to tell him.

The estate wasn't all tough guys or wannabe tough guys, though. Take Daniel, for instance. His life had been made a misery – by his parents, not the other boys. According to my mum and dad, who remembered Daniel growing up, his mother had fallen pregnant at a very late age and had desperately wanted a girl. Daniel disappointed. She took little notice of this fact and dressed her son in flouncy clothes and generally brought him up as a female. By the time he got to school age he was well and truly fucked-up and there was no chance of him ever being able to integrate himself into his surroundings. He was packed off to boarding-school at eleven and his parents grew an enormous hedge around the garden and no one really saw them again. I'd glimpse him when he was a teenager, probably in his summer holidays from school, following his father around the garden with a wheelbarrow as the old man pulled up weeds and threw them over his shoulder. It was highly unusual that a family on Watermead could guard their privacy so tightly and live slap bang in the middle of us yet take no part whatsoever in estate life.

Daniel was a good deal older than I was – there was possibly as much as ten years between us – and I only remember one encounter with him. A filthy river meandered along the road next to the estate. Against all the odds, it supported a population of fish – sticklebacks, tiddlers and redthroats – which we would catch in nets, store in jam-jars and take home to die in tap water. When we outgrew splashing about among the bike-frames, mud and tyres that clogged the stream, we turned our attention to catching and killing the water rats that lived in holes along the riverbank. 'Ratbashing', we called it. We'd take empty Carnation milk cans from the waste bins and brown stockings from our mums' bedrooms and then punch the bottoms out of the cans. The stockings would then be secured to one end of the cans by elastic bands and the other end of the cans placed into the warren of holes in the bank. Finally we'd jump up and down on the earth above the holes until a rat came bolting out, through the can and straight into the stocking. We'd grab the stocking with the rat writhing in it and run to the bridge wall where, with all our young strength, we'd swing and smash it against the brick until we were sure it was dead. It was exciting because it rarely worked. The rats very rarely came out the holes we'd canned, and when they did they'd leap about so much in the stocking you'd panic and drop it. Sometimes you thought they were dead and they weren't. Legend had it that rats had played dead and then, when being shook out the stocking, leapt at the throat. The worst thing, perhaps, was that some of us put our mums' stockings back in her drawer afterwards.

I had a big bastard in my stocking and I was spinning around and thumping it against the wall but I couldn't seem to kill it. A young man approached us. He was carrying two shopping bags and put them down carefully next to the bridge.

'What on earth are you doing?' he asked.

'What does it look like?' I cheekily replied.

'But what has that poor thing done to you?'

'It's a fucking rat, ain't it?'

He was not threatening or aggressive like other older boys and I could sense this. Nevertheless, I allowed him to take the rat from me and shake it out the stocking into the river. I was pleased to see it barely moved in the water.

'Do you like hamsters?' the man asked gently.

I nodded. Sandy, my sister, had a hamster at home.

'Well, rats are the same as hamsters except hamsters don't have long tails.'

I thought about putting a frightened little Hammy in a stocking and smashing him against the wall. I swallowed hard

33

but did not want this bloke to see my discomfort. He proceeded to tell us about man's irrational hatred of rats and the Great Plague and the Pied Piper and all sorts of rat-related things. We listened intently. Unlike the other older boys, he did not wear his hair long or skinhead short, smoke, swear and punctuate his conversation by coughing up greenies. He used his hands expressively as he spoke and I noticed how clean they were. No black under his fingernails. *Melody Maker* poked out one of the shopping bags that he'd rested up against the bridge. Although I sort of knew his face, I couldn't be sure, and I was surprised when he walked into the house with the big hedge in Common Crescent and realised he must be Daniel.

CHAPTER THREE

The Old School Yard

The first day at school. I hated it. It traumatised me. Saying goodbye to Mummy at the gate and realising she really was going to leave me for the first time. It was the first time I 'cried and didn't get'. That's the first blow in life, I reckon, when you're kicked out the nest for your first foray in the undergrowth with all the other insects. Card nametag things were hung around our necks and we stood in the playground, helplessly, like goldfish tipped out of a bowl. Eventually, a teacher gently pushed us into a classroom called the Blue Room and we were introduced to our hard wooden chairs and desks. No cushions here. And there was our own peg to hang our bags on. A lady, much older than Mum, with beads around her neck and wearing a stiff tweed jacket so unlike Mum's soft pink cardigans, told us how our day would be organised. Fear and resentment welled up inside. I yearned to be indoors with *Watch with Mother* on the TV and waiting for my brothers and sisters to come in from school. I cried all morning, as did half of the other children. Lunch – or dinner as it was still called then – consisted of a scoop of mashed potato and two sausages followed by some pink semolina stuff. And first we all had to clasp our hands together and say after the teacher: 'For what we are about to receive may we all be truly thankful.' This was soon amended by tradition to: 'For what we are about to leave may the pigs be truly thankful.' The food was revolting to my little stomach that so far was used only to Mum's lovingly cooked meals, iced biscuits and Marmite soldiers.

The afternoon was slightly more bearable as we were led back to the Blue Room and allowed to play in the sandpit at the back of the class. Finally, we were told to lift our wooden chairs and place them on our desks, but before we could rush out to be reunited with our mothers we were trained to chant the following prayer:

'Thank you for the world so sweet,
Thank you for the food we eat,
Thank you for the birds that sing,
Thank you, God, for everything.'

I hated it from that first day. Torn from my cosy lounge, toys and telly to a red-brick world of fussy women, blackboards, chalk, pegs and pungent plimsolls.

There were three of us who invariably spent each playtime standing on a drain at different points in the playground. The dinner-ladies, who were in charge during break and just wanted to sip their cups of tea in peace, put us on these drains as a punishment for misbehaviour. I can't think what we did to deserve this punishment day in, day out, but that's how it was.

Jacko I recognised from walking to school. He was from the estate but lived around the block in Common Crescent so I didn't really know him before now. Of course he wasn't Jacko then – that came much later. He was Richie Wells and, un-believable as it seems now, always was until he was about seventeen. When we first started drinking and going to pubs, we all struggled to get a pint down. I mean, under what circum-stances does a boy drink maybe six pints of liquid in a three-hour period? But we all fought gamely on to educate our stomachs and digestive systems to accept the volume – except Richie. He just couldn't keep the beer down and vomited the pints up almost as quickly as they went down. After a while he accepted defeat. 'I'll have half,' he said one Sunday lunchtime as we sat in The Wheatsheaf and then looked bewildered as we all collapsed, laughing.

'I'll have half!' we all mimicked.

Richie had unwittingly used the catchphrase of a minor character in a TV sitcom, Jacko, who just sat in the pub in his Mac and cloth cap and whose only words were 'I'll have half' when he was asked what he was drinking. And that was that: Richie was fleetingly compared to this long-forgotten bit-part player in a '70s television programme and was almost never known by his birth-name again.

Richie was born unlucky. He got a dart in the eye once when he opened his back gate while his father was practising in the garden. About a week later, one of the older boys on the estate shot him accidentally in the same eye with an air gun. Later still, when I was with him, he fell out of a tree and gouged his cheek open on a stone. We had been scrumping in the gardens of some rich person's house when he tried to jump from tree to tree, Tarzan-style. He fell on to a sharp stone, leaving a hole in his face. In my panic, I inserted my thumb into it to stem the flow of blood. By the age of eleven his face had a patchwork of smaller scars which, in later life, gave the impression, wrongly, that he was violently inclined. If someone was going to get caught, it was Richie. If the wrong person got cheeked, it was by Richie. If someone was going to fall down a manhole, it would be Richie.

Bob Rees was the miscreant occupying the third drain. He

was also from the estate but I had never seen him out playing up till now. He was a massive five-year-old, twice the size of anyone else. I doubt he had done much wrong but the teachers and the dinner-ladies just didn't know how to deal with him. Little boys shouldn't be that big! Most of us weren't far off toddlers – if we fell over and cut our knee, they'd pick us up and cuddle us before taking us by the hand to the school secretary who would dab our bleeding knees with witch-hazel. They couldn't really do this with Bob. It didn't feel right. And it followed that if Bob had a row with someone, it was always his fault. He was big so he must have been the aggressor. So, almost from the first day, Jacko, Big Bob and I had the drains in common and we became friends.

One morning about a year later, Jacko and I were dawdling to school with Monkey who, being a year younger than us, had just started. All three of us were kicking a stone along the road to break up the monotony of the thirty-minute walk. He supposedly got the nickname Monkey because he looked like one as a baby. His parents obviously didn't disagree with this notion because they called him that too. For some reason, we decided to play truant. I don't think we had any comprehension of what truancy was but we simply didn't walk all the way to school. We stopped under the grandstand of the local football club and decided to stay there until we judged it was time to go home. Judging time was obviously not a skill we had developed in those pre-wristwatch days and we arrived back home a good three hours before we were supposed to and we were, naturally, tumbled. All hell was let loose. Mrs Monkey gave her son a hiding out there in the road and I was sent to bed. The next day at school two desks had been placed out in the orchard and Jacko and I (Monkey was excused on the grounds that we had led him astray) were made to sit out there for the whole day. I guess the idea was to shame us. We were in the stocks, so to speak. But we loved being paraded in front of the school like that. The junior girls who shared the same building kept looking out of their windows and waving. We replied. That day they made Jacko and me a bit special.

'In all my years as headmistress and indeed as a teacher I have never, repeat *never*, had to deal with six-year-old boys playing truant!' ranted the headmistress as we stood in her springy red-carpeted office for the first time. 'And "playing" is the wrong word. Truancy is not, repeat *not*, a game and cannot and will not be tolerated!' She was a bit of a crank. All hairspray, stiff Prince of Wales check blazers and brooches.

And it was a cranky school, too. Take Big Toy Day and Little Toy Day. On these occasions there were no lessons and pupils were encouraged to bring their favourite toys to school and play uninterrupted all day long. Nice idea on the surface but divisive or what? The richer kids would arrive grandly on their new Chopper bikes or babble excitedly into their walkie-talkies. Us lot would be squeaking in quietly on old home-made rusty bikes or clasping the family Action Man. Some kids could only bring in swords crudely fashioned from lumps of wood.

So it was with no great regret on either side when, at the age of seven, we were transferred to the junior boys' school next door. St Peter's was the village school and when we joined it was celebrating one hundred and fifty years of history. Situated in the centre of the old village, it had been educating boys for generations. The transfer there must have gone smoothly, as I have no recollection of first-day horrors.

The hall was the focus of the school. It was the largest room where the whole school would gather for morning assembly. Mr

Ball, the headmaster, would lead us through a couple of prayers and hymns whilst Mrs Dexter banged away, grinning from ear to ear and rocking her head from side to side, behind him on the big wooden piano. She was either trying hard to ingratiate herself with the head or she was mad. The room was dominated by two large mahogany plaques: one listed the names of boys who had gone on to attain degrees at university and the other was a roll call of boys who had perished in the two world wars. No prizes for guessing which was the longer list. I often studied the names. Some were on both scrolls. Others were the surnames of pupils here in the school with me. It was an eerie feeling that boys who had stood on the same wooden floor as me, sung the same hymns, kicked a ball around the same playground and sat on the same lavatories, had died violently in far-off countries we had never dreamt of.

It was a church school but I was not sure what that meant, really. We sang hymns and said prayers in morning assembly, but kids did that at all schools, didn't they? An elderly vicar with a silver Bobby Charlton haircut and a long black robe turned up once a month and mumbled away on the stage about nothing in particular. A couple of times a year we were led through the village to the old church where we sang more hymns and listened to more meaningless and unintelligible garbage.

Another visitor to the school who was altogether more interesting than the vicar was the blind piano-tuner. He tapped his way through the playground and into the hall wearing his tweed jacket with leather patches on the elbows and led by his docile Labrador. Every time he appeared and was left alone at the piano we felt the need to check his handicap was authentic by standing in front of him and quietly waving two fingers in his face.

There were only a handful of teachers. In the first year we had Miss Rich who talked a lot about 'before the war' – and I think she meant the first one – so she must have been knocking on a bit. She was humourless but her great love was nature and when she talked about animals, plants and the seasons we were transfixed. I got my first school smack off her, though, when she caught me and Steve Fletcher reading a comic under the desk, turning the pages with our feet. She got us up at the front of the class and smacked our bare legs.

Mr Vanburgh put the fear of God into us. His reputation preceded him and he delighted in the terror he could see in the boys' eyes when he was around. He was a tall man who reminded me of Eric Morecambe with his tufts of black hair, bald pate and thick glasses, but any similarities with the comedian ended there. In his lesson we sat like scared animals, hands on desks, looking straight ahead, desperately trying to absorb what he said lest he pounce on us and ask us to repeat his last statement. Like all bullies, he picked on the kids he thought couldn't cause him a problem. Well-dressed pupils whose parents picked them up in cars were rarely singled out. Boys like Smith, Brown and us lot from the Watermead were fair game whether we'd done anything wrong or not. Never did a lesson go by without someone being called up to stand in front of his desk.

'Smith, were you talking at the back there?'

'No, sir.'

'Talking is one thing, Smith, lying is another. Which is it to be, Smith?'

'Talking, sir.'

'Right, you know what to do, Smith.'

Smith walked across the room to fetch an adult-sized chair

that stood on a raised platform in the corner of the room. This was Mr Vanburgh's idea of fun. This chair was kept on constant display with a large white plimsoll placed ominously on the seat. Smith handed the teacher the slipper and bent over the chair. Vanburgh took some fast steps backward and ran towards the boy, delivering the shoe down on his little bum like a tennis player delivering a knockout first service.

'Thank you, sir,' said Smith, taking the plimsoll from the teacher and placing it on the chair and carrying both back to their rightful position. The ritual was over for the day and that sadistic bully had had his fix.

We were aged between eight and eleven, most of us four foot something and weighing next to nothing, and yet a fully grown man was permitted to beat us. Parents knew and other teachers knew, yet somehow this man got away with physically and mentally torturing little children. Anyone who did outside the school classroom what that man did each and every day – a grown man hitting a nine-year-old with all his force in the high street, say – would be locked up.

Vanburgh was eventually dismissed. He'd kicked a fat boy called Julian up the arse because the kid didn't move out of his way fast enough. Julian had recently fallen off his bike and ripped his buttock on the saddle and he had fresh stitches in the gash. Vanburgh's kick opened the wound up and blood gushed down the back of the boy's leg. He had to be taken to hospital in the headmaster's car. Julian's parents, understandably, were furious but stopped short of demanding Vanburgh be prosecuted. They did ensure, however, that the sadist never came back to the school.

Mrs Dexter was our next form teacher. I don't think she needed to work. Her husband was a surgeon and they lived at the top of the village in a big house with iron gates and pillars with stone lions sitting on top. She was on a mission. Her 'concern' for underprivileged kids was etched into the foundation that hung like plaster on her benevolent face. She once got us all to write poems and professed to like an effort of mine a great deal. I cannot imagine what I wrote a poem about at the age of eight, but my mum nearly dropped the iron at home one afternoon when the rhyme and my name were read out on *Woman's Hour* on the radio. Mrs Dexter had told me she was going to send it in to some competition or other, but I hadn't taken much notice.

In the fourth and final junior year, or Class Five as it was bizarrely known, a Mr Owen taught us. He must have been near to retiring. The feeling that he was marking time instead of class-work was clear even to us boys. He would set us some reading or writing and then devour the *Daily Express* for the remainder of the morning as the crumbs from the biscuits he crunched loudly fell on to his large cardigan-covered tummy. Sometimes he told us stories about his boyhood in Wales or about his favourite pupils who had passed through the school in years gone by and had cracked it by going on to play for Fulham reserves. When he made a strange rattling noise in the back of his throat we knew that this immediately preceded him walking to the window, summoning phlegm from within and spitting it out on to the ground below. A school legend was that he did this once and, unbeknown to him, Mrs Dexter stood below the window on playground duty – a whistle around her neck and a cup of tea in her hand – not noticing the lump of mucus plopping into her cup.

Mid-morning and the milk arrived, crates and crates of half-pint bottles. The boys eagerly ran to the hall and helped themselves. Some of the bigger lads would knock it back in one while others would take their time, wiping the milk stain from around their lips with the back of their sleeves between swigs. Bob Rees would wait until everyone had had their fill and then drink the milk of those who were not thirsty or those that were absent. Sometimes, during a flu or dysentery outbreak for instance, he was lucky and got through seven or eight bottles.

Dinner was another ritual. Firstly, we were allowed into the playground for a quick runaround before the bell rang. When this sounded the boys would make a mad dash for the hall and queue for their food. A small army of dinner-ladies in white overalls and caps, operating like a factory production line, would slap scoops of the delicacy of the day on to your plate, and you took it off to your seat, which was anywhere you could fit between boys on a long wooden bench. Two rows of tables ran the length of the hall. Very *Oliver Twist*. Lumpy mashed potato, greens, soggy carrots, gravy with a skin on it, apple crumble and rhubarb. The dinners were rank and the puddings were worse. Unlike with the milk, very few – not even Big Bob – asked for more. Most of us bolted it down so we could get back out in the playground to play football, war or British Bulldogs.

I broke my arm when Eddie Richards was giving me a backie home from school on his bike. He lost his balance and we toppled over sideways, the bike falling on top of me. I had a few weeks off school and even when I returned I was excused having to do anything other than listen because my writing arm was in plaster. Jacko couldn't handle this and announced he was going to break his arm too. I think he was inspired by an old British film, which came on the telly regularly on Sunday afternoons. It was a PoW film. I think every other film made for ten years after the war was a PoW story. One of the characters deliberately hit his hand with a mallet in the workshop to avoid some duty or other. Jacko went out into the playground, adopted the press-up position, and invited Bob to jump on him. I winced as I heard his fingers snap as ten stone of Bob landed on his back.

We had our first run-in with the police, or one policeman at any rate, about this time. Jacko was giving me a crossbar home from the rec down the alley that ran alongside it. We actually called it the Cycling Prohibited alley after the signs that stood at both ends of it. 'Cycling Prohibited by order of the Town Clerk, Godfrey Wilkins' it said, but we never read it. I can honestly say that it never occurred to us that cycling was not allowed in this alley. Everyone cycled home down it. It had just got dark and we saw a policeman riding towards us on his bike. He saw us approaching and dismounted. We carried on and, as we drew level, he gave us an almighty shove and pushed the bike and us over. We were barely nine years old and had no idea we were doing anything wrong. As we nervously got to our feet, he shouted at us: 'You are not allowed to ride your bicycles down this footpath! Can't you read?'

'You was riding down here,' replied Jacko, confused, not cheekily.

'I was not, you lying little urchin!'

'Yes, you were,' I chimed in.

The policeman propped his bike up against the wall slowly and deliberately and picked me up by the front of my shirt, lifting me up so my face was almost touching his. My legs were dangling in the air. I was terrified. His eyes were blazing. No man's face had been this close to mine apart from Dad's and that was when he was kissing me goodnight when I was a toddler.

'Have you not been told to respect your elders and betters? Have you not been taught not to answer back?' he hissed.

'No! I mean, yes!' I spluttered.

'Do you know I am a policeman? I can have you put in prison. Do you realise that? Do you want me to come to your houses and see your parents?'

'No!'

He dropped me on the pavement and I was shaking with fear. 'Now, wheel that bike along the rest of this footpath and don't ever let me see you riding down here again. Understood?'

We nodded and meekly pushed the bike away. I started to cry a bit, I was so shaken with the sudden ferocity of what had happened in the last few minutes. I glanced quickly over my shoulder and glimpsed the policeman pedalling his bike down the last few yards of the alley.

*

When my Granddad died I was distraught. My mum's father had been ill ever since I could remember, suffering from emphysema (brought on, my mum assured us, by smoking roll-ups – I'm sure she hoped that if one good thing came out of his death, it would be us kids not smoking – although she and Dad hadn't long given up themselves). But because he had been ill for so long I didn't think he was going to die.

He was a country boy from Kent. He was born around the turn of the century and he still had a soothing country burr. He had been a farmer, a builder and had served in the RAF during the war. I loved just sitting on his lap and asking him to tell me stories about when he was a boy, about how he and his mates would go out at night to where the pheasants roosted and shine torches in their eyes. The birds would be dazzled and then simply allowed themselves to be picked off the boughs and

46

taken home to be eaten. How so much more attractive this was than buying a chicken from Keymarkets.

Mum would take me down to Brighton on the train to visit Nana and Granddad when he was past making the journey up to us. That trip seemed to be such an adventure and undertaking in those days. On Clapham Junction we'd see the *Brighton Belle* fly past in all its glory – 'Dora Bryan's probably on there,' Mum would say – before getting on one of our more familiar drab green trains. At Brighton we'd board a green-and-cream double-decker which would climb the residential streets up to the South Downs where my grandparents lived.

By now Granddad was propped up in bed and I was taken in to see him. Last time I'd visited, he'd still been in his chair watching the wrestling on *World of Sport*, his paper folded open at the racing page on his knee. A tobacco tin and a pen were on the coffee-table next to him. Today he was held artificially upright by cushions and pillows. I was shocked. It was his throat that I noticed first. It had become so thin, bumpy and red and reminded me of a turkey's neck. His eyes bulged but were not seeing.

'Hello there, John,' he smiled, looking at a blank space to my left.

Mum signalled for me to go closer so I stood next to him.

'Hi, Granddad,' I said.

His hand found my mine and he squeezed it hard. I was surprised at the strength of his grip. 'Know any football results?'

He had the right day but the football hadn't kicked off yet. I kissed him on the forehead and was then sent into the next room to watch telly whilst Mum and Nana fussed around him.

He died about five days after our visit. I couldn't take it in. Surely someone could help? Put the clock back a few days and get him cured? Why did he have to die? He was such a good person. Kindness leaked out of him. He was so nice, so kind, so interesting. Yet – and this was the bit that destroyed me – once I was dead no one would even know he had ever existed. What could I do about that? Nothing. I cried for nights afterwards, burying my face in the wet pillow and challenging God.

'Right, if you do exist, how come you let this happen? All right, maybe it was a mistake, just put me in touch with him, so I can tell him how we all love him and miss him, and I'll overlook this one.'

God was not interested in a deal, it seemed.

CHAPTER FOUR

The Young Ones

In that last year at junior school, Hayton arrived. If Jacko and I and the other boys from the estate thought we were the underclass, this urchin soon changed all that. He was introduced to us all as a new boy, paraded at the front of the class. He stood awkwardly with a lop-sided grin as we studied him. His blond hair looked as if it had been cut by himself (it had). He wore a blazer three sizes too big for him with an unfamiliar school badge and short trousers that revealed two knees smeared with dried blood. But the item of clothing that us boys alighted on and which caused much stifled amusement was poor Hayton's footwear. To a boy we all wore black leather Tuf shoes, many of which had compasses or animal footprints embedded in the soles and heels. Some of us wore brown sandals in the summer. This day Richard Hayton wore a pair of yellow-and-black-check bedroom slippers and no socks. I say we stifled our giggling because although his abject poverty was a sight unfamiliar to us, he didn't in any way come over as pathetic. He had a dignity and a defiant confidence that led Jacko and me to befriend him that very first day.

He was from London, he told us. It was only ten miles up the road but to us it was a different world. Boys from London were tough – much tougher than us. That was all there was to it. His dad, he said, was a bank robber but had been caught red-handed and was currently in prison. His mum and his brothers and sisters were waiting for him to be released so he could fetch the money he'd hidden and they could all live like kings. Other boys looked at him disbelievingly, some holding their noses behind his back to signify to the world that he smelt. But to me and Jacko he represented excitement and adventure. Bank robbers and hidden money: *Z Cars* and *Treasure Island* rolled into one.

Another kid, Trevor Brown, joined our little gang. Trevor lived bang next door to the school, yet he still managed to get detention almost every day for being late. Like Hayton he seemed to be very poor although his father was visibly in gainful employment. Perhaps the money he did earn was being diverted elsewhere before reaching the family coffers. What I liked about Trevor was that he never stopped smiling. He was a bit slow on the academic front (he had Tuesdays off to go to a special school for extra tuition) but he didn't care. He was extraordinarily generous too, often inviting us round to his house to view his older sister's tits which she would pull out of her bra cups one by one as if she was introducing us to her pet hamsters.

About this time there was a craze in the school for collecting Soccer Stars – a latter-day cigarette-card type of hobby. These were cards that had a picture of each player in the English first-division teams on the front and a potted biography on the back. Most players were described as 'pivotal midfielders' or 'hungry strikers'. These cards could then be pasted into a large scrap-book-sized album. The pictures came with bubble-gum that could be purchased in all the local sweetshops. The race was on to see who could complete their album first. The manufacturers had shrewdly made some cards very rare to ensure we all kept buying and buying. You couldn't give away Nobby Stiles for love or money but no one had Frank Casper of Burnley or Alex Elder of Stoke City. Our budgets typically stretched to two or three packets of bubble-gum after school, when we would rip open the wrappers to find only Terry Paine, Alex Stepney and Ronnie Boyce.

One afternoon Hayton came with us and watched as we bought our sweets. After leaving the shop he hurried off towards a bridle path running behind the parade. We followed.

'Sit down here,' he grinned widely, emptying numerous bubble gum packs from pockets all over his person. 'If Fred Casper ain't in that lot then I'm a bleedin' chinaman!'

Frank Casper wasn't there, but Hayton's daring raised him another few notches in our estimation. He soon had us spending our dinner-money each day on sweets and fags: 5 Park Drive, washed down with Top Deck shandy and sherbet fountains – which was okay for him seeing as he was on the free-meals scheme.

He was always vague about where he lived until he invited Jacko and me back home after school one day. Half expecting a hostel for broken families, we followed him out of Winhurst up to the big posh houses in Belstead.

'Here it is,' he finally announced outside a six-bedroomed detached mock-Tudor house. We thought it was a wind-up but he pulled a key from his blazer and let us in. Inside, the floors were bare and there was a noticeable lack of furniture. Baby brothers and sisters crawled around the wooden floorboards whilst older family members sat on a solitary sofa watching *Magpie* on an old black-and-white TV with an aerial sprouting out the top.

'Ma, my pals I told you about are here!'

'You can tell them to fuck off then,' shouted a voice from the kitchen. Hayton pulled a face at us as his mum, a small woman with dyed red hair and thick lipstick walked into the room. She didn't even glance at us. 'I told you, you dozy bastard, you don't bring people here.' She smacked him around the head. I wasn't sure if it was serious or playful.

'So, can they stay for tea, Mum?'

'Who said anything about tea? Who says you're having tea? You boys have got tea at home, ain't you?'

She was telling us, not asking, so we left and pondered on the way home how a family so outwardly poor and scruffy could live in a mansion like that. Perhaps the story about the old man, the prison and the stash wasn't too far off the truth.

If the shadow of fathers in prison and the act of stealing from sweetshops was beginning to erode the innocence of early childhood, what happened shortly afterwards was to shatter that naïvety completely. In the wake of the Moors Murders, all our parents had drummed into us not to take lifts from strangers or even to talk to them. 'Even if someone you know offers you a lift home, you mustn't accept. Do you understand?' Mum had her serious face on.

I nodded but she must have thought I wasn't taking it in. 'Even if it's . . . say . . . Uncle Charlie?' says Mum.

'Uncle Charlie! Is he a sex maniac, then?'

'No, of course not, don't be so saucy.'

Sometimes the messages from parents were so confused. Poor Charlie, my dad's brother, had four children – my cousins – but I never regarded him the same way again.

(The other parental message that remains in my mind even

now was a strange one: don't put plastic bags over your head because you might suffocate. What was that all about? I was always baffled about that one but never really queried it, thinking perhaps there was some tragic death way back in our family history involving a Waitrose bag or something. I was even more bewildered when Jacko told me that his parents kept warning him about the very same thing.)

Trevor, Hayton, Jacko and I were playing around the railway line after school one day when Trevor got into conversation with a man who had crossed the railway bridge. The bridge was a fairly busy one that was on a main route from the estate to the school. Trevor left the man and came back to us triumphantly smoking a cigarette. As he spoke the fag went up and down in his mouth like Popeye. 'That man gave it to me,' he said. 'Have a lug – it's minty.'

We all took a puff and, sure enough, the fag had a novel peppermint taste. We had, by that time, all experimented with cigarettes: Mum's Guards and Dad's roll-ups, or 5 Park Drive from the sweetshop sold to us by the owner who pretended he believed they were for our fathers.

The man smiled at us from the railway bridge as we sucked in the smoke. Eventually he walked over and pulled a green-and-white packet of Consulate from his jacket pocket. 'Here, have one each.'

We took the long white cigarettes and, with the exception of Trevor, carried on with whatever we were doing in the trees and bushes around the railway line. Soon Trevor was calling us over to a copse where he had disappeared with the man.

'Look at this!' he howled as he pointed to what looked like the outline of a truncheon in the man's trousers. 'It's his winkle!' Trevor pressed the shape for our benefit.

The man stepped under the cover of a tree and unzipped his fly. 'Yours will be this big when you get to my age,' he said in a matter-of-fact way.

We were aghast. None of us had ever seen an erect penis before. There was this rocket-like piece of flesh jutting skyward from the man's trousers, all pink and shiny. We looked at one another and giggled.

'Touch it if you like,' invited the man as if he wasn't that interested. We all stepped forward and poked it, jumping back as it sprung back into position.

'Yours can go big, too,' the man said. 'I can make it go big for you.'

The three of us stepped backwards as the man gently tugged Trevor towards him. He slipped his hand up his shorts and began to fumble away inside whilst rubbing his own penis faster and faster with his other hand. Suddenly and unexpectedly, a milky fluid came shooting out of the man's penis and landed very near where we were stood. We screamed as if a rat had tried to crawl up our leg, and ran. We knew something was happening that wasn't quite right but we didn't honestly give it a second thought. It was just something else that happened in those eventful hours between finishing school and going home when dusk fell. We didn't even worry when we stopped running and noticed that Trevor wasn't with us.

But he was at school next day. He proudly produced a load of silver from his pocket and told us the man had given it to him. We thought no more about it.

Apparently that afternoon Trevor set off to meet the man again and innocently told his Mum where he was going. I can imagine old Trevor – he wasn't the brightest of kids:

'Where you off to, son?'

'I'm going down the railway, Mum, to see this man. He gives me money if I rub his willie.'

Trevor would have been careful not to mention the Consulate, though.

His mum contacted the police and before we knew it we became the centre of a drama we could not have imagined. The police arrived at our house and questioned me for ages. They chided me for calling a penis a willie. They asked what the penis looked like. Was it bigger or smaller than my father's? Why the fuck did they want to know that? They wondered if the man had kissed my penis. Did I kiss his? Did Trevor kiss it?

What was all this? We were four boys mucking around and now we were being questioned and doubted in front of our horrified parents. We were taken out separately in police cars and driven around the town in an effort to try and find the man. Finally, our parents were told to keep us off school for a few days so the four of us couldn't meet up and discuss our statements. Why? We couldn't work out what we'd done wrong. Then my mum insisted I keep away from Trevor and Hayton. I really didn't understand that. Like me, they were innocent parties in all this.

The man, we were told, indecently assaulted a kid some days later and was caught. He confessed to the incident with us and was imprisoned. None of us ever spoke about it, either to each other or anyone else. More happened to Trevor than we knew, though. He smiled a lot less after that.

There must have been a lot of these guys around. I met up with another paedophile only a year or so later, only they weren't called that then. 'Strange men' was the term our parents used in front of us, and 'child molesters' when they were alone. The older boys on the estate called them 'nonces'.

I had a crush on a girl called Jill who was two years my senior. She was the first girl I'd ever had a crush on. These were my pre-wanking days so there was certainly no sexual desire involved. It was pure child love. I'd hang around the park just to catch a glimpse of her. If I saw her my spirits lifted, and if I didn't I became depressed. Clinically depressed at ten! Everything about her captivated me. Her dark complexion. The way she shook her hair. When she first spoke to me it was the biggest landmark in my life up to that point.

'Why do you keep looking at me?' she said as she jumped off the swing and strode past me to head homeward.

'Because I love you.'

She studied me for a second or two like I was deranged and then threw back her head and laughed. 'You're only ten! How can you? I'm twelve, for Christ's sake!'

'I can't help it,' I went on pathetically. 'I'll always love you.'

'You're bonkers.'

But she allowed me to walk home with her and at one point as we said goodbye she brushed my hand.

When she was with her senior-school pals she ignored me but when she was on her own she played and flirted with me. I just wanted to hurry up and catch up with her age-wise.

We'd been down the rec, laughing and chatting on the swings. Night began to fall – nine o'clock or dusk was our curfew time, whichever came first – and we knew we should set off home. As we climbed the steps of the railway bridge a man was coming down, carrying a bike on his shoulder. I wasn't alarmed when he ruffled my hair. I was small, cheeky and blond. Grown-up men often ruffled my hair and grown-up women sometimes pinched my cheeks. But he tugged it violently as I kept walking yet somehow I shook free. Almost in one movement he lifted Jill up, pulled her navy-blue school knickers down and liberated his penis from his trousers. In his excitement he let the bicycle crash to the ground. I was not as shocked as I might have been, perhaps because the last bloke had been nice in a funny sort of way and I was becoming an old hand at this lark. But this man was much more urgent and frenzied. Jill didn't scream. She didn't say a word as the man prodded around her lower region with his hard dick. I picked up a crumbling house brick and, because I was a few steps above him, was able to bring it down on his head as hard as I could. It didn't really hurt but it was enough to distract him and make him relax his grip on Jill and let her make a bolt for it. She ran across the main road with her knickers around her knees and only stopped to pull them up when she was safely out of reach. I put my arm around her as we walked home. I remember how chuffed I was that she'd let me cuddle her.

This time I told my parents and Dad rode his bike straight round to Jill's house. She hadn't told her parents. Again, though, it was like I'd done something wrong. Jill was never seen at the rec again and soon after the family moved away completely. She wrote me a lovely little letter with a picture of me and her and a little love heart on it which I kept for years, but I never saw her again after that night. I pined for what seemed like months but was probably only a few days. The bloke was caught almost straight away, as we were able to give the police a good description of him and his bike. I think they knew who he was anyway.

*

'That's the bank,' whispered Hayton in hushed tones as we stood in the wasteground that separated our school playground from the back of the High Street shops. 'If we start digging here, sooner or later we'll hit the vaults. We creep in, nick the money, hide it here and fill in the hole.'

It all seemed so easy to us ten-year-olds. Jacko, Big Bob and I had all borrowed our dads' spades and hidden them in the undergrowth. Hayton had brought nothing; garden tools were not among the few household implements stored at the big empty house. The idea was to sneak through the fence at play-time and dig until we 'hit the vaults'. We'd all seen *The Wooden Horse*, *Albert RN* and countless other escape films on Sunday-afternoon telly, and this latest adventure dreamt up by Hayton had really caught our imagination.

We didn't bank on Mr Owen looking out the upstairs class-room window and seeing us digging away furiously on the other side of the wooden fence. He came down and demanded to know what we were up to. No one answered. We all looked at Hayton. What could we say? We're tunnelling into the Williams & Glyn Bank, sir?

'Well?' demanded Owen.

'We were trying to escape, sir,' volunteered Hayton eventually.

'*Escape?* Escape from what?'

'Trying to escape from school, sir.'

'Why didn't you walk out the school gate like anyone else?'

'We thought it would be more exciting to tunnel out,' Hayton replied.

Owen felt uneasy, we could tell. There was something not quite right. He knew Hayton was not the full ticket but the sight of us digging a tunnel with our spades on private property had unnerved him.

'Come with me,' he commanded.

He took us to Mr Ball, the headmaster. Hayton went

through the same story as we three stood with our hands clasped behind our backs, looking down at the floor. Ball took us back out to the wasteground to inspect the tunnel, which of course was only a ditch, and collected up the spades. He said he was considering calling our parents down to the school but would leave it up to them how they dealt with the borrowing of their garden tools.

He had decided to cane us, however. One by one he leant us over an armchair in the study and whacked our arses. Hayton was first and Jacko, Bob and I shot glances at each other, trying to suppress laughter as puffs of dust rose from Hayton's shorts. Ball told him to leave the office as he bent Big Bob over. Safely outside, Hayton made himself visible to us through the window in the door. He put one hand around his neck and then with the other made out he was trying to pull the first hand off. Because we could only see his head and neck this looked like he was attempting to stop someone strangling him. I nudged Jacko and he couldn't help himself from snorting with laughter.

'You think this is funny, do you, Wells?' Ball was trembling.

From the corner of his eye, Jacko could see Hayton sliding down the door as if he were succumbing to the strangulation and he was laughing so much inside but with his mouth tightly closed he emitted no more than a farting noise. Ball grabbed his hair and hauled him towards him and then started swiping his legs with the cane. He lost control for a minute.

The upshot of all this was that we crossed another divide that day. Fear of the cane was worse than the cane itself. The worst thing Ball could have done that afternoon was cane us because once we'd had it, and we realised it wasn't that bad, it was no deterrent. The school's ultimate punishment held no fear for us. By the time we came to leave and prepare for our respective senior schools, Big Bob, Jacko, Hayton, Trevor and I were a regular feature of the morning assembly: our names being called out and told to stand outside Mr Ball's study to answer for some misdemeanour or other.

Ironically, Hayton was going to Watermead Boys School when we left the juniors, and we weren't. The new all-boys school that had been built next to our estate had already established a bad reputation because older boys like Steve Langton and Andrew Halliday went there. Our parents had put us down for Crowley Lane, a mixed comprehensive a mile or two up the road. I needed to be sure that I did go there along with my friends, and, as there was no chance that Jacko would pass his eleven-plus, I had to ensure that I failed mine. We weren't supposed to know when we were sitting the exam but it was fairly obvious the day they sat us all at single desks and gave out the papers. I answered all the questions facetiously just to make sure they didn't give me marks for trying. 'Where was Jesus born? Bethnal Green' – that sort of thing.

Jacko was a few desks behind. At the close of the exam, Mr Owen called him over. 'Richard, why have you written "X" on your paper as your middle name?'

'Because that is my middle name, sir.'

'X! X can't be your name, Wells. X is not a name. X is a letter.'

'Well, that's my name, sir.'

Owen looked over his half-moon glasses at this boy answering him earnestly. *Maybe*, I could see him thinking, *maybe*. Boys who try and tunnel their way out of school might just have parents who give them X as a name.

'X isn't your middle name, is it?' I asked Jacko as we ambled home that afternoon.

'Yeah, it is,' he replied, getting defensive now over this sudden interest in his name.

Back at his house, I just had to ask his mum. She threw her head back with laughter as she dried a cup with a tea-towel showing the map of Spain. 'You soppy sod!' she squealed at Jacko. 'Your name is *Lex*!' She turned to me. 'Almost as bad, isn't it? I had a real thing about this film star when I was a girl. Lex Barker. You wouldn't have heard of him. He played Tarzan at the pictures. I named Richie after him.'

Jacko reddened but his mum hid his embarrassment by pulling him towards her and pushing his face into her chest. 'My fault for giving you such a stupid name. Forget it son, you ain't got a middle name.'

Hayton stepped out of our lives when that last summer holiday ended. We heard years later that he set fire to the headmaster's study at Watermead after being expelled. The big house went. I noticed on the few times I passed it that flowers grew in the garden, the lawns were mown and a shiny car stood in the driveway. We glimpsed him just the once not long after we had left school altogether. He was with another boy and they were smashing the side windows of cars, leaning in and ripping out the eight-tracks from the centre consuls. He wanted to stop and chat but we felt decidedly nervous standing talking while his jacket bulged with recently acquired stolen goods. We never saw or heard of him again.

Something happened that summer break between junior school and senior school, another incident that served to close further the curtains of childhood. The Miles brothers and I were idling away a Saturday afternoon at the football ground behind the estate. We often did this: got through a hole in the fence, clambered up the grass bank and watched the match.

The oldest Miles brother smoked his fags and enjoyed the on-field strategies whilst we younger three tumbled around on the grass, playing and fetching the ball for the players when it came over the top of the bar. We got into a lark with three other boys we didn't know, teasing them and calling names and such. One, the smallest and youngest, was giving back as good as he got.

We walked over to them when this small one said to me, 'Do you like ice-cream?'

Before I could reply, he said, 'Lick this!' and booted me straight up the arse. This took the whole thing on to a different level. I was only eleven but this was a challenge to any credibility that I thought I had. If the Miles boys hadn't been there I could have walked away and no one would have been any the wiser. But they were. I had to react.

Earlier we had been playing splits on the grass, splits being a little game where boys stood with their legs apart in front of each other and threw a penknife into the earth between the legs. I can't remember how a game was won or lost – I suppose the thrill was that the penknife might impale your foot into the ground or a misjudged throw might take half your scrotum away. I took my penknife out of my pocket and jabbed at the smaller boy's stomach. To my horror, he fell to the ground and writhed around in apparent agony.

'I didn't touch him,' I said to the Miles brothers, but they had gone and were running as fast as they could back to the estate. I followed, chucking the knife into the river *en route*.

Within thirty minutes the estate was alive with police cars, their sirens wailing. I was sitting inside my house watching Frank Bough perched on the edge of a table, presenting *Grandstand*. The knock on the door reverberated around my bowels. Two policemen sat with me, watching the football results together in silence, until Mum and Dad returned home from their Saturday shopping. Before that, two more policemen turned up with my victim's parents. What Mum and Dad thought when they arrived, I don't know. It turned out that my thrust had ever so slightly broken the skin of the boy but no way was he stabbed. His parents, very reasonably, decided not to press charges and the police cautioned me with the adult audience all looking intently at the delinquent in their midst. I sat there sobbing throughout.

Later, when I was in bed, Dad came to my room and sat next to me. 'Don't worry too much,' he said. 'It was just one of those things. Put it behind you. I've done worse in my time. When I was a kid, we'd cop a cuff round the ear – none of all this police malarkey – and it would be forgotten.'

I was glad he'd said that, because I was lying up there feeling different – feeling like a bad person.

But word got round the estate and people treated me a bit differently after that. Not much, but a bit. I had had my baptism of fire with the police and I became the one who stabbed that boy at the football ground – a label I was not quick to deny.

CHAPTER FIVE

Skinhead Moonstomp

The boys from St Peter's stood in a bunch, nervously eyeing with a mixture of suspicion and curiosity the other groups of boys forming in the playground. Crowley Lane seemed huge compared to our little village school. It was a comprehensive, whatever that meant. We were smart in our blue blazers and our caps and felt very grown-up in long trousers for the first time. There had been a uniform at St Peter's but it was adhered to only according to financial ability. Jacko and I, for instance, wore a school tie occasionally. Hayton and Trevor, on the other hand, wore absolutely nothing resembling a uniform. Some boys had the full monty, down to the red tassels on their socks, all bought from Hedges, the 'department store' in the village.

Inside the school hall we were told our class numbers and filed off with our new classmates. Eddie Richards, who was from the estate, and I were designated to 1A, which I soon found out was the grammar stream, and Jacko got 1R. The R stood for 'remedial'. Very subtle. You might as well as have had a 1C (Clever Kids) and a 1T (Thick Kids). Jacko may not have excelled at school work, but he was as sharp as the next boy. Our new classroom was a hut made from wooden slats balanced on four big breeze blocks. Eddie and I, stupidly, scrambled to a pair of desks at the front of the class. A teacher followed us in.

She placed her black shiny handbag on the desk and glared at us all. We looked at her. She was the ugliest woman I had ever clapped eyes on. Her face was covered in large warts. She had a long nose with another wart hanging off the end for good measure. This gave a final focal point to what was a very pointed face, as though her head had somehow got sucked into a vacuum cleaner and had been prised out, like in the cartoons. She had straight black shiny hair and she wore a chiffon scarf around her neck. She always dressed as though she would later be handing out prizes at the church fête; as if the nice clothes and the feminine scarf could compensate for the fact she was pig ugly.

'Good morning, young ladies and young gentlemen. My name is Miss Douglas-Spark.' (*Miss* – I might have guessed.) 'I am your form teacher for the next year. I will also be teaching you music once a week. As your form teacher, we will be seeing a lot of each other. We have a lot to get through but I think it would be instructive if each of you were to stand up, tell the rest of us your name and a little bit about yourself – what subjects you like, what your hobbies are and anything else of interest.'

She looked down at me, 'We'll start with you . . . stand up then, boy.'

'My name is John Hay. I don't like any subjects and my hobby is watching telly.'

The class convulsed with loud laughter.

'So you're the class comedian, are you? I'll talk to you later. Next.'

A couple of days later she captured me in her music lesson when I was pretending to sing by opening and closing my mouth like a fish but emitting no sound. She stopped playing the piano and peered over the top of it. 'Hay, I don't think you

are singing,' she said. 'I think you should come to the front of
the class and sing for us all. Don't you?'

I stayed put.

'Hay, come up here and join me now.'

'I ain't singing, Miss.'

'Ain't? I'm sorry, I don't know any word like "ain't". What
does "ain't" mean, Hay?'

'I am not singing, Miss – not in front of the class.'

There was no way I was either. And she knew it. She also
knew that this wasn't the one to fight me on. Forcing someone
to sing in front of the class was not something a teacher could
argue was absolutely necessary.

'Well, if you don't want to sing in front of the class, you
make sure you sing along with the rest of the class. Understood?'

'Yes, Miss.'

She had lost face and she knew it. I had defied her and got
away with it. I'm sure she resolved that day to fuck me up one
way or another. And that was the start of my strained relationship with that grotesque woman.

Eddie and I were the only boys from the estate, or any
estate, in this class. I'm sure when they streamed the children it
was done by address over any academic ability, unless your old
school had made some sort of representation on your behalf.
This is what I reckon had happened with me and Eddie. St
Peter's must have said that we were capable but were mixing
with the wrong crowd: *give 'em a chance and they'll shine.* We
didn't know anyone else at all. The boys had names like Hugh
and the girls were Rowena or Philippa. They rode to school on
polished Claud Butler bikes and zipped open pencil cases to
reveal an enviable selection of protractors, rubbers, pencils and

posh fountain pens. They made no effort to befriend us nor us them. The only ones we bothered with were Keir and Colin Hubbard, identical twins with brown Beatle fringes and wide smiles. They lived up on Winhurst Heath deep in the stock-broker belt and their father was a doctor, a surgeon I think. They were soon to make quite an impact on me. Eddie was loyal but he was a quiet bloke by nature. He kept his head down whilst I established myself quickly as the class rebel and wag. The Hubbards didn't say a word either but I could tell they relished my cheek and antics. Soon they were making sure they sat near Eddie and me in most lessons.

It was on the second or third day that it really hit us all that life was to be different at Crowley Lane; that we were now living in a rougher world. We were in the first lesson with our new history master (who was known as Jesse on account of a finger-clicking and pointing movement he employed that reminded us of a Wild West gunslinger) when the door burst open and in walked Ben Smith, the thirteen-year-old brother of Sid. We knew Sid was married now and lived on the estate, but Ben was still with his parents on the permanent caravan site that lay just on the other side of Crowley Lane, and he was, in those days, unknown to us. Lanky, dark-skinned, long black hair and surly-looking: you could tell he was Sid's brother. He strode up to Jesse, put one arm around his neck in a stranglehold and with his free hand pushed Jesse's arm up his back.

'What d'you say about me?' demanded Ben.

'Ben, I've said nothing. Please unhand me.'

Ben jerked Jesse's arm up another notch. The teacher grimaced as we sat transfixed and a little bit scared at the drama being played out in front of us.

'You say anything else and it'll be my brother or the old man down here.' He let Jesse go and, as he strolled out of the classroom, he pointed backwards with his thumb. 'Don't take no notice of 'im. 'E's a tosser.'

Jesse brushed himself down and composed himself remarkably quickly. It occurred to me that this wasn't the first time something like this had happened to him.

'That was Ben Smith,' he explained to the class. 'He rarely comes to school but when he does he can be rather difficult. He is a problem pupil, I'm afraid.'

Careful what you say Jesse – you don't want it getting back to Ben.

Keir Hubbard leaned forward and whispered in my ear: 'I bet he comes from a broken caravan.'

That first summer at Crowley I became aware of two things for the first time, really: fashion and girls. Skinheads and skinhead fashion had swept the country like a bush-fire. I have no idea how and where it started but suddenly the entire youth of Britain seemed to be swaggering around in Fred Perry shirts, braces as thin as elastic bands, Levi's jeans and shiny Dr Marten army boots. The hair was cropped, hence the name, and reggae music was the religion. I can remember buying my neatly folded Levi's from Millets, the camping shop, and a tartan Stradbroke (the poor boy's Ben Sherman) off Sid the Yid at the market. I managed to cadge old black boots off an older boy on the estate who'd just been bought a new pair of burgundy highups for his thirteenth birthday.

There was even a version of the uniform we could wear to school and get away with it. A neat blue Ben Sherman, with the button-down collar, underneath a sleeveless jumper, and shiny Levi sta-prest or a dark pair of tonics as trousers and Ivy

Brogues or Royals on your feet. And don't forget the yellow socks. The skinhead cult consumed all. It formalised the social structure we operated under and it gave us our meaning. We got Saturday jobs to buy more clothes and records. We learned who all the older skinheads were and worked out where we fitted on that social ladder. History has overlooked how big and widespread the movement was. At our school, I would estimate that seventy per cent of the boys were skinheads, or at least seventy per cent followed the fashions. It was no minority fad and it lasted a good three years, which in the teenage frame is a long, long time.

The older and more committed skins descended on Hastings, Margate and other seaside resorts on Bank Holidays just like their older brothers, the mods, had done five years earlier. We watched it on the news: the police searching the youths as they alighted from train after train at Brighton station and making a pyre of the steel combs they took from almost every one. We got very excited one day when Paul Dowson, a boy two years above us, made the front page of a national tabloid christening his Cherry Reds on a prostrate greaser.

It didn't take long for the skinheads to cotton on to the fact that these beanos and mass displays of power and style could be had every other week at Chelsea, Millwall, Arsenal, Spurs or West Ham. The seaside invasions became a thing of the past. The ones that followed with subsequent mod or skinhead revivals were really only exercises in nostalgia, as unreal compared to the first time around as a tribute band.

Those coastal invasions were a sight to behold. Mum and Dad somehow managed to scrape the money together to take us kids down to Hastings most years and it was there, as I played on the West Hill when I was about eight, that my mum pointed and almost shrieked, 'Look at that!'

From the height of the West Hill you could look down and view the sea front and beach clearly. As far as the eye could see was a moving mass of black, like a swarm of beetles or a massive oil slick trickling away from the East Hill. We could make out little police cars edging alongside them at walking pace.

'Rockers,' Mum informed us.

Soon they were disappearing out of sight as they headed up towards the pier. My brother and I quickly scampered over to the other side of the hill where we could see further up the promenade. There was a similar mass of people here but not dressed in black and they were moving our way.

'Mods,' I breathed.

I probably hadn't been so excited since Mum had allowed me to go and see *A Hard Day's Night* at the Odeon with a bunch of my sister's screaming friends.

The two armies clashed but we couldn't see much as it was directly below us and the hill sort of overhung it. But we could see the rockers scatter in retreat fairly quickly like ants being dispersed by water. The full account of the 'Battle of Hastings 1966' was in the papers the next day. According to the journalist, a lot more seemed to have gone on and lasted a lot longer than what we had witnessed. I learned two things that day: one, that newspapers tend to exaggerate; and two, not to become a rocker when I got older.

The girls got into the skinhead thing almost as much as we did. Their hair was cut short on top with longish wisps left at the sides and at the back. Often these wisps had slides in to hold the strands in place. They'd wear a Ben Sherman, Brutus or a Fred Perry and a skirt and tights. At school they all carted their books and other paraphernalia around in wicker baskets. Whilst the fighting, football and seaside trips didn't hold the same fascination for them, they probably embraced the music more than the boys did. Reggae topped the list of likes, with Jimmy Cliff, Desmond Dekker and the *Tighten Up* albums prominent among most bedroom record collections. But Motown was almost as popular. It had to be black. It's strange that skinheads have been presented retrospectively as universally violently racist.

The fair on Winhurst Downs was where the local skinheads and youths of all other persuasions could display themselves to each other and the opposite sex. The fair came twice a year to coincide with the two big race meetings held on the Downs. It started on the Sunday night and climaxed the following Saturday. As dusk fell each evening, families and younger children would drift off clutching their goldfish won on the hoop-la and be replaced by youths from all over Winhurst and beyond.

I adored the fair as a little kid. I remember being amazed after it had left how the grass had been literally worn away in just a week, just through people walking around. I knew all the rides so well: the Dive Bomber that went so high you could see the Post Office tower when you were up there; the Rotor where you were stuck to the wall with no floor beneath you; the bumper cars, the Big Wheel and the newer rides where you were flung about in little cars on the end of long, mechanised arms. Then there was the Wall of Death, where one of our local skins rode a motorbike furiously round and round the walls of a deep cylinder. There were also the strip shows. The one I remember was a Wild West affair where a decrepit old man fired a gun and an item of the lady's clothing fell off until the tent was full of smoke and the girl stood there completely naked apart from a cowboy hat and false smile.

I remember, when I was an apprentice skinhead, passing a tent with a sign that read: 'REAL-LIFE WEREWOLF – COME INSIDE AND SEE THE LAST CAGED WEREWOLF IN ENGLAND – IF YOU DARE!' Real-life werewolf, my foot! But like a mug I handed the last of my pocket money to an old man sitting on a stool outside the tent and entered the dark space. In the middle was a cage and in the middle of the cage was a chair. Sitting on the chair was a perfectly still werewolf dressed in a Marks & Spencer shirt and trousers. What a con! Half a crown to look at a waxwork dummy! I ventured closer to the bars and must have snorted with derision, when the dummy suddenly sprang into life and roared. He parted the bars like they were rubber (which, obviously, they were) and chased me screaming out of the tent. I noticed the old man chuckling as I shot like a rocket into the safety of daylight and moving crowds of people. It took me a good five minutes to compose myself. I looked around me furtively to see if anyone I knew had spotted me.

A ring of trailers enclosed the fairground area. On peering inside any of them I would see luxury such as I had never come across before: china ornaments stood on polished walnut surfaces and lace curtains hung at the windows. You didn't get rooms like this on the Watermead. And in the middle of the floor was a large colour television. No one I knew had colour TV then. We'd seen them in the window of Granada – I'd even joined the crowd of about sixty people one Saturday afternoon pressed up against the shop window watching Ann Jones play tennis at Wimbledon. '*Look at that green grass,*' gasped the adults around me. Anyone would think the real world was in black and white then, not just the telly.

The last night, the Saturday, was when the fights were meant to happen. The fair would be winding down and couples would hurry across the road for the last bus back into town. All that would be left was a large gang of skinheads and a large gang of greasers eyeing each other as the dodgem men covered the cars with tarpaulin. In all the times I was there, I saw no more than a few insults exchanged, but local folklore told of running battles with the greasers using bicycle chains for weapons and the skinheads employing knives and clubs. Even though the evidence, or lack of it, was before our eyes, we never questioned whether these things really happened.

*

The first girl I had a crush on at the new school was Paula Harris. She was in my class and I soon established that she lived in a pleasant tree-lined road of old but spacious Victorian houses which were on the route home from school. I took to riding my bike up and down this road in the early evenings after school in the hope that I would run in to her – which, of course, I did, many times. Each time, naturally, I just put my head down and rode straight past without saying a word. Eventually a boy came out of the house next door to Paula's. I recognised his face from school. He was one of the gang, one of the boys, in the year above. In reality there was only a matter of months' difference in age between us but at that time, when seniority of years was an important and envied attribute, it could have been a decade.

'What the fucking 'ell you doing?' he demanded.

'What?' All innocent.

'You've been riding up and down past my house every night for the past fortnight looking in the windows. D'you fancy me or something?'

I don't know how I spluttered my way out of it, yet Vic Lewis and I somehow became best mates. The big house and the road were a bit misleading. It turned out his family were the only ones who were tenants. The house belonged to the mental home where Vic's dad worked as an administration manager, and it was theirs to live in as long as Vic's old man stayed in the job.

Vic was a real little skin. I went with him on the train to buy his 'made-to-measure' Crombie overcoat from a stall on Petticoat Lane. Fourteen pounds, his dad paid, an absolute fortune and certainly more than his father's weekly wage at the time. I stood next to him hundreds of times as he groomed his hair (there was none of it) in the gilded mirror in his hallway and adjusted his red silk handkerchief in the top pocket of the treasured Crombie. It wasn't until many years later that I let on to Vic the real reason that whenever he glanced out his bedroom window he saw me cruising past one way and then the other, leaning back on my back-rest and gripping my apehanger handlebars as I shot sneaky glances over in his direction.

The real skinheads went to the Methodist Hall in Winhurst every Friday night and this was second only to the Chelsea Shed in the league table of forbidden places we would love to go but weren't allowed. The Methodist was a green wooden hut-like building in the middle of town that held dances (rapidly becoming known as discos) on a Friday night. This was where records were first heard, new clothes displayed, boys met girls and girls met boys, but also where, most importantly, reputations were won and lost. Fighting, or one's ability to fight or not, soon became an indicator of where you stood on the social ladder and the yardstick of the respect your peers held you in. It was a point of great discussion as to who could 'do' or 'have' whom. Some clever people got away with having one fight and living off it for the rest of their youth. They may even have lost but comments like 'He's not that hard but he don't half have a go' or 'Don't start on him 'cos even if you beat him he'll always come back for more' were enough to deter potential attackers. Others were even cleverer, rising to the top of the ladder without ever having a fight. Somehow they sent out subliminal messages that it would be a mistake even to challenge them, and got away with it. Others survived and sometimes flourished simply by having older brothers who were well respected or sisters who went out with the faces who were well respected. Having said this, though, what was on offer at the Methodist, week in week out, were the local skinheads establishing their reputations the hard way by viciously fighting one another.

Vic, who had already got in at the Methodist with his older sister, persuaded me to lie to my parents and go there with him one Friday night. I was twelve and he was thirteen and I told my parents we were going to see *2001: A Space Odyssey* at the Odeon cinema. Vic told me the story to the film in case they quizzed me. Only afterwards did he admit that he'd never seen the film either and the story he'd told me was a complete fabrication. Instead of going to the pictures we hopped on the bus, smart in our Prince of Wales check Harrington jackets and stinking of Brut aftershave, and set off for the big night. Outside we joined the queue and looked in awe at the local legends milling around. There was Dave Green, 'leader of the Winhurst', Vic whispered in my ear, Pugsley Pullinger and Bernie Walsh. Pugsley even came over and spoke to Vic, an acknowledgement that, in our eyes at least, boosted our credibility no end. 'Pugs', as he was known to his mates, was a chunky, thickset boy who had been given his unflattering nickname because of his likeness as a child to a character in TV's *The Adams Family*. He was only in the year above Vic, but by fighting boys and men years older than him, he had established a fearsome reputation already. He was still only fifteen but he knocked around with Dave, Bernie and the others, all of whom had been out at work for some time.

As we passed through the entrance and paid our money a huge man covered in tattoos and wearing a dangling earring stamped our hands and then shone an infra-red torch on them to check the stamp had worked. He looked down at Vic and me and smiled. 'Right, you two – no trouble, okay?'

Everyone laughed. Vic and I weren't sure how to respond to the piss-take.

A big girl in a two-tone tonic suit said, 'Leave 'em alone, Lou – they're really sweet,' and she ushered us through to the main hall.

'*Never-been-a-sinner,*
I've-never-sinned,
I-got-a-friend-in-Jesus'

The words pulsated out of two massive speakers at the top of the room. A group of girls were doing a dance that involved standing in a ring and doing a few synchronised steps that culminated in them all making one final stride into the middle of the circle they had formed, as the verses of 'Spirit in the Sky' reached their climax. Plastic orange bucket chairs lined the four walls of the hall and it was around these that the majority of people stood or sat. A makeshift bar dispensed cokes and fruit drinks – the place obviously wasn't licensed – but almost everyone was puffing or holding a cigarette.

The hall darkened and the DJ activated his new disco light show, which consisted of a searchlight, throwing off coloured

rays, that he could swing around the hall when he remembered.
A record began that started with the demand:

'Come on all you skinheads,
Get up on your feet,
Put your braces together,
Put your boots on your feet.'

Everyone was up on the dance-floor doing a strange little
writhing movement on their own and barely moving from the
same spot. I'd never heard music this loud. I'd never seen so
many 'famous' people in one place. I'd never been so elated just
standing around looking at people and listening to music.

Because I was eagerly drinking in everything that was going
on around me I think I was the first inside to notice the two
dozen black youths pushing through the main door into the
hall. Nearly all of them wore black Crombie overcoats on top
of white Ben Sherman shirts. They all had close-cropped hair
with partings cut in, and they were making a lot of noise. The
big doorman was remonstrating with two or three of them at
the desk but the others had just pushed through and stood, feet
apart, backs to the wall, facing the Winhurst skinheads who
were by now beginning to turn around and size up the situation. These guys were definitely not local. The only blacks in
Winhurst were from Beechurst, the children's home at Belstead,
and everyone knew them all. This lot were here for a reason and
their body language made it pretty clear what that was.

A fairly inoffensive bloke called Chris Fitt walked past the
group as he crossed the dance-floor. Chris's antennae had not
picked up the vibes. One of the black guys stepped forward and
nutted him. I had never seen the human head used as a weapon,
either in real life or on the TV. It struck me as so much more
graceful than punching or kicking someone. Poor Chris collap-

sed to the floor, holding his bleeding nose, as the strangers stepped forward and laid in to the shocked Winhurst skins. Girls
started screaming and people began running in all directions.
Problem was, the visitors were bunched around the door, the
only way out. Vic and I stood up on our chairs. This gave us a
clearer view of proceedings whilst at the same time hopefully
sending the signal that we were clearly not in this fight and also
showed that we were only nine and a half foot tall between us.

The blacks were showing the Winhurst lot a thing or two
about fighting, when a couple of things happened that tipped
the balance. Firstly, Lou the doorman, who was by far the oldest
person present, steamed through the mêlée, laying out one after
another with his huge mallet-like fists. Secondly, Pugsley Pullinger grabbed their leader, the boy who threw the first head-butt,
in a headlock and ran him across the dance-floor, smashing his
face into the wall like some human battering-ram. There were a
couple of brothers, the Wheatleys, there, and tonight was the
night their reputation was established. Up until then they were
known but they hadn't seemed too interested in climbing the
social ladder. One of them picked up an empty Coke bottle,
smashed it against the wall and jabbed it into the face of the big
black youth who was trying to wrestle Pugsley off his leader.

Girls screamed as blood spurted through the boy's fingers as
he covered his face. Vic and I held each other's forearms and
almost forgot to breathe. Fear and excitement stiffened our
bodies. Ryan Wheatley smashed a bottle over another bloke's
head and knocked him out.

The black boys started to run out of the Methodist and over
to the station to catch a train back up to Clapham Junction or
Vauxhall or wherever they had come from. By the time the police
came charging in, truncheons drawn, all that was left was

splattered blood, broken glass and a bunch of young skinheads. They stood in the middle of the dance-floor, shoulders heaving, fists clenched but smiling and acknowledging the congratulations of the less brave or reckless among their number. Steve and Ryan Wheatley had taken the fight to a level no one had really seen previously, and Pugsley had shown the stamina and bottle to take on anyone. They were never to be viewed in quite the same way again. That night they eclipsed Dave Green who, at twenty years of age, was the skin that everyone else looked up to. Pugsley and the Wheatley brothers became the nucleus of 'the Winhurst lot' who, as they grew older, became increasingly violent and feared.

Fortunately, I was not there a couple of weeks later when those London boys came back. This time there were more of them. The Wheatley brothers ended up in hospital; one had a fractured skull and the other had been cut up his back with a long knife. This served only to enhance their reputation and deepen the legend that was rapidly growing up around them.

Against this backdrop of gang and individual violence, it was natural that we would soon want to flex our own young muscles. We did this mainly with small groups of boys of our own age, when we were careful not to really hurt each other, or in the occasional playground brawl. Jacko was the first one to take it a little bit further.

Besides Bob, he was the biggest among us and had started to fill out first, but I always thought of him as having not a violent bone in his body. On Saturdays we had a ritual of strolling into Winhurst and visiting Boots, where there were three booths where you could stand and listen to a record you were thinking of purchasing. The staff at Boots got tired of us, hogging these booths, knowing we had no intention, or means, of buying anything. Jacko had asked to hear 'Storm in a Teacup' by The

Fortunes and I could see him nodding his head in time to the beat and mouthing the lyrics:

'*One drop of a rain on your window pane,*

Doesn't mean to say there is a thunderstorm coming . . .'

as I flicked through the album covers. Keir Hubbard had briefly shown me a Jimi Hendrix album with nude women on the front and I was keen to find this. Then the manager appeared. He was a little bloke of about twenty-five whose face we knew well from his constant patrols of the store. In case anyone thought he was a kid dressing up, he wore a badge on his lapel with the word MANAGER written on it in big red letters. 'Come on, you boys, clear off. You've been here long enough.'

I stopped my search and turned around in preparation to leave and maybe give the bloke some lip on the way out, but Jacko continued to drum his fingers against his thigh and listen to the music. The manager signalled over to one of the sales girls to take the record off the turntable. When the music stopped suddenly, Jacko sarcastically said thanks to the manager, took his earphones off and we both turned and headed for the down escalator. In a stupid attempt to underline his authority to his sales girls, or maybe because we were leaving so obediently, the manager gave Jacko a little shove in the small of his back as we passed him. Before I knew it, Jacko had swung round and hit the manager on the chin with a force I couldn't have imagined. It lifted the guy off the floor and sent him flying backwards into a rack of Kodak film. We leapt down the escalators and ran laughing hysterically out into the High Street. I don't think Jacko understood what he had done. He was as puzzled as I was when we went over and over the course of events as we walked home. We'd barely reached our teens and hadn't really got to the stage of answering adults back let alone knocking them out.

CHAPTER SIX

Victims

Back in school, as my hair was getting shorter, the Hubbard twins' hair was growing longer. I got along fine with them but they had less and less to do with anyone else bar each other and a few blokes from other classes who shared their interests and increasingly rebellious outlook. These interests consisted mainly of going to the Harlequin record shop after school and listening to new albums by Jimi Hendrix, Janis Joplin or Jefferson Airplane. As the terms went by, their musical taste became more and more obscure and I found it hard to take them seriously. It was they who had lent me *Sgt Pepper's Lonely Hearts Club Band* when we first met and then *Ogden's Nut Gone Flake* with its threepenny-bit cover. Later they put me on to Neil Young and the new mellow Cat Stevens. But soon they were raving about bands I'd never heard of. When we first met, it was our mutual love of The Beatles and The Stones that had drawn us together but the people they told me about now I had never listened to. *Melody Maker* and *New Musical Express* were bulging with features on these mainly American bands but I had not taken any notice. They handed me an album by a band called Grand Funk Railroad. 'Listen to this man, it'll really turn you on.'

Man? Turn me on? Their Afghan coats and their long hair

were turning them weird. The bulk of the school had decided to pin their colours to either the T Rex or Slade mast. As it happened, the girls generally followed Marc Bolan and the boys plumped for Noddy and company. Personally, I couldn't take seriously anyone who wrote lyrics like 'She ain't no witch but I like the way she twitch' or 'Jungle-face Jake, Jungle-face Jake, make no mistake about Jungle-face Jake'. I took the Hubbards' LP home and played it on my brother's new tinny stereo. As I suspected, it was absolute shit: a con. In my book this whole progressive music thing was a con on a par with modern art, nouvelle cuisine and French avant-garde films. I was surprised the twins had been taken in by it.

'You can't honestly say this is as good as say . . . *Abbey Road*,' I started off diplomatically.

'John, Grand Funk are going to be much, much bigger than The Beatles,' they replied earnestly. It was at that point I knew we really were growing up in different directions. They were hippies and soon became the focal point for the few other boys in the school who had rejected the skinhead street culture. They sat at the bottom of the school field, keeping themselves to themselves, smoking (normal cigarettes, I think) and discussing music or laughing hysterically over the previous night's *Monty Python's Flying Circus* episode, the more extrovert members of their group re-enacting sketches and impersonating dead parrots to great shared hilarity. They were reading George Orwell and Aldous Huxley when the rest of us, if reading at all, were being weaned off Enid Blyton and the Jennings books. They had a racket going hiring out *Knave, Forum* and other sex mags they had pinched on the way home from school the previous day. By the third year they were regular dope smokers and by the fourth they were dropping acid. They won the admiration of the whole school when they famously poured another kind of acid over one of the teachers' cars and then managed to splash themselves with it whilst running away. One boy was badly burned and never returned to the school.

I was horrified when the twins became a target for the school bullies. It started almost innocently but developed into something quite nasty. A boy called Campbell had joined the school. I suppose he was only trying to make friends but he had a rather stupid habit of inviting people to punch him as hard as they could in the stomach. He was able to tense his stomach muscles to such a degree that even the hardest punch seemed to have no effect. Indeed, when I tried it, I hurt my hand. He was displaying his bizarre party trick on the school field one day to the Hubbards and company when Kenny Baird, renowned as the best fighter in the school but a bully to boot, strolled up with his mates in tow. 'Can I have a go?' Kenny said.

Campbell braced himself. Baird stepped back and then punched Campbell with all his force straight on the chin. The younger boy was knocked unconscious. Baird and the others carried on walking and laughing across the field towards the shops for their lunch-time chips when Keir Hubbard, I think it was, shouted after them: 'That wasn't very fair.'

Baird stopped and turned. His entourage stopped and turned. Hubbard's crowd stopped trying to comfort Campbell and backed away. All eyes were on Keir with a 'you shouldn't have said that' look.

Baird stood in front of Keir and stared at him. 'What did you say?'

'I said that wasn't very fair.'

'D'you want to make something of it?'

'No, I don't. I just said I didn't think that was very fair.'

Baird brought his knee up and thrust it slowly but surely into Keir's groin.

'Cunt!' gasped Keir as he lurched forward.

Baird grabbed the twin's shirt, pulled Keir towards him, lined him up and headbutted him cleanly on the nose.

'Cunt,' said Hubbard again, barely flinching, and looking Baird in the eye. Baird then attempted to kick Keir's legs away but lost his balance and almost fell over. The older boy then threw a punch that missed. Keir remained silent and still.

'Don't ever cheek me again!' snarled Baird, signalling that was the end of the incident and walked off.

Keir Hubbard came out with some dignity, having remonstrated with the so-called hardest boy in the school. He had stood his ground although he hadn't hit back. Baird, I believe, was a bit spooked by him but this began a series of confrontations between the older boys, Baird's bullies, and the Hubbards and their long-haired, peace-loving followers. As the twins were identical, whatever trouble one got in had to be faced equally by the other.

My behaviour in 2A was getting worse. I resented being in a class where we had a curriculum to follow and were expected to work towards some sort of O or A level, when my pals were in classes where the idea was containment not attainment. Nothing was expected of them and they came and went almost as they pleased. I was forever being berated with the line: 'Hay, you may not want to learn but the rest of people in this class do', and suchlike.

In one lesson that revolting old bag Douglas-Spark took exception to something I did. 'I'll have you demoted to the B stream, Hay, if you continue to misbehave!' she threatened.

'Yes, please, Miss, I'd like that very much,' I replied, and so began a negotiation between the school, my parents and me that ended in my demotion to 2B.

We really were a shower of shit. The worst boys in the school were in this class, Sloan and Higgs, especially. Jacko and Big Bob were here now too, Jacko having fought his way out of the humiliating R class. We did no work and the school had a full-time job just preventing us from preventing the school functioning. We didn't really become uncontrollable until the third, fourth and fifth years, but even then, at the ages of twelve and thirteen, we must have been a nightmare.

Mr Pelham, our form teacher in the third year, summed up the scenario when he introduced himself to us on the first day of a new term: 'Right, let's get a few things straight. You are young adults and I will treat you with respect, but I am an old adult so I would like you to treat me with respect. I know many of you are just counting the days until you can bugger off out of here but there are some who want to work and you must treat them with respect. I have to earn a living and unfortunately this is what I've ended up doing, so let me get on with it and I'll let you get on with whatever it is you want to do. If you walk out of this place having learnt respect for other people, that'll probably get you further in life than any maths I can ever try to teach you.'

It was a strange little speech from a strange angular man with a whining nasal voice. But he was as good as his word. He never set those of us who were not interested any work; he just pulled a few of the girls and boys over to one corner of the classroom and gave them close tuition. We were almost jealous.

Not all the teachers were so pragmatic. We still had the charade of a music lesson once a week with Miss Douglas-Spark. Her frustrations with our total disinterest and rowdiness got the better of her one afternoon. She slammed down the walnut piano lid. Her face was never uglier.

'Have any of you ever thought of what you are going to do when you leave school? When you have to make your own way in the big bad world?'

Before anyone could respond, she went on: 'No, I thought not. Well, take it from me, no one owes you a living and it's hard out there. All this you're getting for nothing . . . what's so amusing, Hay?' She had seen me smirking. 'Well?'

I was loath to answer but my brain was furiously working out a way I could set a trap for her. She was in a temper and was vulnerable. 'Miss, be honest: how is music going to benefit any of us lot? How many of us are going to be music teachers?'

The class sniggered but she rose to the bait and went for me with her tongue. 'Hay . . . yes, Hay,' she drawled like my name had conjured up some unpleasant taste in her mouth. 'And what do you think you're going to do when you leave school? What do you want to do when you leave school?'

I didn't answer at first but she said something about a cat getting my tongue.

'Actually, Miss, I do know what I want to be when I leave.'

'Really. Please enlighten us, Hay. What is it? Brain surgeon? Nuclear scientist?' Her tone was weighted with heavy sarcasm.

'No, Miss, I want to be a dustman.'

The crowd laughed aloud and I could see Douglas-Spark's plumage fan out. 'A dustman. Well, what an illustrious career that is, Hay. You want to throw your life away clearing up other people's rubbish, do you?'

She was walking into this so easily.

'What's wrong with being a dustman?'

'What is wrong with being a dustman?' she repeated slowly

and looked at the class and then looked at me and then looked at the class again, hoping this was holding me up for public ridicule.

'Yeah, what is wrong with it, Miss?' I replied, pretending to be offended, 'Higgs's dad's a dustman – ain't he, Jeff?'

Jeff Higgs nodded. Douglas-Spark was literally speechless. I smiled up at her as she went bright red. I'm not sure if she was embarrassed for herself, or maybe Jeff, or whether she was incandescent with rage that I had suckered her into rubbishing one of the pupils' parents.

When I was in the third year it was time for Vic to leave and enter the working world. I would have to stay on for another two years as the school-leaving age had just been raised to sixteen. We were called ROSLA (Raising of the School Leaving Age) year. Vic was in the last rump of those who could be let loose at fifteen. He had signed up to be an apprentice painter and decorator with a local firm. Vic was not at all nervous. Even at that age, he was one of those people who didn't give a shit about anyone or anything. His capacity to be rude to people, whether they were adult, family or friend, astounded me. What was in his head just came out of his mouth. He couldn't help it. Like me, he strongly resented authority, but with Vic it didn't stop there. He was racist, sexist, facist – almost anything -ist. He called a spade a spade but more often than not a coon or a black bastard. He was also a really nice bloke. Remember, these were the days when Jim Davidson was soon to make his living by impersonating an over-the-top West Indian, and when one of the top TV sitcoms was *Love Thy Neighbour* which featured a white man abusing his 'Sambo' neighbour for half an hour every week. These were the days when large swathes of the country were paralysed with fear by Tony Benn, and later

Arthur Scargill, and their apparent communist agenda. Being racist and right-wing was, at that time, politically correct.

Ronnie Matthews was just about the only black boy in the school. He was from Beechurst, the local children's home that took in orphans and 'unwanted' children from inner London. As a young boy he'd had to tolerate being approached by adults in the street, usually women, who wondered if he minded if they touched his hair. ''Ere, Renee, feel this! It's like cotton wool!'

Even my own grandmother was guilty of this type of insensitivity and ignorance. I took Ronnie on the train one day to Battersea to a reggae shop on Lavender Hill and we dropped in to see her. She made us both a cup of tea and offered me a sandwich. 'Do 'e want a banana?' she said in all seriousness as if he wasn't in the room.

Ronnie took it all in his stride, though. We became great friends. My mum doted on him. He was so genuinely polite with all our parents – unlike most of us, who had to make a mental note before entering someone's house not to spit. Maybe his institutional background was responsible, but his pleases and thank-yous were heartfelt. He never wanted to go back up to Beechurst at his curfew time, preferring to sit in our lounge, jammed up on the settee with all of us watching *The Newcomers*, but Mum would gently urge him to go and catch his bus. 'I think we might as well adopt you, Ronnie, the amount of time you spend around here,' she joked once, but failed to notice Ronnie's attempt to force eye-contact.

Shortly before Vic left, a cascade of bullying took place that I somehow got roped into. Vic had punched Rodney Reynolds, a boy in his year. Rodney used to be teased endlessly because he was what was then called a 'poof'. All that description meant at the time was that he did what teachers said, produced home-work and wore a school uniform. Then, in our circles, 'poof' had no sexual connotations. I think Rod the Mod, as he was known, bit one day and turned on Vic. To save face, Vic beat him up. I wasn't there but I don't believe he hurt him badly. Like me, Vic was only small and not very powerful.

Reynolds could play football well and he was in the school team with Kenny Baird and others. Kenny heard about what had happened and one lunchtime pulled up Vic as they ate their chips outside the fish bar that had become the main meeting-place at lunchtimes. 'If you want to pick on someone, pick on me,' challenged Kenny, which was a bit rich coming from the master bully.

Vic was never short of a reply. 'You're twice my size, Kenny, I'll fight you with a mate and that'll be fair.'

Kenny agreed and Vic put my name up, in my absence, as his partner. Thanks a bunch, Vic. The rendezvous was made for after school that evening and I suddenly found events over-taking me. When Vic told me, I could barely breathe that after-noon as the clock ticked away to three-thirty. I contemplated feigning sickness or running away from home – anything to get me off the hook. I knew in my heart that the two of us stood no chance against this street-fighting lump.

The fight was scheduled for four in the park and when the school gates opened it seemed like everyone was heading in one direction. This was the biggest attraction since Ronnie Corbett had turned up at our local football club in the Showbiz Eleven match.

Like true boxers we walked to the venue together past the running track and the brick toilet block down to the river. Our entourages were of fairly equal size but there was no banter. No one wanted to identify too closely with either side, most of them, unbelievably, not being sure who would come out victorious. I badly wanted to fart but didn't dare: shitting myself was becoming a squelching reality. Vic didn't seem too worried. He either hid it well or he had an unreal confidence in our joint fighting ability. Whilst he was chatting with others about last week's episode of *Budgie*, I was contemplating my very existence. I was finding it hard not to cry. We reached the rope swing over the river and some young boys already there swung across to the other side of the bank and ran off. The crowd of around sixty boys stepped back to make room and the three of us just stood there in the middle, looking at each other.

Vic, never one to hang around, charged at Kenny like a bull, head down, and punched blindly in the air. Equally, like a matador, Kenny sidestepped him, grabbed his passing head and held him in a headlock. I jumped on Baird from behind and attempted to pull him over backwards. But he wouldn't go. I was hanging around his neck like a kid getting a piggy-back from his dad whilst he was punching Vic's framed head.

'Okay, I've had enough,' cried Vic.

The bigger boy let him drop to the floor. He shook me off and I stepped backwards towards the river. Baird's boot shot out and caught me in the upper legs. I made more of the impact than it actually was and allowed myself to tumble down the bank into the water. A huge round of applause and laughing went up. Then he turned around and booted Vic full in the face, almost taking his head off. Vic started to cry as the blood filled his mouth and spilled out between his lips.

'You've had it, Baird – you're a dead man!' he spluttered through the claret, teeth and tears.

To my shame, I was taking my time getting out of the river

in case I got the same. Kenny Baird took a cigarette from one of the spectators and lit up. 'You're out of your league, Vic, and as for you, Hay, do yourself a favour and stay in the river.'

More laughter. He turned, and fifty-five of the sixty-odd audience followed him, swaggering out of the park. Jacko, Big Bob, Tony Bond and a couple of others helped us up and generally comforted us, shaking their heads and trying to make us feel better as they contemplated the terrible fate that was awaiting Kenny Baird. I'd got off lightly, though. It wasn't blatantly obvious I had bottled, but I knew that basically I'd taken a dive and I think Vic knew but he was too good a mate to say anything.

Keith Nelson, who we all assumed was one of Kenny Baird's entourage but was a quiet boy who kept himself to himself, stood there with us for a while. We weren't sure why. 'You did well standing up to him,' he eventually said. 'I should have helped you.'

Why he should have helped us, we had no idea. Neither of us knew him particularly well. 'I hate fucking bullies,' he added. Keith became a firm friend and from that day on he knocked around with us a lot. He was always the quiet one. Didn't say much, just looked on and laughed at our antics, but was always fiercely loyal.

The following Saturday me and Vic were examining the latest Oxford bag trousers on Sid the Yid's stall in Winhurst when Pugsley Pullinger came along. By now Pugsley was legendary in the area. He had filled out even more and his face was beginning to show the signs of a seasoned fighter: flat nose, puffy eyes and small scars all over. He noticed Vic's still bruised lips and missing teeth and we told him what happened. Pugsley said he'd pay a visit to our school on Monday at 3.30. I didn't take too much notice of this. Really, we were nothing to Pugsley.

I'd almost forgotten about his promise when from my class-room window a bike and a flying white coat flashed past my line of vision. Pugsley delivered wet fish and here he was slamming on the brakes of his trades bike in the centre of the playground. When the bell went I ran out of the classroom and approached him.

'All right, John? Where's Vic? Where's this Kenny Baird geezer?'

Quite a few people in the playground recognised this brawny youth and they were nudging one another and looking over. It was as if Peter Osgood had appeared in our midst. Vic soon arrived in the playground. He looked at me as if to say, 'Oh-oh, what have we done here?'

'Where's Kenny Baird?' Pugsley demanded, aggressively scanning the faces of all around him.

'Thanks for coming, Pugs, but maybe leave it, eh? There was two of us on to him, after all.'

I could see Vic was questioning the wisdom of this escala-tion. Unfortunately, Baird appeared before anyone could answer. He knew Pugsley even if Pugsley didn't know him. And when he saw the town hardnut with us, he knew the score straight away.

I thought about the sound of Kenny Baird's boot leather as it connected with Vic's mouth. 'That's him,' I said, pointing.

Pugsley called Baird over with a flick of his head. 'I don't like bullies.'

It was getting surreal now. Pugsley made a slight circling movement of his head as if he was uncoiling his neck, and smashed his forehead down on Kenny's nose. Kenny fell to his knees as blood streamed from both nostrils like someone had turned the taps on.

'Get up, you cunt!' screamed Pugsley.

Kenny stood back up, careful to keep his hands by his sides so as not to antagonise his attacker. *Crack! Crack!* A left to the jaw and then a right putting his jolting head back in the upright position. He then performed his party trick: holding Kenny's collar and his jumper, he ran him in to the toilet wall, like we had seen him do at the Methodist Hall, time and time again until Baird collapsed in a puddle of hair, blood and teeth on the ground.

A teacher approached as Pugsley was mounting his bike. 'Gangway! What is going on here?' he demanded as the crowd slowly parted to let him through.

'Fuck off, mate, or you'll get some too,' jeered Pugs as he steered his bike past the teacher and swerved out of the playground with a cheery wave.

It's frightening to think how bad the bullying was at Crowley. In some cases, boys had been secure only a matter of months earlier, at schools where they'd taken watercolour paintings or gaudily daubed papier-mâché ashtrays home as gifts to their parents, in houses where they'd sat indoors among cushions and toys and watched *Blue Peter* whilst Mum prepared tea in the kitchen. And then they transferred up to senior school and their world was blown apart but they couldn't tell anyone. Because, truth is, only the bravest or most foolhardy kid ever tells their parents they are being bullied, and nine times out of ten the bullies only go for the kids they know won't tell their parents. That is a big blow, perhaps the biggest, on the path out of childhood – the moment you realise that your parents can't actually protect you when it comes down to it. It is on a par with sussing out Father Christmas doesn't exist when you're six or the realisation that your mummy or daddy might die one day.

Take Mancub. What happened to him troubles me still. He appeared in our class in the fourth year. Pelham told us a little about him before he actually appeared: 'Next week a boy called Thomas Wolf will be joining the class. Now, I am appealing to you to treat this boy with respect. He has had a difficult time, a very difficult time. He's been at Watermead School but has suffered at the hands of bullies and his parents have decided to send him to us. Now, you lot are a load of things, but one thing you are not is bullies. I know that. And that is why I suggested to Mr Bradfield that we take Thomas in to this class. I'm not asking you to give him any special treatment. Welcome him, accept him, respect him . . . under no circumstances are you to ask him about his experiences at Watermead.'

This was quite an introduction and aroused our curiosity no end. Living on the Watermead, it wasn't hard to find out more about Wolf from the boys on the estate who attended the local school. One of the Miles lads explained that the older boys at Watermead had beaten the kid up on a regular basis and that he had been off school for months.

'Why?'

'Why what?'

'Why did they beat him up?'

'Don't know. Some people reckoned he smelt, some people reckoned he's queer. Don't know, really. They just all picked on old Mancub.'

'Mancub?'

'Yeah, Mancub. That's what they call him. They say he was brought up by Wolfs, so he's a Mancub – you know, *Jungle Book* and all that?'

I suppose I was the first bloke at Crowley to do him a dis-service because I told everyone in the class he was called Mancub and why before he even arrived. When he turned up you couldn't help but pity him. He had the most pronounced twitch for one thing, and he was noticeably ragged. It reminded me of the time Hayton was first paraded in front of us at junior school some six years earlier. But, unlike Hayton, Tommy Wolf did not have the same presence or confidence. He hung his head and studied the floor as Pelham introduced him. His com-plexion was a grubby brown, like he needed a good wash. On his upper lip grew a noticeable bumfluff moustache that made him look older than his years. His clothes were a mixture of the Watermead and Crowley uniforms. Right jumper, wrong tie. Grey first-day trousers rode up his leg to reveal thick red-and-white woollen football socks, and for shoes he wore open-toed sandals, 'Jesus bashers' or 'Jesus boots', the boys called them. They were the ultimate in 'sissy' clothing in this fashion-conscious school where your life was barely worth living if you wore a Tesco shirt to school rather than a Ben Sherman or a Brutus. People like Mancub had long ago abandoned any stab at trying to compete in the fashion stakes.

He sat down at the front and from behind all I could see was his head twitching away and his fringe bouncing up and down as his head spasmed. Of all the places to send him, I thought. He didn't speak unless spoken to and when you did make conversation he chose his replies carefully. He looked no person in the eye – boy or girl – and mumbled out simple mono-syllabic answers. Mancub wasn't taking any chances, thinking that sooner or later one of us was going to turn on him. He lived up Winhurst Heath way, a pocket of the area where rural Winhurst still survived. Heath people still lived off the land to an extent and the kids went out with nets and ferrets and caught rabbits. The adults drank in The Heath pub and the main families all seemed to be inter-married – a community within a community.

Mancub was a bright kid. He knew better than to volunteer answers to the teachers but when he was forced to explain something he could. Sometimes he'd help some of the others out with their homework. One day, at our insistence, he brought his ferret in to school and dazzled us by putting it down his trousers. We didn't go overboard but we allowed him to become part of our group, a fringe member but nevertheless a part. His twitch started to disappear or maybe we just noticed it a little less.

Tony Bond teased him endlessly but then Bond teased everyone and Mancub knew this and didn't take it too person-ally. The belief that Mancub had homosexual tendencies fol-lowed him from Watermead to Crowley. There was absolutely no foundation for this, his desire to survive overriding sexual urges of any kind, I would think. The *Jesus Christ Superstar* musical was out at the time, and Bond adapted the words to the title song as follows:

'*Tommy Wolf,*

Superqueer,

How many bums have you had this year?'

Mancub would just smile a sad smile and get on with whatever he was doing.

Shortly before we left school, most of the boys in the class arranged a night sleeping out on Box Hill. I asked Mancub if he wanted to come.

'Are you sure?'

He was shocked that he'd been invited. He came along and

amused us by not bringing a sleeping-bag or any food and finally falling asleep in the moonlight with a knife the size of a small sword strapped to his hip.

If we had such a thing as a head pupil, Nigel Lassky would have been it. He was in the 'A' stream and was destined to stay on long after all us lot had gone. He excelled at games, playing for the district football team and running for the county. He was big and strong and among his peers was much admired and looked up to.

I suppose if you had split the school into social groups for analysis there were three obvious ones: the louts, the hippies and the swots. We were the louts: troublemakers with no academic interest, followers of skinhead and suedehead fashions, supporters of Chelsea, Fulham or Palace, and the children of manual workers, we were by far the largest group in the school. The hippies, typified by the Hubbard twins, were quiet and surly but perhaps as rebellious as the above group. They were intellectual but not necessarily hard-working, liked heavy rock music and soft drugs, supported CND and were the children of professional people. They made up the smallest of the three groups. The swots were Nigel Lassky's group. They wore school uniform, were good at games, tried hard at their school work, steered clear of both other groups, supported Arsenal (because they'd won the double) or Manchester United or Liverpool, and were children of white-collar workers and aspiring middle-classers. This was the group that the school *wished* made up the majority.

How Nigel Lassky and Mancub crossed paths initially I don't know, but I'll never forget the day Lassky did what he did. We were queuing outside the Art Room to enter a lesson as the other class – Lassky's – filed out. Nigel towered above all the others and he spotted Mancub leaning up against the wall. It all happened so quickly. I just saw Lassky's fists raining down on Mancub as he slid down the wall. He must have thrown ten punches in five seconds and Mancub was lying on the floor. Lassky walked off and we rolled him over. Tommy Wolf's nose was crushed and blood pumped from his mouth like a small oil well. His whole body jerked like he was having a fit. The blood ran down the corridor towards the Art Room door. Two teachers appeared and carried Mancub away. It was the last time we ever saw him.

I hated myself afterwards because I knew I could have done something. Nigel Lassky may have been big and strong but he was in the wrong social group. He'd never have attacked me if I had tried to stop him – not because I was any match for him physically, but because I knew people, people he would not have mixed it with under any circumstances. The thought of Pugsley Pullinger coming down to see him, for instance, would have prompted him to consider suicide. There was, maybe, a tiny chance that he would have turned around and battered me too, and I was sufficiently scared, truth be told, not to take that tiny chance. Not long before I had gone down the rope swing to fight the feared Kenny Baird with Vic because I couldn't have faced Vic otherwise. Facing Mancub was not an issue.

The bullying didn't just extend to boys, and it wasn't just physical. Cheryl Wilde suffered in a way that no person should suffer. I'm surprised she didn't commit suicide and wherever she is now I am sure the horrors of her schooldays remain. I hope not, but I am sure they do. Cheryl came from a poor family and dressed very shabbily. The boys (and some of the girls) called her 'Gypo' but if she really had been a gypsy they wouldn't have dared do this. The point was a lot of the kids came from poor families and wore hand-me-downs and the like – Cheryl was one of many. She was ugly, or at least that was the theory, but again there were girls in the school who were as 'ugly' as her or worse. So I don't know why she was singled out in the way she was. My guess, and this makes it worse, is that it was one of those silly nasty things that just escalated. I reckon someone started giving her some stick – *Don't sit near me, Wilde, you stink* – and a few others copied and then it became a school thing. An in-joke for everyone except Cheryl.

As she walked down the corridor boys would jump out of her way, screaming as if she carried some contagious disease. In class no girl would sit next to her lest they become victims by association. In the playground, people routinely pinched their noses as she passed to signify a bad odour, and eventually a noise evolved that was emitted when 'Wilde was around'. It was like the honk of a seal, and wherever the poor girl went in the school it was to the accompaniment of this cruel and grotesque noise. Her name slipped into the school language. You could be discussing another boy, for example:

'Has he got a sister?'

'Yeah, but she's right ugly.'

'What, worse than Wilde?'

'Oh no, not as bad as Wilde.'

Like Mancub, in my eyes, she had a real dignity. She never bit, never cried (at school at least), and turned up to lessons every day. She ignored the jibes and the honking and not in a haughty way. It was as if none of this was aimed at her. She bravely tried to carry on as if all this was not happening. I expect that was the advice that had been given to her by well-meaning or desperate adults – *Ignore them, Cheryl, they'll soon get fed up*. But they didn't.

I saw her a few times after we left school, shopping in Winhurst, a clutch of small children clinging to her Sainsbury shopping trolley as she wheeled it through the town. I hoped they too were not the victims of what her mother had been through. It was a small town and I could imagine that some inconsiderate parents had told their children about the mother in the ill-fitting coat waiting at the school gates and her sad history.

Even fifteen years after any old pupil had seen her, she would crop up now and then in conversation. Some of the boys might be reminiscing over their school days and one might say to the other: 'Do you remember when you were going out with Cheryl Wilde?' to hoots of laughter and disgust. Three men in their thirties sitting in the pub honking like seals.

CHAPTER SEVEN

School's Out

With Vic and Kenny's year gone, here we were at the age of fourteen the most senior kids in the school. Ours was the first school year to be affected by the raising of the leaving age from fifteen to sixteen. Resentment about not being able to go out to work was high, and what little discipline there was completely collapsed. The headmaster, Mr Bradfield, was a daft old sod. He was another with a rampant social conscience. He only saw the good in people and was forever making excuses for why we were the way we were. This was Winhurst, for God's sake, not Broadwater Farm! Only now do I realise how unfair it was on the kids who would have liked to have been educated, and how 'caring' teachers like Bradfield did not do those people any favours at all. Far too much time and effort was expended trying to 'help' the so-called problem pupils.

Respect from your peers at the school did not stem from sporting excellence or academic achievement. People admired you for your 'hardness' or your propensity to cause trouble or be a rebel. Applying yourself academically only made you a target for bullying or ridicule. At Crowley Lane the culture was all back to front. Impressionable adolescents do not like to stand out from the crowd and will normally try and fit in with the dominant peer group. At Crowley there was a clear hierarchy and everyone knew their place in it. Some tried to climb the ladder, others were content with their position. All manner of things counted towards your placing in the hierarchy: your own ability or perceived ability to scrap; the positions of your older brothers in the hierarchy; the amount of trouble you and your family had had with the law; what older boys your sisters went around with; what you wore and so on. It seems childish now but that's how it was.

The first time I got sent to Bradfield he invited me inside his study. 'I don't want to cane you, Hay. Basically, you're a decent, intelligent boy. You're running with the wrong crowd, that's all.'

'Well, sir, if you don't want to cane me – don't.'

His sympathetic features hardened a little. 'And how do you suggest we deal with persistent offenders?'

'I don't know, sir. But caning doesn't work, does it? I mean, you have the same people waiting outside your office every morning. It's not modifying behaviour nor is it a deterrent.'

He raised an eyebrow as this young upstart in front of him articulated his innermost doubts. I sensed the discussion moving in my favour. I was wrong.

'Just because you don't know what the alternative is – is that a just reason to continue with a form of punishment you know doesn't work? That's a bit stupid, isn't it?' As the last words tumbled out of my mouth, I knew I'd overstepped the mark.

'Hand out!' he roared and bought down the stick, which resembled a large, fat Twiglet, down on my hand.

'Thanks, sir, see you tomorrow,' I said as I walked out of the study clenching my teeth.

There was one teacher we were all wary of. His name was Mr Wallace. Legend had it that he'd been a Japanese prisoner of war and had been a victim of all sorts of terrible tortures. When he spoke his mouth barely moved and the prevailing myth was that his lips had been sewn together by the Japs. There was an air about him. Unlike a few other teachers who tried to throw their weight around and ended up getting shown up, Mr Wallace said very little and rarely raised his voice. It had been passed down from school year to school year that 'if he goes . . . he goes', but no boy wanted to test this little bit of historic advice. Until Harris unwittingly did.

Harris was a diamond. He could neither read nor write and he would do whatever we told him – not because he was bullied or intimidated but because he loved a jolly-up and could rarely think of any wind-ups himself. He revelled in the anarchy of the school and was up for any prank. He was never touched by the boys but was forever getting knocked about by the teachers.

Mr Wallace happened to deputise one lesson for a teacher who was off sick – one of the many who had given up and was basically just going through the motions. Harris, assuming that this particular teacher would be taking us, bowled into the classroom some time after the lesson had started, having had a smoke and a chat with another boy in the playground. Harris just opened the door and casually walked down the aisle to his desk.

Wallace's eyes followed his progress. 'BOY!' he boomed.

Harris looked nonchalantly around.

'Where have you been? You should have been here ten minutes ago!'

'Why, what happened?'

Wallace went ape-shit, scattering over desks in his haste to get at Harris. The man's impact knocked the boy to the ground. The redness of the teacher's face worried us. He grabbed Harris's wispy hair and began to bang his head against the wooden floorboards. 'Never [thud] never [thud] be [thud] impertinent [thud] to me [thud]. Understand [thud]?'

On the other hand, Mr Endecott was a master of whom we had no fear at all. We could smell nervous breakdown on him and went for the kill. He taught Religious Education, which with us lot was akin to trying to sell George Cross flags to Welsh nationalists. I decided one day to take him on but first made sure I had the support of the entire class – which I did, save one or two.

'. . . and Jesus walked on the water . . .'

I shot my hand up. 'How could that be, sir? How did he walk on the water without sinking?'

Endecott looked at me incredulously. 'It was a miracle, Hay.'

'Yeah, but how do you know it's true? It's a lot to ask us to believe – that this bloke actually walks across the sea. It sort of devalues the rest of it.'

'It was a miracle and it is here in black and white in the New Testament,' he punched down on his bible.

'Yeah, but how do we know that's true? Some book written thousands of years ago? I mean, is there any proof that any of these things actually happened?'

'Hay, we all know you're a cynic – an atheist, probably. But I will not allow you to impress your view on everyone else.'

'Isn't that exactly what you're doing?'

His neck was reddening and he was clenching his fist as he tried to control his temper.

'To be honest, sir, we're not having it. If you can't back any of this up we might as well start believing Enid Blyton is gospel.'

'Shut up!' he roared. 'Okay, Hay, you are excused from my lesson. You can tell your parents that you have opted out of the

Religious Education syllabus. Now get out and let the rest of us get on with our lesson.'

'Problem is, sir, no one wants to do this pointless lesson or the pointless exam.'

'Really? I'm sure the class appreciates you making decisions about their future on their behalf. Hands up those, besides Harris, Higgs, Wells and their motley crew, who would like to opt out along with Hay.'

Thirty-seven hands drifted up. Endecott gathered his bible and briefcase and turned around and walked out of the room.

Unbelievably, the school kept up a pretence of normality as its social fabric crumbled away. There was a national shortage of teachers. The ones who stayed were counting the days until they could retire and the rest of the staff was made up of an ever-changing roll of relief or student teachers, some of whom were barely older than us. In the fourth year space was so scarce that the canteen doubled up as our classroom. It was disgusting, sitting among squashed carrots and regurgitated potato, and hardly conducive to learning. Again, I lobbied the class, girls as well, and one break we sat in the field and refused to come in when the bell rang for afternoon lessons. Our form teacher came out and asked what was going on.

'We're protesting, sir, about our classroom being the canteen. How can we be expected to learn in those conditions? It's not on.'

'Because you're really interested in learning, aren't you, Hay? We'll see what Mr Bradfield has to say about this.'

As he turned and stalked off to the main school block, some of the others got twitchy.

'What's he going to do? Fuck all. He can't cane forty of us, can he? Imagine if the papers got hold of it. Don't worry.'

Bradfield arrived and was unusually aggressive. 'Whose idea is this?'

No answer.

'Fair enough. Hay, come with me. We will discuss this in my office. The rest of you, go to your classroom. If you don't, I will discipline each one of you individually. You'll find out who is bluffing.'

Harris, bless him, stood up. 'It wasn't John, sir, it was my idea,' he declared.

Bradfield looked at Harris disbelievingly, knowing the boy had never had an idea in his life.

'No, it wasn't Harris, it was my idea.' Jacko was up now and then Big Bob and then Tony Bond and then Norma Sutton. Everyone stood up and owned up to it being their idea. Maybe it was coincidence that *Spartacus* had been shown on TV the previous weekend. Fucking brilliant.

Later, a pupil swap was arranged between a French school and ours. Naturally and understandably, no one from our crowd was despatched across the Channel but we suddenly found this bunch of twenty French boys and girls sharing our classrooms. We took an instant dislike to them. I can't remember whether or not it was prearranged, but during assembly Steve Fletcher let off a smoke bomb and in the ensuing mêlée we all rushed across the hall to where the French contingent stood. When the smoke cleared, some of the French boys could be seen lying on the floor, clutching their torsos. Others wiped blood from their faces with their sleeves. In a few seconds we had launched an unprovoked and horrible attack on these children who didn't even want to be here.

By the time I was in my final year, the school was full and more wooden huts had to be lowered on to the breeze blocks to accommodate the growing numbers. We got one of these huts as our last classroom. There wasn't even a form teacher for us. We had no timetable and it was clear that the school preferred it if we played truant. Some of the boys were involved in a project to build a car, which kept them occupied. Jacko, for one, loved this, and I can remember him triumphantly driving it around the school field with the master's blessing. Others were sent out on errands in the community. The idea was probably to get them used to the community service the school obviously felt they would inevitably be doing in later life. Mowing old ladies' lawns was one we liked. Very often the old dears would tip us.

I knew it was all coming to an end when I arrived one morning and my classroom had gone. It was simply not there. All that remained was a black stain on the school field and the breeze blocks. It transpired that Gary Langton, Steve's younger brother, and Ricky Vetch had burnt it down the previous night. Why our classroom, I don't know. Maybe it was the only one they could get into. They had done a thorough job, bringing petrol and helping the fire spread. They went on the run and a couple of days later we saw from the main school window as they were led out of the playground – having returned to bask in their notoriety – by two policemen. One policeman pushed their heads down and shoved them into the back seat as the other got into the driving seat. As the first policeman then eased himself into the passenger seat, Gary and Ricky simply opened up the door on the other side and ran off again.

One of the saddest figures was Mr Byrne, the Games master. Before the war he had played on the right wing for Aston Villa, Derby County and other first-division football clubs. After the war ended, his career as a footballer was over and he took the job as Games master at Croxley Lane. Judging from the news-paper cuttings he once showed me after I had asked to see his scrapbook, there was considerable local excitement about the arrival of this sporting celebrity at the school. His early teaching career was distinguished, with the school team regularly win-ning trophies and some boys going on to reach professional level.

By the time we got to him, however, he was nearing retire-ment and had been battered and beaten by an increasingly rebellious and uninterested pupil intake. Physically, he could no longer run around and would delegate match organisation and football practice to prefects or enthusiastic pupils. He wore plimsolls and a whistle hung permanently around his neck on a bit of a string to indicate what he was meant to be doing, but his involvement in physical education extended no further than that. Tragically, his daughter had died a couple of years before from a drug overdose and his spirit was visibly crushed.

He soon became a school sport himself – a sport of the most abhorrent type. It became the challenge to gob or spit on to his back. Boys would pass him in the corridor and, like a reptile flicking its tongue, would spit out a well-aimed greenie on to his jacket as soon as they were out of his line of vision. Some boys did it more openly and others, more cautious, would spit on to their fingers first and flick the spit on to him. Some days I'd pass him and take a peek at his back and there would be green phlegm and saliva hanging all over him like obscene fairy lights.

Fights caused great excitement and were often scheduled for after school. The buzz would go from classroom to classroom that so-and-so was fighting so-and-so on the field at four o'clock. The ones that were evenly matched could be bloody affairs and the spectators got into the spirit of the thing by rhythmically chanting 'Fight! Fight! Fight!' as the blows rained down. One such match was arranged between a boy in my year called Derek Flynn and a boy from the year above called Phil Hayes. Hayes had picked on Derek and Derek had shown him up a bit in front of his mates. To save face, Hayes challenged the younger boy to a fight after school. Derek was an unassuming boy; good at sport and work but also comfortable with the disruptive element, he was able to cross the social divides within the school with ease. In short, he was popular. Phil Hayes was one of Kenny Baird's gang who had been one of the few from that year to stay on and take exams. He still put himself about a bit even though Kenny and company were no longer around to provide his much-needed muscle.

Outside the school, boys and girls hung around the gates, trying hard not to look like a baying mob, whilst the teachers swung their cars out on to the road and drove away. No.6 fags were handed around as we all chatted in excited anticipation at the spectacle awaiting us. Finally, Derek rolled his sleeves up and stepped out the throng and put his fists up Queensberry-rules style. Phil Hayes, who I think was hoping that it wasn't going to come to this, took off his watch, dropped it into the wicker basket of one of his female admirers and slowly screwed his cigarette into the ground with his shoe. He then rushed Derek and tried to nut him. Derek withdrew his face just in time but returned with a solid punch to Phil's stomach. Phil was winded but Derek did not press his advantage and allowed him to recover as he trained his eyes and fists on him. Hayes came in again and Derek simply stepped back and planted a combination of punches on and around the older boy's head. Hayes seemed to be fumbling around his lower body as he kept his head down at Derek's chest level. Suddenly Hayes jumped backwards and Derek let out a loud gasp and looked at his opponent and then at us lot watching. His look was one of complete horror. Hayes was waving a long sharp knife at Derek.

'Want some more?'

Derek stood and looked down at the black stain that was appearing on his jumper. He felt the sticky blood and looked at his red fingers as if to make sure. 'You've stabbed me,' he said, staring wide-eyed and incredulous at Phil. For the first time he looked angry.

Phil Hayes pushed a boy from his bike, jumped on it and rode away at speed. One girl started to scream. Other spectators turned their bikes around sharpish and rode off. Many walked away hurriedly. Another girl ran back into the school and knocked on the caretaker's door and shouted at him to call an ambulance. By the time it arrived Derek was sitting up against the fence, the girls holding towels over his wound, and he seemed to be drifting in and out of consciousness.

Derek did recover, although he was off school for some time. The headmaster conducted a very grave assembly the following morning, stating that Derek would recover but that had the knife wound been half an inch higher, he would almost certainly have died. He criticised us all for not intervening. He unwittingly lightened the proceedings when he accused us of lacking 'spunk' and seemed genuinely confused when half the school put their hands to their mouths and tried to suppress giggles. Phil Hayes never appeared at school again.

My undistinguished but eventful school career ended a few weeks later, some months before I was due to leave officially. The school knew we were to go shortly and they were attempting to draw a line under us and start again. We were the

ROSLA year. A freak. Nothing could be this bad again. A younger headmaster and headmistress were scheduled to take over from Mr Bradfield on his imminent retirement. A new gymnasium had been built and the post of Head of Games had been created. David Willis was recruited to revitalise the school's physical education faculty now that Byrne had finally been pensioned off. He was a minor celebrity, having played professional football for Brentford before a cartilage injury cut short his career. That was his story, anyway. He probably just wasn't much good.

He caused a stir when he joined, marching around the school buildings in his tracksuit and sporting fashionable shades. He was thirtyish, very fit, muscular and good-looking. The girls swooned over him and he loved it. His energy and enthusiasm were almost tangible. Why he chose to challenge us, I cannot fathom. He could have ignored us for a few more months and not risked his credibility and saved a good deal of hassle.

Games was a double period when some boys brought kit to school and played unstructured football on the field. The rest of us sat around smoking and chatting. Most of us had not possessed a football kit for a couple of years.

David Willis came out on to the field and rounded us all up. He led us into the new gymnasium and asked us to sit down on the new shiny five-a-side floor. 'I don't know what you guys are used to here but as far as I am concerned that is all in the past. I am paid to ensure you take part in physical recreation and physical recreation is what you will take part in. Am I clear?'

No response.

'Am I clear?' He looked down at Harris. 'Why are you not wearing kit?'

'I ain't got one,' drawled Harris.

'Well, you'd better get yourself one, boy. Now, listen carefully. Next week I expect each and every one of you to turn up here with kit and I expect you all to play games. There is plenty of choice. I am not going to tolerate slovenliness or disobedience. If any of you cannot find or obtain kit or for any reason cannot take part in these lessons, I require an explanatory letter from your parents. Am I clear?'

The only thing clear in our eyes was the stupidity of the man.

Frankly, we forgot about it. The following Friday a handful of the boys had managed to throw on some ill-fitting shorts and T-shirts and joined the others who were out on the freezing field enthusiastically kicking a ball around. As for the rest, I suppose there must have been fifteen of us, lolling around chatting when David Willis trotted past us and barked: 'You boys follow me into the gym.'

We followed him, continuing our conversations and stamping out our cigarettes on the concrete outside.

'Have you forgotten our little conversation of last week? Why are you not suitably attired?' He swung around and faced Big Bob.

Bob Rees was by now six foot four inches and wide and strong. He was not a bully or really even a troublemaker. He continued to knock around with us but although he had the physique and sheer physical presence to be a leader, he was not interested. But those who did not know him often thought otherwise. I guess that was David Willis's strategy. If he could make an example out of Big Bob, it would send a message and short-circuit the rest of us.

'Rees, where is your kit?'

'I don't have a kit. I've never played games,' answered Bob in a slow, matter-of-fact way. It was true. He had never played games, even at the juniors. Maybe he felt self-conscious, but none of the other teachers had ever really put any pressure on him to take part. He wasn't disruptive. Leave him be.

'Can I see your note then?'

Bob shook his head. 'I don't have a note.'

Willis was stiffening. I could see a vein running down his neck beginning to become more visible. This was becoming interesting. A few of the boys wearing kit had begun to congregate around the doorway to watch the unfolding situation.

'You don't have a note? Why not?'

'Because I didn't ask for one. I told you, I don't play games.'

Willis reddened. He bent down and picked out a pair of smelly shorts and a Crystal Palace team shirt from an open holdall on the floor. 'You play whatever you are told, Rees,' he spat, throwing the shorts and shirts at Bob's face. 'They're clean. Go to the changing-room and change – now!'

Bob picked off the shorts that had landed on his shoulder, tossed them to one side and began to push himself away from the wall he was leaning against.

'Where do you think you're going?'

Willis and Big Bob were now facing each other. The teacher stepped forward suddenly and Bob instinctively jerked the top part of his body backwards and clenched his fists.

'You think you can take me out?'

This from David Willis, the master, who was by now as red as a beetroot. His eyes were bulging and he was pushing his face into Bob's, noses almost touching.

'I'm going home,' declared Bob and turned his back on the teacher.

'You go home, Rees, and never come back. We can do without the fat useless likes of you. Next time I will not be able to restrain myself and I'll knock you into next week.'

Willis had misjudged Bob turning his back as a climbdown. His mistake was trying to underline that with his last comment.

Bob stopped and slowly turned back to face the teacher again. 'Come on, then,' he said, calmly beckoning the man towards him.

There was no going back for David Willis now. It couldn't have escaped his notice that there must have been thirty boys and a smattering of girls in the vicinity. It was almost laughable as he put his fists up and bounced up and down like a boxer in the ring. He stepped forward and jabbed at Bob's head. Bob parried the blow with one arm and brought the other fist up, almost from the floor, in an uppercut that landed squarely on Willis's chin, lifting him off the ground in the process. Big Bob then simply fell on to the teacher, pinioning his arms to the floor with his knees.

'Stop this here,' breathed Bob.

But Willis knew his whole credibility and career at Croxley Lane was now in the balance. He was fit and wiry and managed to thump his knee into Bob's back, jolting him forward. Then Willis got an arm free and walloped Bob straight in the bollocks.

What had been an almost calm, restrained duel now turned seriously nasty. Bob growled like a bear and volleyed the Games master in the face as he tried to get to his feet. He gave him another boot in the stomach and then another one in the face. Blood pissed from Willis's nose and mouth. Bob didn't stop kicking and the teacher curled in the foetal position to protect himself. A pool of blood was beginning to silhouette his body. Jacko looked at me and I looked at him. *We're having some of this*, we thought. I kicked him time and time again in his kidneys whilst Jacko was kicking and jumping on his head in a frenzy. We had no worries about being caught. David Willis was already unconscious.

It seemed fitting that that was effectively our last day at school. Bob, Jacko and I had started school together and now we had finished together. Bob was expelled and never came back. To David Willis's credit, although he was hospitalised and he too never came back, he did not involve the police. Our cowardly involvement in the fight, whilst widely known, was never mentioned.

I did come back to the school for one day, mainly out of curiosity, to attend an appointment with the visiting careers officer. His name was Mr Roughton. He shook my hand as he welcomed me into the study he was using. The handshake didn't feel very natural. It was a way of saying welcome to the adult world. He asked me a few questions and studied the patchy records that existed of my academic progress. Finally, he locked his fingers over his belly, sat back in his chair and studied me. 'What would you like to do?'

'Dunno.'

Silence. Then, 'Have you considered the GPO?'

'The GPO?'

'Yes, the Post Office. Have you considered becoming a postman?'

I'm sure he had said this to half the boys he saw that day. Making the best of a bad bunch, he was thinking. What a wanker, I thought. I knew something – I didn't want a poxy job like his for fuck-all. He filled my pockets with leaflets and application forms and I stepped out in to the world of work.

CHAPTER EIGHT

Wild World

I had no intention of becoming a postman whatever that careers man said. Wear a uniform? No thanks. Postmen in those days looked too much like policemen for my liking. I had no idea what I wanted to do. Well, the truth is, I didn't want to do anything. Jacko had got fixed up at the sheet-metal works down on the Watermead Industrial Estate. Vic was an apprentice painter and decorator, which meant he went around painting houses with lots of men but the apprentice bit meant they could pay him far less. Tony Bond was working in the laundry at one of the mental homes that surrounded the estate: 'shaking the turds out of nutters' trousers' is how he described the stark reality of his new job to me. Big Bob was learning how to lay bricks and Harris had taken the postman option. Keith had joined the navy. None of this attracted me.

'What do you want to do, then?' Mum asked, exasperated when I still had not found work weeks after officially leaving school.

'Get rich,' I replied, to which she would tut and re-immerse her hands in the washing-up bowl.

I suppose I was good at English at school. It was the only subject I was good at. Writing essays and reading, I really enjoyed. Dad got to thinking we should try and think along the lines of journalism, although an A level in English was a pre-requisite even for the local paper. Finally, he spotted an adver-tisement in the *Evening News* for a messenger boy on the *City Telegraph* in the City of London.

'Not really a reporter, though, is it, Dad?'

'You have to start somewhere. Anyway, who says they'll offer you the job?'

Dad helped me compose a letter and we mailed it off. A few days later a reply arrived inviting me up for an interview. Mum whisked me off to Kingston where she bought me my first suit, complete with a waistcoat, from C&A.

On the day of the interview I had butterflies as bad as the day Vic and I walked down to the rope swing to fight Kenny Baird. I was particularly traumatised about any of my mates seeing me all scrubbed and suited up on the walk to the station with Dad who, bless his soul, had taken a day off work to come with me.

Fern House, home of the *City Telegraph*, was an imposing glass building on the edge of the Square Mile. We sat on a bench across the road as we had arrived early. Pigeons alighted hopefully around our feet. I really didn't want to go in, know-ing my life was about to change forever.

'Go on,' said Dad eventually, gently pushing me and giving my shoulder a loving squeeze. 'Just ask at reception for Colin Moore and say you have an interview.'

I pushed the double-doors open. Sitting at the reception was the most ridiculous-looking man I had seen outside the psychi-atric wilds of Winhurst. He was perched on his chair in his commissionaire's uniform and spoke in the most over-the-top posh voice. I thought he was taking the piss and almost res-ponded in the same old-English butler voice to get into the spirit of things.

'Good morning, sir, how may I be of help?'

Even at this time of personal crisis I found it hard not to laugh. He had a little pinched face with a tiny but noticeable hook nose that made him resemble a budgie, but the *tour de force* was the little sandy wig which seemed delicately balanced on his head. I didn't realise that real people wore wigs. I thought they were merely props for comedians or party pieces. Take the lift to the third floor, he told me. I had never used a lift. Wigs, lifts – what next?

On the third floor a nice girl ushered me into Colin Moore's office. Mr Moore did not look up on my entry and introduction. He continued to write furiously on a pad in front of him.

'John Hay. Winhurst, Surrey. Sixteen years old. Happy with the money?' finally broke the silence. 'Fifteen pounds a week – you happy with that?'

Of course I was happy with that. Vic was on thirteen and he'd been at work two years. Some of the boys were on twelve or even ten.

'Take the travelling into account, though – that'll cost you.' He scribbled some more. 'When can you start? Monday? Okay, wait here.'

He got up and flew out of the room, clutching the pad in his hand. I hadn't said a word in the whole 'interview'.

The nice girl came back in and gave me some forms to fill in. 'Kevin will be in to see you in a minute,' she said sweetly.

Kevin? Kevin appeared. He was tall, wearing a red granddad vest and bell-bottom trousers. His hair was curly and bounced around on his shoulders and he sported a long Mexican-style moustache. 'Hi, John, I'm Kevin, I'm the NATSOPA rep here.'

He could see I was none the wiser.

'NATSOPA is the trade union you'll be a member of and

I'm the union representative for this department. You will be deducted 17p from your weekly wages to the union funds and we in turn look after you.' He winked and shook my hand. 'When do you start?'

'Monday.'

'Great, look forward to it. You'll like it here, but let me give you a little tip . . . don't wear a fucking suit.'

On my first day I was introduced to Peter, a tall man of about twenty-five who came from New Cross. Pete was to be my mentor. He was pleased to see me because, it transpired, my post as Library Messenger was a new one that allowed him to stop doing the demeaning tasks that were part of his daily routine. These centred around delivering special-interest magazines and letters to journalists on a daily basis and running library files all around the building to them as and when they requested.

Pete would fling open the office doors of the editorial stars of the *CT* and toss their magazine or paper on to their desks without even entering. The ritual must have been quite well established because most of the journalists didn't even look up from the big black heavy typewriters in front of them as the bundle of paper crashed down, surely breaking their concentration.

'Don't they mind? Won't they report you?'

'Nah, they're all too pissed.'

I thought he was joking. Pete took me to The Dandy Roll pub for my first lunchtime 'session'. This was obviously another well-established ritual as the pub was packed with pinstriped suits and red faces. George Macrae's 'Rock Your Baby' drifted out of the wall-mounted jukebox and cigarette smoke hung thick in the air. Conversation was limited, the object of the exercise being, it seemed, to drink as much as you possibly could in the hour or two you could get away with for lunch.

'What you having?' asked Pete as he barged his way through the crowd with me following sheepishly in his slipstream.

What am I having, indeed? I had barely tasted alcohol.

'Brown Ale, please.'

I'm not sure where that came from. I'd seen Grandma drink it at Christmas. Pete passed me a pint mug of frothy Forest Brown Ale and it felt like a jug in my hand. Pete drank six pints and I had three and he had to hold my arm as we negotiated the zebra-crossing on Queen Victoria Street as we returned to work.

At the end of that first week I received my first pay packet of fifteen pounds. I had to buy next week's rail ticket for three pounds and Mum accepted another three for housekeeping, leaving me with nine pounds. I rang up Vic, who had been keeping me in family bags of Maltesers and cans of lemonade shandy for two years now, and told him a night out to the pub was on me. I was still only sixteen, and a small sixteen at that, and my attempts at gaining entry to pubs had not been successful thus far. The best I had done was when Tony Bond and I had strolled into The Magpie in Winhurst. We'd been told that the couple who ran it were elderly and it was easy to get served. Attempting to learn by our mistakes, we strolled confidently to the bar. Tony placed a bunch of keys on the bar in front of him to give the impression we were driving.

'Pint of Guinness,' said Tony authoritatively, 'and . . .' he looked over to me

'I'll have half a light and bitter,' I ventured.

The publican's right eyebrow rose quizzically over his glasses. 'Come back in a year, lads,' he smiled.

But tonight we were off to The Wheatsheaf in the village. Big Bob had been a regular in here since he was fourteen and Vic had the confidence of a regular pub user. To top it all, the licencees, Edie and Harold, were old and deaf. We had no problem getting served and got legless on mild beer at 17p a pint. Somehow I made it home and to bed. I remember the room swimming and wishing I was dead. Vomit squirted out of my mouth like a geyser as I lay flat on my back, and Dad came rushing in and helped me to the toilet. I smothered his pyjamas in brown sick as he cradled my head over the toilet bowl. I didn't surface until the Saturday afternoon and lay wide awake in bed, dreading going downstairs and facing Mum and Dad. Eventually I did and not a word was said. I guess they hoped I had learnt an important lesson.

Back at work a whole new world was opening up for me. Far from being the bastion of bowler-hatted gentility I had imagined the *City Telegraph* to be, it was turning out more like an asylum. Not a day went by without new revelations and experiences unfolding. After a while Pete had confided to me that he had been in borstal for pulling a policeman off his horse at a Sheffield Wednesday versus Millwall fixture. Tony Fachetti, who worked with me and was a real Caledonian Road wide-boy, had served time in Dover prison for his involvement with a King's Cross gang that had been caught paki-bashing. Mike Straker, our immediate superior, had also served time in a military prison for desertion. These three were my first main influences in the working world. Out of the frying pan into the fire.

They called Straker a spiv at work. He was forever on the make. If you wanted anything, Straker could get it. He became genuinely annoyed if you purchased anything from the shops on nearby Cheapside. 'Why didn't you ask me first?' he always demanded.

I never saw him smile but he had real poise. He always wore a neatly cut suit and shiny loafers. His blond feather-cut hair fell neatly on to his collar and his moustache was well groomed. Mike resembled a cross between Rod Stewart and Jason King. The manager, Colin, got on well with him and turned a blind eye to his activities – probably because he was benefiting from them.

I know Mike got into a bit of trouble over a scam once. It was a good one and I always meant to have a bash at it myself when I could put the money together. It went like this: Straker put small ads in the tabloid press advertising a 'sex kit'. This included 'blue films from Sweden, near-the-knuckle magazines and your own surprise sex toy, all for £3.99'. Punters were encouraged to send a cheque for this amount made out to Blue Crest Ltd to a PO Box number and await their goodies. Thing was, there were no goodies. Straker banked all the cheques and then sent out a letter saying, 'Due to unforeseen massive demand, we are out of stock and I therefore return your £3.99.' Problem for the punter was that the return cheque was made out on the 'Sex Toy and Blue Movie Company Ltd' bank account and most of them were too embarrassed to take the risk of banking it. Straker was left with thousands of pounds in the Blue Crest bank account and hundreds of red-faced punters were £3.99 poorer. Trading standards got on to him in the end but not before he had made a nice few quid.

Another time he placed ads in the papers offering 'The Lazy Man's Path to Riches', a get-rich-quick scheme for 99p including postage and packing. When the punters responded, he simply sent them a letter saying, 'Place an ad like I have.'

Tony Fachetti was less subtle than Mike. He took me over Cheapside one lunchtime and said he needed a new pair of shoes. 'Got to be Church's or Loakes,' he told me. 'They last for years.'

He showed me the brogues he had his eye on as we stared in the window of Russell & Bromley. They were fifteen quid, as much as I earned in a week.

'Start walking up the road,' he said as he slipped into the shop. 'And don't look back.'

Three minutes later I felt a gust of wind and noticed Tony fly past me, swerve left into Bow Lane and vanish. I got back to the office and he was sitting at his desk with his feet up on a chair, displaying a shiny pair of Loakes. 'Did anyone chase?' he asked.

No one had as far as I had noticed. Tony had simply walked into the shop and asked to try on a pair of shoes. He'd walked round a bit in them and suggested he probably needed the next size up. When the assistant went to fetch them, he bolted, leaving his smelly old pair on the floor.

I saw him do the same with coats, strides (as he called them) and shirts. When he needed something new he just strolled over Cheapside and nicked it. He was very generous with his plunder, too. I just mentioned once that I wanted to buy *Venus and Mars*, the new LP by Wings, and it was on my desk the next day. He never encouraged me to follow suit either.

Tony never did any work at all. His job was to file the cuttings from the national newspapers that mentioned companies with names beginning with A to F. He got into the habit of paying me five pounds a week to do this for him. It was a doddle and I fitted it in between my file-running errands while Tony sat around the library desks reading the sports pages and answering the telephone occasionally. 'Who's calling the Golden Shot?' he would say as he put the receiver to his ear. How he got away with it, I don't know. On the rare occasion he was forced to do something, he would mutter: 'I thought slavery had been abolished.'

One afternoon I was pushing his trolley around the filing lanes, sticking the British Mohair Spinners cuttings in the correct file, when Lewis Poole loomed up in front of me. Lewis was a big man of about thirty. He wore round John Lennon glasses and that was about all you could see of his face as a mass of black curly hair and a great bushy black beard obscured the rest of it. He wore a denim shirt and loon trousers. Like a kid, he adorned his denim shirt with badges displaying all manner of slogans: 'Save the *Daily Herald*', 'Make Love Not War', 'Mrs Thatcher – Milk Snatcher', and so on.

'What are you doing?' he demanded.

'Filing.'

'Whose filing?'

'Tony's.'

'Right – stop now.' He led me around to the desks where Tony and the others sat. 'Tony, why is young John doing your filing?' he challenged.

'Because he wants to.'

'You should know better, Tony. It's not on. We can't have juniors doing Library Assistant work without getting paid for it. You know that.'

'Fuck off, you commie bastard!'

Lewis fucked off and Tony told me not to worry, that Lewis Poole was a troublemaker and no one took any notice of him. But Kevin, the softly spoken union rep I met at my interview, came to see me later and advised me nicely that I shouldn't do other people's jobs even if they asked me to. He said words like 'precedent' and 'demarcation'. I didn't know what he was on about but I did know that I was a fiver a week worse off.

Over the months I became aware of the power of the unions. Management had effectively abdicated in favour of them, at least in the newspaper industry. NATSOPA, the union I found myself in, was one of the least powerful and least militant, probably because unlike the printers and the journalists it was not within their gift to hold the newspaper to ransom. The printers were a law unto themselves and a breed apart. I only ever came across them in the company-subsidised bar where they lined the walls in their boilersuits drinking bottles of Heineken and puffing on fat cigars. Their union was the National Printers' Association (NPA) and their officials appeared to be closer to Mafia bosses than left-wing idealists. In fact, they seemed to me to be apart from the trade union movement. Their agenda was to protect and develop their vested interests. Print jobs were handed down from father to son, like pitches on Petticoat Lane. These jobs were fiercely protected and had long waiting lists. In all my time, for example, I never saw one black print worker. Sometimes they would go through the motions of spouting left-wing ideology but if truth be told the NPA members were out only for themselves.

And who could blame them? By flexing their muscles over the decades they had exposed and subsequently caned weak managements up and down Fleet Street. By the 1970s, the peak of their power, ordinary members were earning two hundred pounds per week when I was on twenty and the national average wage was, say, forty. The FOC (father of the chapel) was reputed to spend weekends shooting with the chairman on his country estate, and at night Fleet Street was lined with black cabs – because the printers had negotiated themselves deals whereby most of them only worked two or three days a week, they were able to launch parallel careers, and driving taxis was a favourite.

I earwigged a conversation once in the *CT* bar between two writers on the influential 'City Watch' investment column. They were bemoaning the situation that existed, saying it was surreal that they were being asked daily by the printers for advice on where to park their money and which shares were worth buying. 'I wish I'd put him into Court Line,' joked one, referring to a travel operator that had recently gone bust.

They hated it, the journos. Public-school-educated most of them, some with the snazziest double-barrel names imaginable, and here they were having their noses rubbed in it by tattooed, beergutted, boilersuited upstarts from Deptford.

To assuage any damaging jealousy problems from the other trade unions that operated in closest proximity to them, now and then the NPA would throw us some snippets. 'Casual work' was one such sop to the plebs. Us clerical workers could put our names down for the casual rota and usually you would get called in once a fortnight. It involved turning up at one of the papers on a Friday night at nine o'clock and presenting yourself for 'work'. Your name would be registered and you were told to come back at 1 a.m. We'd find a pub on Fleet Street that operated after hours, get pissed and then at one o'clock present ourselves in, say, Bouverie Street, and assist in that night's production of *The Sun*.

My job was to sit on a stool. As the papers came down a production line, I had to scoop up each choir (the machine automatically fanned out every twenty-first copy) and place them in piles next to me. Someone else came along and picked them up.

Every ten minutes or so the operator would press the red button and stop the machine for a 'blow'. A blow was a break for a fag. They all seemed to smoke as they worked so why the fag break was needed I wasn't sure.

I made a big mistake on my first session. The papers were coming down the line thick and fast and I lost my rhythm. To catch up, I did as I had been told, and threw batches over my shoulder until I could get ahead and resume the rhythm. When the next blow took place I got off my stool and began to scoop up my discarded papers.

'Oi! What d'you think you're doing, young fella?' shouted a grey-haired man with a roll-up perched behind his ear and an array of pens clipped on to his overall pocket. 'Who are you?'

'John Hay.'

'No, not your name, Einstein – which union?'

'NATSOPA.'

'Well, that's RIRMA work you're doing there, fellahmylad. You'll be the cause of a walkout, you will. Use your noddle,' he shouted above the background noise of machinery, tapping the side of his forehead to emphasise whereabouts in the body the brain resided.

At 4 a.m. we went home, but not before collecting our brown pay-packets with four crisp ten-pound notes folded inside. Forty quid for three hours' work! That was twice my weekly wage. It was ridiculous. There was no need for casual workers – there wasn't enough work for the permanent payroll, let alone us lot. These were keeping-the-peace payments from the NPA to the lesser unions, but, naturally, using the newspaper proprietor's money rather than their own.

It must have been pretty demoralising for the journalists, who felt they were the papers' most valuable asset, but there were plenty among their number who were also taking the piss big time. Many of them would turn up around eleven in the morning, rewrite a press release or two and then adjourn to the pub at one. They'd wander back in at around four, walk meaningfully around the newsroom, and then be back in the pub by six or seven.

There was a strange office called the Gold Room. One of my jobs was to go down there and file their cuttings for them. Apparently they needed their company files in their office and not in the library like everyone else. I think it was because most of the time they were too drunk to pick up the phone and send for them. There were three of them, two old boys approaching retirement and a young guy. Maybe once, when the gold-mining industry was at its height, these two were rising stars, but as these companies with strange-sounding names like Driefontein Gold Mines (1929) Ltd became less relevant to the British investment scene, they became less important to the newspaper. They went from having a couple of pages of news a day to a smaller and smaller column. They probably didn't notice, though. When I was down there, the oldest one was always asleep and the other two just clattered around among the cabinets in a drunken stupor.

James Burgess was another mad drunk. He was apparently a talented young writer but something had sent him along the vodka path. He looked like Robinson Crusoe in a tweed jacket and corduroy trousers. At one time his job was to write the Foreign Exchange column and reply to readers' letters of a technical nature. I made myself busy in his room when the news editor, an ambitious young man called Huntley, came in to bollock him. 'James, what are we going to do? You haven't answered a reader's letter for months,' he said, pointing to the pile of envelopes like a mini mountain rising in Burgess's in-tray.

'No other newspaper answers readers' letters,' complained James.

'But we do, we are the *City Telegraph*. James, I have to tell you, I'm at end of my tether.'

Before he could go any further, James put his head in his hands and began to cry aloud. The news editor motioned for me to leave the room.

By now Audie had joined the library. At first I thought he was a nutter. Perhaps the *CT* had a social scheme to employ mental defectives? He was six foot four inches tall and all he did was laugh. 'Hello, Audie,' I'd say and he'd throw his head back in manic laughter. Sometimes he laughed so much he cried and snot would shoot out his nose and spit would fly around the office. He wasn't stupid at all, though, and like me, he was fascinated by the unusual characters who surrounded us. He came from a council estate in Wandsworth and life, especially work, was one big laugh for him. His mum obviously had a sense of humour, too, naming him Audie after her favourite film star, Audie Murphy.

One day he walked through the newsroom and shouted out, 'Brezhnev's dead!' He creased up when the sleepy reporters jumped out their seats and went running to their Reuters machines. He wasn't. This became his catchphrase and every time he walked through the newsroom he'd shout it out. Some of the editorial staff smiled, others shook their head in pity at this poor buffoon and the rest gritted their teeth. Audie considered it his greatest personal achievement when the *CT* was the only UK national which did not report Brezhnev's actual death in their early editions.

Audie was a good-looking bloke but he just didn't hang together right. He wasn't shy but seemed to have great difficulty with girls. I think the madness that sparkled in his blue eyes put them off. I was astounded one day when we sat around a table drinking coffee in little brown plastic cups from the vending machine when he asked Tony Fachetti's advice on how to attract women.

'In pubs, Tone, they talk to all my mates, but once I speak to them they just laugh or piss off.'

I could see Tony trying to keep a straight face. 'Have you tried the spunk-behind-the-ear trick?'

'What?' laughed Audie, splurting out coffee.

Tony leant forward to underline he was being serious. 'No, it's true. It's a primitive thing. Don't ask me why, but the crumpet just can't resist it. Next time you have a wank, just dab a little bit of Harry Monk behind the old ear 'ole and you watch: they'll be all over you.'

Audie looked over at me and I just shrugged. 'I'll try that,' he said, but we weren't sure whether he had fallen for it or if he was just humouring Tony. We found out a few days later.

Audie called me over as he pushed his trolley down the filing alley. 'I think it could be working,' he declared triumphantly. 'You know, Harry Monk behind the ear and all that. Last night I got chatting to this bird down The Jolly Gardeners and I'm taking her out Friday.'

'Well done,' I said, as I tried not to stare at the knotted and crusty ringlets of hair all around his ear.

At first I loved the power of the unions. Seeing Lewis Poole and his followers walking around the building causing trouble appealed to the rebel in me. Not only was the paper paying them all not to do any work, it was paying them to cause trouble. I saw it as school all over again: we were the pupils and the managers were the teachers. I loved the one-day strikes in sympathy for nurses, coal-miners and other groups of genuinely deserving cases. I couldn't believe my luck when Lewis chose me to join the deputation to go over to Grunwick and join in a siege at a photo-processing plant that was played out on the news every night. This lot were football hooligans in corduroy trousers and 'Save the Whale' T-shirts. In fact, their keenness to steam in to the Old Bill was worse than anything I had seen at football. All of it stirred that working-class thing inside me.

Lewis took me to his flat in Streatham where he smoked a fat looking cigarette and stretched out on his sofa. *Tubular Bells* tinkled away in the background.

'What does your father do for a living?' he enquired.

'He works in a hospital.'

'Doing what?'

'Clerical.'

'I bet he's exploited. The health service is corrupt from top to bottom.'

'He's never said,' I replied innocently. 'What does your dad do?'

Lewis laughed and laughed and laughed. 'You'll never believe it,' he said finally. 'My father is the chairman of British Engineering.'

'British Engineering! We've got a company file on them.'

'I know. BE is one of the biggest companies in the world.'

I mused on this awhile as Lewis raided his fridge, saying he had the 'munchies'.

'You must be rich then,' I said, when he had returned and settled again on the sofa.

'My family are rich. I'm not.'

'But you'll get it all one day, I suppose.'

'I doubt it. I don't want it. They won't give it to me, anyway. They know I'd just give it away.'

'Give it away? To who?'

'I'd give it to people who deserve it, John. The workers. People like us. The downtrodden. People like your dad.'

His eyes were sparkling and his beard bristled as he went into a tirade about the redistribution of wealth and the exploitation of the working classes. Much as I was seduced by his charisma, I couldn't help thinking that he hadn't done a day's work in his life. He wasn't working class and he had a fucking cheek painting my dad as some sort of servile pleb. A penny started dropping.

I started to look at the other union activists around me; almost without exception they all came from middle-class backgrounds, were university-educated and didn't do a stroke. Yet they were representing us – people who needed to work, people who didn't have family money to fall back on, people who weren't necessarily going places, people who couldn't afford to taunt the management for a few years until they felt like they ought to 'get on'. They were spouting on about 'poverty', 'workers' and 'solidarity'. But the real meaning of these words was as alien to them as the words 'thesis', 'inheritance tax' and 'dinner-party' were to me. I started to resent their patronising manner and their snobbery. Their self-important, meaningful conversations began to grate:

'I went to see the new Fellini film last night. It's so intense. Have you seen it?'

'No, but I saw Bruce Lee in *Enter the Dragon* on Saturday. It was fucking brill.'

Just as at school, though, it was a case of the predominant

culture prevailing, and it took some serious thought if you were going to kick against it. I'm sure Tony Fachetti and the others all saw through these people too but had decided that good money was coming in; humour them and make hay while the sun shines. But basic commonsense told me this couldn't last. Something had to give. The newspaper was a commercial organisation. Profits had to be made to keep the thing going – even I could work that out. In my department there were forty-odd people. Thirty of them did nothing. The newspaper failed to make it to the streets ten or twenty days a year when the printers walked out. Printers were earning more than politicians. Managers were not allowed to manage. Most of them were taking the piss too. But it just seemed to roll on and on and my pay-packet bulged and bulged.

Like stumbling upon a fellow Resistance member in occupied France, I got friendly with Maurice. He was about twelve years older than me and had been identified by someone somewhere as management material. He was the deputy manager of the whole department, wore a suit and tenaciously tried to control costs and maintain some order in this very cynical and anarchic organisation. Somehow, I confided in him my frustration and fears and he told me he felt the same way. He had done his national service and had joined the paper straight after. He was not academically qualified and had wanted a career. He wasn't yet thirty but he seemed so wise. 'Look, all you can do for now is keep your head down and get on with your work,' he told me. 'When the crunch comes you'll be okay. Take it from me.'

He didn't mince his words and he gave me great encouragement. 'You'll do very well in life,' he said to me once. 'Half the people are stupid – not in an academic way but in the way they think – and the other half are bone idle. So if you're smart you'll do well or if you're a grafter you'll do well. If you're both, you'll fucking well clean up.'

Maurice moved me through the organisation as quickly as he could. My age and background were against me. Men and women in their twenties, fresh out of university, do not take kindly to scruffy teenagers organising or eclipsing them. However, if someone else was going to take responsibility or help them with what little work they had, they were happy. Eventually Maurice was made the manager of the whole library and he took a chance by promoting me to be section head of a research bureau staffed almost exclusively by graduates.

But his next move astounded me: Lewis Poole was appointed his deputy! Maurice's story was that by appointing Lewis, he was removing an obstacle in the workforce. He was making the old union/management confrontations a thing of the past, and said that Lewis was a great negotiator and thinker. Yeah, he certainly spent a lot of time thinking. Lewis himself seemed embarrassed and got out of it in a wink-wink sort of way. He wanted people to think it was part of some sort of master plan of infiltration. No one dared question Lewis's motives. My cynicism for both the unions and the management deepened that day and any trust or admiration I'd had for Maurice crumbled.

CHAPTER NINE

What's Love Got to Do With It?

Horizons were being broadened in other areas, too. I had not been at work long when I lost my virginity. Since about the age of ten I'd been having a sexual relationship of sorts with Jean Winter who lived around the corner. That's not as grand as it sounds because so had most of the other boys on the estate. But I like to think we had something a bit more special. We were the same age but in matters sexual Jean was light years ahead. One sunny afternoon before we got to senior school I was over the fields with her. I reckon we were nine – ten at the most. Spending time over the fields was quite innocent – those fields behind the estate were our playgrounds. She was wearing a flowery mini-dress with a zip at the front. She grabbed the ring on the zip and pulled it sexily down as far as it would go.

'Do you like these?' she said, looking down at her own tiny but developing breasts.

'Yes,' I replied decisively, studying them as if it were her collection of birds' eggs that I had been invited to inspect.

Impatiently, she took my hand and put it on one tit. 'Squeeze it, then.'

And that was the start. Over the next five or six years many more of these encounters were to take place, but only when Jean could fit me in, was bored or fancied a laugh. You see,

Jean's sexual appetite was strong and it emerged early. Within a couple of years she was going out with blokes of eighteen and by the time she was thirteen she was having regular sex with a series of adult boyfriends. We remained good mates throughout and walked home from school together most days. She delighted in telling me about her latest sexual exploits and watching my subsequent frustration.

'Me and Tim did it sitting on a chair last night.'

Tim was a dirty, filthy greaser who cruised in and out of the estate in a big American car.

'I keep telling Tim to use a Johnny but he says it's like having a bath with a raincoat on.'

Tim this, Tim fucking that. But it didn't stop me having a good old wank over her, Tim and a chair when I got home.

I'd blown my chance of a fuller sexual relationship with her about a year before Tim came on the scene. I suppose we were thirteen. Same fields. Lying on our backs, chewing grass, looking up at the evening sky.

'Can I have it away with you?' I blurted out, having planned this for a few days.

She looked at me and laughed. That was good for the confidence. Eventually she responded, 'You'll have to get me excited then.'

How? Talk about Christmas or what she might get for her birthday? I went to kiss her but she kept her lips shut. Again, she had to lead the way by taking my hand and rubbing it vigorously on her crotch through her jeans. 'Like this.'

I obliged but there were precious few traces of excitement on her face. I moved on to her tits where I felt more at home. They had grown a lot in the last couple of years and were now her main feature in many eyes. 'Jean, show us your lils!' older boys shouted to her sometimes and she feigned embarrassment but stuck her bust out that little bit further.

I had them out of the blouse and was busy rubbing my face in them, like an excited puppy, when she pushed me off. I thought that was it again – but not quite. She was wriggling out of her Levi's and now her knickers were kicked off so they hung from one foot. The bottom of her body was so grown up! I'd been down there before with my hand and got a 'smelly', as we called it, but to be frank I couldn't see the attraction. On the contrary, I thought this practice quite revolting. My old class-mate at school, Tony Bond, delighted in stuffing his finger under my nose in lessons. 'Whiff that. Pure Norma Sutton,' he would purr, then smell it himself and roll his eyeballs like he had just inhaled some magic powder or tasted a rare, delicious exotic food.

But looking at Jean and that forest of pubic hair was too much for me. I practically ripped my trousers and pants down and launched myself on top. I laid my penis on the mound and gently rocked up and down. 'Oh, that's good. That's good,' I moaned – and that was before I'd ever seen a blue film. I rocked away whilst slobbering over her breasts with my cock squashed between my lower stomach and her pubic mound. Looked up to see what sort of ecstatic state Jean had reached. She was inhaling deeply on a No.6.

Nevertheless, she was a good old sort. One day shortly before I left school for good, we were walking home. Tim had gone and her new boyfriend was another big, black-haired, square-jawed grebo nicknamed Sparky. This one was in his late twenties and he'd young kids of his own. She was telling me how much like Alvin Stardust he looked. I told her it was my sixteenth birthday.

'Come round tonight – Mum and Dad are at bingo. I'll give you a little present,' she said.

I didn't hold out much hope of anything. She and Sparky were experimenting with more positions than Brian Clough was at the time and she quite often whiled away an evening with me when her parents were out and Sparky was otherwise engaged.

Last of the Summer Wine was on the box, a strange little comedy that had just started running and which held no appeal for me. Jean's riding boots did, though. She saw me looking at them, thigh-high with her jeans tucked inside. Jean's other hobby was horse-riding.

'What's up?'

'I'd like to see you naked with just them boots on,' I breathed. Well, she did ask.

'You should be so lucky.'

We got to kissing and this time she did open her mouth and stuck her tongue down my throat.

'I just gotta go to the toilet.' She jumped up and bounded up the stairs.

Last of the Summer Wine had finished and *Top of the Pops* had started. I was beginning to feel distinctly uneasy because Alvin Stardust was on singing about jealousy. He was looking straight at me and the way he clasped the microphone made me think of Sparky gripping my neck.

'Get yer clothes off, then.'

I looked up and she was standing there, naked except for the riding boots. *She is beautiful in every way and now I love her. She is God and this is a vision. A masturbation fantasy has come to life.* I stripped off – it crossed my mind to leave my Ivy loafers and socks on – but I thought better of it. I was trembling. My mouth was dry and my insides were churning.

'Calm down, there's plenty of time.'

Jean lay on the settee. Pulled me by the knob towards her. Drew her knees up almost to her chin. She wasn't taking any chances this time because she put my penis surely and firmly inside her.

'Now, go up and down slowly,' she instructed.

I did so but couldn't help speeding up. We rolled on to the floor as Roberta Flack was killing me softly in the background and I came my lot.

'Happy Birthday.'

*

It never rains but it pours: I wait sixteen years for a real bunk-up and then only weeks after the anguish of virginity is ended I get ravished by an older woman. I was into reading biographies at the time and a common theme was how the subject got himself seduced by an older woman whilst in his mid-teens. David Niven, if I recall correctly, in his *Moon's a Balloon* book, was deflowered by the busty matron at his public school. I know that I do recall having numerous wanks over this passage in the book anyway. Having seen similar accounts elsewhere, I concluded that they were all lying old bastards. Why mature women would force their attentions on dirty, spotty, immature youths was beyond me. Until Brenda.

As a new boy at work I had all the customary tricks played on me: directed to the ladies' toilets, bogus phonecalls from imaginary journalists requesting 'every file in the library just to see what you've got' and so on. One afternoon I got a call from Nick Gardener, then an up-and-coming writer on the Diary column, who asked a number of questions that I was able to answer competently.

'Do you smoke?' he asked suddenly.

I lied that I did.

'Well, you've been so helpful, I've got a packet of cigarettes here for you if you'd like to pop down and fetch them.'

What a nice geezer. I trotted down the stairs and presented myself in the Diary office. I stood there smiling. Nick Gardener and his two colleagues glanced up at me and then looked back down at their typewriters.

'Hi, Nick, I'm the person you were just speaking to from the library.'

Nick looked up again blankly.

'The cigarettes,' I ventured.

Nick started to look puzzled and I fell in. Back upstairs Tony Fachetti and the others were strewn across their desks in uncontrollable laughter.

So it was no surprise that when they told me to be careful of Brenda the tea-lady I took no notice. They said she was a nymphomaniac and had a penchant for young boys. She certainly looked the part. She had a mound of black hair, black painted eyelashes, black lacy top, black mini-skirt and black 'kinky' boots. You could have been forgiven for thinking it was Fennella Fielding pushing the cake trolley around Fern House. She had no tits to speak of, though. There was something there but no sign of a cleavage. No matter, the rest of her more than made up for it to my hungry eyes. When she sold the cream buns she flirted heavily with the boys and they all had a laugh with her over the length of the chocolate fingers and so on. 'Never get in the lift alone with Brenda,' warned Tony.

I got in the lift alone with Brenda as soon as I possibly could just in case it wasn't a wind up. Immediately, she gently pushed the corner of the trolley into my groin area. 'Sorry, petal,' she lilted in her distinctive Cornish accent that seemed strangely at odds with her tarty appearance. She lunged over and squeezed my crotch tightly. I nearly ejaculated there and then. But all this happened between the doors closing on level three and re-opening on four – about fifteen seconds. She clattered the trolley out, winked, and left me hot, flushed and with a pulsating erection.

For the next couple of days I repeated the process. In fact, I went to work each morning with butterflies of anticipation in my stomach that intensified as 'trolley time' – ten past three – approached. Each time Brenda did the same thing, although now she didn't bother pushing the trolley into me first.

On the third day, she said, 'I do the South Block last, petal. Go over there at about four and we'll have some fun.'

The South Block was a sparsely occupied part of Fern House. The rival *Daily Times* had some space in one part and in the other was a handful of out-of-favour or elderly journalists and managers occupying ridiculously large offices. The paper didn't really fire people then so I think they thought it best that staff who had so obviously outlived their usefulness should be put out to grass somewhere it wouldn't affect morale or give people ideas.

The problem for me was that the anticipation was now unbearable. I had to have two wanks between ten past three and five to four just to prevent myself from passing out and keep down the rampaging hard-on pressing against my trousers. As I got there she was just rattling out of old Walter Goldberg's office. Walter's claim to fame was he had interviewed Hitler before the war. She shoved the trolley away from her down the corridor and with a flick of her dyed hair commanded me to follow. She stopped by a cupboard door, looked up and down the corridor to ensure the coast was clear, and stepped inside the cupboard motioning for me to follow. Inside, in the near dark, I stood bolt upright next to a mop, which was almost as tall as I was. She dropped to her knees and unzipped my trousers. My penis needed no encouragement to find its way out the opening of my Y-fronts. She rubbed the length of it a couple of times and then popped the whole lot into her mouth. Then she began to move her lips up and down, leaving a smudged gloss of lipstick in her wake. I didn't touch her hair or hold her head. I didn't speak or groan. I just stood there rigid, hands by my sides, looking down at this unbelievable thing that was happening to me. It was like I was watching a nurse lancing a boil which, in a way, was what was happening. At one point she looked up at me but for obvious reasons was unable to speak. Now, I think she was thinking: how come this boy don't come? Of course she was not to know I had more than expended the contents of my scrotum in the past fifty minutes. I was running on empty. Then, I knew no better. I didn't really understand that this sex act had a natural course and on my part it was not going to plan. Finally, she withdrew her mouth and patted my penis, which was her way of saying 'put it away', laughed her deep laugh and nipped back out the cupboard. When she wiggled her arse as she led the way towards the lifts, rattling her trolley, I felt a bit uncomfortable. I had a strong image of a Dick Emery TV character in my mind – the one with him dressed as a woman who exclaimed, 'Oooh you are awful!' and then shoved her male interviewer over with the strength of a man. Something about her didn't add up.

The type of relationship boys and girls had were very clearly defined in our strand of society. 'Getting off with' – that was stage one. All it really meant was that you had broken the ice

WHAT'S LOVE GOT TO DO WITH IT?

and perhaps kissed and fondled a girl or vice versa. Rarely did it mean that any serious intimacy had been achieved.

'Going out with' was the second stage. Now you really were boyfriend and girlfriend and you went around each other's houses. After a while you were likely to be at it. Sometimes, you even went out with each other.

'Going steady' – that was next. An extra commitment from just going out with. I suppose it meant that at some time in the distant future you would marry. This sometimes led to getting engaged, getting married and, in many cases via separation and divorce, getting single again.

Jacko, Vic and I tended not to go in for this regimented procedure although we were as desperate as anyone else for sex. Our lifestyles didn't really allow proper boy–girl relationships to develop. Take Vivienne. She was Big Bob's bird. He'd got her young. I reckon she was about fourteen when he first started shagging her and he started bringing her to the pub when she was just sixteen. I didn't consciously take her off Bob. I wasn't really interested in her, but I could tell she was interested in me, and during one of the lulls in their long-standing relationship I moved in. We started 'going out'. This meant she came to the pub with me instead of Bob and some days I managed to shag her in gardens or in the park on the way home from the pub. I steered well clear of going to her house or bringing her to mine.

There was little conversation between us and I would be lying if I said our relationship was based on physical attraction. I never really saw her body, nor she mine. We had sex maybe a dozen times and not once was it indoors or with any lighting. It was a strange union and soon fizzled out. But she did introduce us to Wendy. I rang Jacko one evening and said that Vivienne had a mate called Wendy and asked if he wanted to

meet her. Jacko would do anything, at any time, anywhere –
that's why I rang him – and he came with me to meet the two
girls. Wendy was a small, brunette, pretty girl who, although a
little chubby, prompted us both to look at each other and think
the same rude thought. We walked over to the park, found a
secluded alcove and lay down with the girls. I didn't waste time
and started to fuck Viv. To my amazement, within minutes,
Jacko was riding Wendy, a girl he had only just met, and in
front of me too, whom she had never met before either. Wendy
was wearing suspenders and I spent more time looking at them
as I absent-mindedly pumped away on Viv.

The upshot was that Viv drifted back to Bob but Wendy
became fixated on Jacko. Whilst he didn't mind shagging her,
there was no way he was going to have her as his girlfriend. She
was immature (not her fault – she was only sixteen), a bit slow
on the uptake and very clingy. Even when Jacko blanked her,
she'd turn up. Poor girl, she wasn't demanding – she was just
there. All the time. She took to finishing work and coming on
to the estate and if Jacko wasn't in, or he had got his mum to
pretend he wasn't, she'd come and knock for me. One day she
knocked and I was the only one in, so I thought I'd try it on.
Without a word, she obediently took her knickers off and lay
back on our new leather settee. Again, time was rushed as fear
of the family coming home was uppermost in my mind, but it
was more like a household chore for her than electrifying sex. I
could see why Jacko had tired of her so quickly. 'She's better
than wanking – just,' he'd said to me once and now I knew
exactly what he meant.

A pattern emerged and a strange three-way relationship
developed. Wendy became our girlfriend. She was loyal to us
both but we were not necessarily loyal to her. Sometimes I went

out with her, sometimes Jacko did and sometimes the three of us went out together. There was absolutely no jealousy and, over time, the two of us began to like her a bit more. She never tried to play us off against each other or expressed unhappiness about her lot. She confused sex with love and because we both regularly had sex with her, she thought we loved her, even though we accommodated her only on the most selfish terms.

Then she fell pregnant. She rang me up at work. 'Guess what? I'm pregnant. Three months pregnant.'

I was stunned as I stood in my office listening to the excited chatter of this now seventeen-year-old girl. As if I was being questioned by the police, I chose my words carefully, not wishing to incriminate myself. 'Whose is it, Wendy?'

'Yours.'

'Mine?'

'Yes, yours and Jacko's.'

'It can't be both of ours, Wendy.'

'Well, I've traced it back to Sunday the 5th and according to my diary I had a shag with both of you that day.'

The conversation had become surreal and I said I would go round to see her that evening. Firstly, I went to see Jacko.

'I haven't fucked her for ages,' Jacko declared.

'Neither have I.'

'Good, then it's not one of us then,' we lied.

But it wasn't as easy as that.

Jacko refused point-blank to see her, or discuss the baby at all. 'Look, if she has that baby we'll be lumbered with her for life. You'll have to get her to have an abortion.'

'Why me?'

''Cos you can talk to her better than me.'

I took Wendy down to the curry house and as we walked

down the hill she slipped her hand in mine and rested her little head on my shoulder. A shiver ran down my spine as I could feel her smiling sweetly up at me. I wanted to hold her and tell her I loved her. Problem was, I didn't. I knew I had to be strong. For me. As I looked at her across the poppadoms and pickle tray, she looked so young and innocent which, of course, she was.

'Wendy, you can't have this baby.'

'Why not?'

'Because we don't know who the father is, do we?'

'So what? It's you or Jacko, isn't it? Do you think I've been sleeping around or something?' She was offended now.

'No, but he's not going to want to bring up a kid that he doesn't know is definitely his and neither am I, come to that.'

She started to sob. Not a teenage girl's manipulative sob, but a real sad crying from deep inside. Her shoulders heaved and I could tell she couldn't control it. The sobbing was coming from deep, deep down. I looked around guiltily to see if any of the other diners had noticed. We walked home but there was no comforting her.

Jacko never heard from Wendy again, but I did. She rang me about a week later and said that her GP had arranged for her to have an abortion at the general hospital and she was going in that evening. Would I come and see her the following day? She had told her mum and dad she was staying the night at Viv's. I walked on to the ward the next evening and judging by the looks I got Wendy had told all the ladies in there about her predicament. I sat by her bed and made small talk.

'How do you feel?'

'Weird.'

'What do you mean, weird?'

'I feel like I've had a big lump taken out my tummy.'

Once it was over I thought it would be business as usual but Wendy had other ideas. We sat in her back room a couple of evenings after she had come out of hospital, watching TV on a little black-and-white portable. Her parents occasionally came through, heading for the kitchen to make a cup of tea.

'I don't want to see you or Jacko again after tonight,' she said quietly and calmly as she took another sip from her coffee cup. I didn't ask why.

CHAPTER TEN

I Don't Want to Go to Chelsea

During our childhood years most of us didn't get off the estate and its immediate environs very much at all. My brothers and sisters and I were lucky because our parents managed to take us on holiday most years. The palaver of getting to and from our destination was unreal and involved brown leathery suitcases, mini-cabs and long train journeys. It took a whole day to get to the south coast and settle in to our holiday house. Now people commute twice that distance without blinking.

For most boys on the estate, the first significant venturing further afield would be to football: Fulham, Palace or Chelsea. The first time Dad took me to a match it was to Selhurst Park to see Crystal Palace against Norwich City. Both clubs were newly promoted to the First Division and there was a crowd of about thirty thousand. Skinheads had faded out a bit, at least the cropped hair had, but still I'd never seen such a large display of turned-up Levi's and polished Dr Marten high-ups. After the game we saw Norwich fans chasing Palace fans around the streets of Selhurst. I was mildly interested.

Dad obviously wasn't too perturbed about the charging hordes because soon after that game he allowed me and Vic to make the trip to Palace unsupervised. We soon got right into it. Even though Crystal Palace were not the sort of side you boasted about supporting at school, there was something about them that was quite attractive. It was a friendly club and it was safe and for those couple of seasons anyway the football was as exciting as anything else on offer.

John Jackson was a goalkeeper who put Gordon Banks to shame, it seemed to us. We stood behind the goal so we knew: if it wasn't for that man Palace would have been relegated every season. Stevie Kember was the boy wonder, the local kid who would so obviously soon join a big club. But the main attraction was a long-haired, moustachioed winger called Don Rogers. Palace had picked him up at Swindon after he had dazzled the nation in the League Cup final when the little club had beaten the mighty Arsenal. He was awesome on the wing, cutting in, swerving past defenders and then dummying the keeper and slicing the ball into the net. Don Rogers was different gear. For a while his form was so electric that the rumour (down at Palace, anyway) was that Alf Ramsey was going to abandon his policy of not playing wingers and draft old Don into the England squad. When Don went off the boil the club stumbled on barrel-chested Peter Taylor who, although a different sort of player, pleased the crowds no less. He did make the England side but the story of his career was that he could only really do it for Palace.

Vic and I headed over Croydon way for the big fixture – Crystal Palace versus Manchester United. There was a crowd of fifty thousand in town for this one. Bobby Charlton was playing, as was Denis Law. Alas, there was no Georgie Best – probably on a vodka binge somewhere. Manchester United fans filled the ground but they were mainly good-humoured. To everyone's amazement and United's horror, Palace thrashed the big side 5–0. Shortly after, it was the turn of Chelsea to visit and Vic and I made our way to the ground with a certain amount of trepidation.

Chelsea had a big reputation as *the* skinhead club. We'd been raised on folklore about Chelsea and the 'football hooligans' as they were starting to be called. One story that did the rounds at our school was so obviously an urban myth that we were surely the only people who believed it: a mother takes her young son to Stamford Bridge. He wants to go to the toilet and she waits outside the public conveniences for him. After a while she becomes concerned that he has not reappeared and enters the toilet to find him. Inside she sees her little boy in a pool of blood on the floor. He is alive but some Chelsea skinheads have cut his testicles off with a knife and have been rolling them around the floor like marbles.

How these more ridiculous urban myths started and survived is baffling. Some of them came from a book called *Chopper* that was, for a summer, prized currency at school. I remember one story that concerned the skinheads' natural enemy: the rocker, the greaser or the Hell's Angel. It described the initiation ceremonies of a Hell's Angel gang: the biting-off of chickens' heads and the gang-banging and the urinating over new members but the story that did the rounds was true and all the more chilling. (When I say *true*, it was always told in confiding tones and the teller knew the person who knew the victim.) A lone skinhead bumps into four girl greasers who offer him a sex session. He accepts and they go to a local park. After some horseplay they pin him down and start to wank him off. Everything seems fine except that they carry on and on and on, even after the skinhead has climaxed. Eventually he is ejaculating blood and he dies.

These stories were never told jocularly. It was as if we'd been let into a terrible secret. As impressionable eleven-, twelve- and thirteen-year-olds, we never wondered why these stories never made the papers but simply passed them on with equal authority. There were a couple of greaser girls who lived in Common Crescent; whenever I passed them as I swaggered down to the shops in my Fred Perry and tonic trousers, my scrotum tightened.

This day against Chelsea the local rail network was awash with blue-and-white woollen scarves streaming from the train windows. The Chelsea fans sang songs with words like:

'With hatchets and hammers,
Carving knives and spanners,
We'll show those Tottenham bastards how to fight.'

or

'We don't carry hatchets,
We don't carry lead,
We only carry pick-axes,
To bury in your head.'

Vic and I were in no doubt they meant what they said. We 'knew' that people were routinely hit with axes and iron bars at Chelsea. We'd even heard that at Millwall there was a bloke who carried and occasionally fired a shotgun at opposition fans.

At Selhurst station we alighted from the train and tagged along with the Chelsea crowd towards the ground. I was looking for the leaders. We'd heard so much in the playground and on the estate about Danny Gardner, the fearsome warrior, and Bulworth, the so-called leader of the Shed. Dave Elmer, an older boy from Watermead, had told us that Bulworth wore a suit and bowler hat to games, just like the bloke on the *Clockwork Orange* film posters. I was so excited at the prospect of just clapping eyes on one of these mystical characters that I failed to notice that two older boys had fallen into step with Vic and me, one on either side of us. We knew something was up. They veered us off into a side road as the main crowd continued onwards.

'Give us your jacket,' said one menacingly. He was eyeing Vic's Budgie jacket. This was his pride and joy – a black-and-purple thing with a long pointed collar that had been made popular by Adam Faith in the TV series *Budgie* about a cockney wide-boy.

'And I'll have your sheepskin,' said the other, nodding at my dirty but much-prized coat. Time seemed frozen for several seconds. We were of course shitting bricks, but giving up our precious items of clothing was something else. Seeing that we needed convincing, one of the boys turned the side of his leg towards us and tugged slightly on his Levi's. Tucked inside the woolly grey sock that was visible above his Dr Marten boot was what looked like the top of a sheath knife. I began to unbutton my coat.

'All right, Terry?' shouted Vic.

He had spotted Terry Baker, from the estate, at the top of the road passing along with the moving masses.

'Vic! John! What you doing down there? Come with us!' And he beckoned us towards him. We stepped away from the older boys and hurried up to join Terry and his mates. Our would-be muggers pressed on ahead of us. For some reason we didn't even mention to Terry what had happened.

Terry was only a couple of years older but he did seem to know a lot of this Chelsea crowd. He knew all the words to all the songs, which is more than we did, and we felt a bit like at school when you're paying lip-service, literally, to the hymn being sung in morning assembly when the teacher's beady eye is on you as we joined in.

'Bring on Tottenham or the Arsenal
Bring on spastics by the score
Barcelona, Real Madrid
Tottenham are a load of Yids
And we're out to show the world we can score.'

These were the words they seemed to be singing as we filed into the White Horse Road end. They seemed to be singing a lot of songs about Tottenham, whom they weren't even playing.

This time Palace got thrashed 5–0, but for me something had changed. Despite the frightening experience before the match, I was absolutely intoxicated by the atmosphere and excitement of the day. Shopkeepers, railway ticket-collectors, ordinary people and even coppers seemed in awe of the Chelsea crowd, and I'd been one of them. I hadn't seen the famous leaders of the Shed but I had seen scores upon scores of boys and young men all dressed alike and doing exactly what they wanted. Vic wasn't so taken with it, so it was with Peter Smith, a Chelsea fan from school, and Ronnie Matthews, that I tagged along to visit Stamford Bridge and the Shed the following week.

Chelsea were playing Sheffield United, who were far from being a glamour team. They had Tony Currie, who was being hailed as a 'creative midfield genius' but the player that impressed me was their winger, Alan Woodward. I think a couple of seasons watching Don Rogers had conditioned me to focus on the wingers in any side. I believed they were the most important players on the pitch. Because they didn't get as many goals as the other forwards they didn't get as much glory, but I got more pleasure from watching them than any of the others. Most of the big clubs had wingers and they each had a unique style: Dave Wagstaffe at Wolves was said to be able to cross a ball on to a sixpence; Peter Thompson at Liverpool; George

Armstrong at Arsenal; Alan Hinton at Derby; Eddie Gray at Leeds; and Mike Summerbee at Manchester City to name but a few.

Peter and Ronnie had been before and they led me into the cauldron of young bodies that was the Shed. I still couldn't believe that we could just walk into this exclusive club. Who were we, anyway? Five-foot nobodies. Yet we were able to become members of the most notorious football crowd in London just by turning up.

The Shed was not really a shed. It was a partly covered end of the Stamford Bridge ground where the home fans gathered. I learned years later that the fabled leader of the Shed, Bulworth, had kicked off the singing at Chelsea in response to hearing other clubs' fans becoming vocal on *Match of the Day* and the like in the early 1960s. Originally he and his cohorts stood down at the side of the pitch but Bulworth soon realised that if they gathered under the tin roof of one end their vocal efforts were substantially amplified. This they did, and each week more and more fans joined in. Bulworth and friends also searched for a name that would give the end an identity in the same way that Liverpool had done with the famous Kop. The Shed was born.

To be inside was exhilarating. The place had a force of its own. Peter told us to get as near to the middle as possible, which was easier said than done when ten thousand other boys were trying to do the same. You ended up lost in a mass of flesh, bones, scarves and bobble-hats. During the course of the game the natural movement of the mass caused you to be gradually carried all over. Pimply teenagers just smiled at you as you came crashing into them after the latest surge. They were loving it as much as you were. There were no adults around and the police rarely intervened. It was like on the school field when we would shout out 'BUNDLE!' and all go charging in to one another and roll around the grass, except this was on a massive scale.

'If I catch you wanking,
I'll saw your legs right off,
Knees up, Knees up,
Don't get the breeze up,
Knees up, Mother Brown.'

This strange ditty always triggered a mass friendly free-for-all whereby you pushed and shoved the people in front of you and they did the same to you. From a distance it looked like a land-slide. From close up it was a lot of innocent fun.

There didn't seem to be an obvious cheerleader but the songs came thick and fast. Who made them up? Some of them had detailed words and rhythms. They couldn't just have tumbled out of someone's brain and mouth during a match. I tried to picture some big skinhead sitting in his study, sucking on his pen, and waiting for inspiration:

'Who's that lying on the tarmac,
Who's that lying in the snow . . .'

That particular one was sung to Manchester United fans and referred to the Munich air disaster in which many United players perished. A strange sort of lyricist indeed had dreamt that up, but someone did. It was a sick song but its intended unkindness had got lost somewhere along the way. I doubt if half the boys singing it knew what it was about or, if they did, really meant what the words celebrated. It was like another one, which, when I first heard it, made me cringe. Directed at Spurs fans (who, according to the *Urban Myth Guide to Soccer Fans*, consist solely of members of the Jewish community), it opened something like this:

'*Spurs are on their way to Auschwitz*
Hitler's gonna gas 'em again . . .'

Sick or what? I worried about some little old Jewish lady, alone at home in her armchair, who happens upon *Match of the Day* one Saturday night and hears that being sung in the background. What would she think, having lost her family in the Holocaust and seeing out her final years in a civilised, sympathetic society, realising that fifty thousand young men are singing a song about marching Jews to the gas chambers. Of course, the political and emotional significance of these songs was lost on all but a handful of those singing them and, believe it or not, the Spurs fans, for example, didn't take them personally. But the skinhead, or whoever, at home with the blank lyric sheet – well, he did spook me.

Up at the back of the Shed I got a glimpse of the darker side. The back row was raised up and this is where the older boys stood and sat, draped over the crash-barrier, looking down on the dark walkway that was a chicken run through the end. They were not watching the game – they couldn't possibly see the pitch from there. I found it frightening to walk along with my head dead level with thousands upon thousands of shiny leather Dr Marten boots and all eyes on me. That's how it felt. But there were more police officers here mingling with the crowd. The youths perched on the barriers at the back didn't wear bobble-hats nor were they flourishing scarves or singing. They sported sideburns and many had tattoos covering their muscular arms. Unlike most of us, their tattoos were not in the first flush of colour.

The tattoo thing was another aspect of the skinhead fashion. At school we started experimenting with Indian ink and a needle, puncturing our arms to make crudely drawn letters and symbols. As soon as we could lay our hands on enough money we traipsed in our hundreds up to Wandsworth to have our flesh decorated by Rick Richards: tattooist to the underage or inebriated. Swallows, scrolls with the inscription 'Mum and Dad', flowers, swords and the Chelsea lion were the order of the day. Some of the more daring or reckless among us left there with eagles or sunsets adorning our little hairless pigeon chests as well as a hangover.

I sneaked glances up at their hard faces, wondering which ones might be Bulworth or Danny Gardner or even Hicks, a reputed one-armed man I had heard so much about. But for the time being I was content to grab my pie and return to the carnival atmosphere in the Shed centre.

For all the violent and hate-filled songs, I saw no fighting at all in my first season of going to Chelsea (Palace had soon become a distant memory that I kept close to my chest). I couldn't imagine that any opposing supporters would be fool-hardy enough even to consider going to Stamford Bridge. The next season, though, I literally stumbled into my first experi-ence of football fighting. It was against Tottenham, and Peter, Ronnie and I had left our customary five minutes earlier to avoid the queues on the Underground we needed to catch back to Wimbledon. As we scurried past the North Stand entrance, where the away supporters would eventually be let out, we couldn't help but notice groups of older youths standing around by the flats opposite. A group of Spurs fans came hurry-ing out – perhaps they too were keen to beat the rush. The six or seven pockets of youths who were hanging around the flats sprang into action and attacked the Tottenham fans. They were outnumbered and soon fell to the ground as the Chelsea lot sur-rounded them and mercilessly kicked away. I sprinted towards the mêlée and landed my unchristened boot into the back of a Tottenham fan whom I'd judged wasn't getting up for a while.

'What did you do that for?' asked Ronnie as we stood on Fulham Broadway station.

'I don't know,' was my honest reply.

I was in the Shed when it fell to West Ham one Boxing Day and I realised that it wasn't all one-way traffic. Merely being a Chelsea fan didn't protect you from the nasty realities of life. That afternoon, as I saw West Ham supporters flourish their scarves and start singing,

'We took the Shed,
We took the Shed,
Eee I Adio,
We took the Shed '

I noticed many of those youths and young men who had frightened me so at the back of the Shed suddenly looked pretty scared themselves.

I learned about the pecking order in football just as I did on the estate and in the playground. West Ham and Millwall were our superiors, Tottenham were our equals and pretty much everyone else was inferior.

With Peter I ventured not very far across London to Loftus Road, home of Queens Park Rangers. Chelsea had pretty much overrun the ground and there was none of the fighting between fans that we had hoped to witness. However, there was a fad at the time for throwing coins at the opposing team's goalkeeper and Chelsea fans were busy chucking their spare shrapnel in the direction of the pitch. Some police officers waded into the throng and started to bundle out those they thought might be responsible. One of these coppers was a young boy, really. He had grown a little beard to make himself look older but his eyes betrayed his fear as he grappled with a stronger boy he was trying to cart off. These were the days before CCTV which can pinpoint within seconds any incident in the crowd. He was the last of the policemen to be pushing his way back out of the crowd with his catch, and his unease was obvious. Someone kicked his legs away and he toppled on to the concrete steps. *Thud.* A steel toe-capped black army boot caught him in the lower back. And then they were on him like ants. I pushed my way through and kicked him as hard as I could in the back of the head and then made my way back out of the crowd.

I had no qualms, no guilt. In fact, I was disappointed when an army of black uniforms charged back in and rescued him. I would have been quite happy if he'd been kicked to death. I wasn't unusual in hating the police – they were the natural enemy of young boys and men who indulged in anti-social behaviour. With me, though, it went deeper. I had been brought up to respect them. They protected decent people. They came into our schools and gave talks on road safety. They stood in the streets and directed traffic in their nice friendly uniforms and helmets. Dixon of Dock Green, with a face like my Granddad, saluting every Saturday night under the street-light in the drizzle, gave me a warm feeling. The police were nice people looking after us. Then slowly I started to meet them and get to know them.

There was the incident in the cycling prohibited alley, and then as teenagers we got collared one day riding a stolen moped around the fields. They wanted to know which one of us had nicked it and they drove us to the station but no one would say. We were put in the cells for an hour or two. Finally, a plain-clothes officer came to my cell. He stank of alcohol and his cheeks and nose were speckled with broken blood vessels. He seemed quite ordinary in his suit and tie and with a rolled-up copy of the *Daily Mirror* in his hand.

'Okay, John, I've no time to be fucking around. Tell me who stole the bike and you can go. I know it wasn't you.'

I protested I didn't know and *whack* he had whipped me across the face with the newspaper. Then again and again and again. Okay, it was only a newspaper, but it stung and it hurt. I was thirteen or fourteen and we were talking a stolen moped, not gold bullion.

That was just one of many experiences my friends and I had of bullying at the hands of the police. I was soon to discover they were not above lying, racism, stealing and just about every other vice. Like us, really. But they were using it against us and with the blessing of society – the society we didn't belong to, the society we offended against.

Once we got out to work and had access to money, Peter, Ronnie and I were tagging along with older boys like Terry Baker, Barry Duckett and Steve Langton to games outside London. This was a different world: the Chelsea hordes gathering at St Pancras, Euston or Kings Cross for trips north, swigging from beer cans, singing, shouting and swearing, we would outnumber all other travellers by ten to one. There was a carnival atmosphere. Friendships were forged on the 'special' trains that transported the most over-exuberant of over-exuberant youths around the country. I always thought it ironic that the government-owned rail network every Saturday was a willing participant in facilitating the transport around England of mobs of youths hellbent on destruction, aggression and sometimes violence. It couldn't have been lucrative for them – the tickets were so cheap. Indeed, for some seasons, football boys notched up thousands of miles simply from collecting vouchers from their mums' Persil packets.

I finally got to meet the legendary Bulworth on one of these away trips. I'd come across the famous Danny Gardner and Hicks when they'd entered our railway carriage some months before when Tony Bond and Peter Smith had had a fight and broke the train window. Bulworth was there then but he kept in the background as Gardner ticked us off like a cross father. On this trip, though, I managed to sit opposite him on the train and observe the legend at close range. He spoke sparingly in gruff tones and his staircase nose told a hundred stories from a previous decade. He was dressed in a suit and tie, which was unusual garb for a football fan to say the least. Alas, no bowler hat. He looked like he'd been to a wedding, got pissed and turned up for the game after having slept the night in a field in his suit. Everyone who passed down the corridor either spoke to him or took a long look.

He was a true Chelsea fan and I couldn't help feeling that he was a bit like Dr Frankenstein in having created something – the Shed – that had turned into a monster. He was having a friendly argument with two or three of the other lads, who didn't seem to be showing him the respect I thought they should. Then again, they were more his age. They were discussing the motives of the seven hundred or so men travelling on the train.

'They're all here for the ruck, Mick, believe me.'

'I don't think so,' opined Bulworth. 'Some are, but most are true Chelsea fans here for the football.'

He decided to settle the dispute by conducting his own opinion poll up and down the carriages. Forty-five minutes later he was back and started counting up the ticks he had marked in a small notebook. He shook his head in bewilderment and mumbled: 'Four hundred and twenty-seven say they are here for the ruck, ninety-six for the football, seventeen asleep.'

The excitement, the feeling of notoriety, the adrenaline rush of arriving mob-handed with Chelsea in a strange town was more powerful than any drug. Once you'd tasted it, you needed it again and again and again. Platforms cleared, shoppers stopped and customers clambered up to the pub windows – pubs with the doors safely bolted – to catch a glimpse of us as we were escorted through the city streets to the football ground. This was the nearest our generation was going to get to being in an invading army; the only time many of us would be held in awe; the only time we ran the show and made the newspapers. The feeling of comradeship was immense. The cocktail was irresistible.

So irresistible that Peter, Ronnie and I made the trip up to Carlisle, the furthest-flung football ground in the English league. The special was only half-full – maybe three hundred chaps rather than the usual seven hundred. And I doubted if there would be many others making the trip by coach or car. The journey seemed endless and there was great excitement when someone spotted snow-peaked mountains from the window. The train finally pulled in at Carlisle at 2.15 p.m. allowing almost no time for the ritual pre-match drink. We decided, along with five blokes we'd met on the train and knew vaguely, to slip the inevitable police escort and try and find the first pub away from the route. No one knew whether Carlisle was dangerous or not. Had this been Newcastle, for example, we would not have dared split off from the main contingent. But none of the boys, including Bulworth or Danny Gardner, seemed to have been here before so there were no dire warnings about the locals being 'naughty' or not. On *Match of the Day*, grazing cows could be seen in a field next to the ground so, subconsciously, I think, we believed we were dealing with people in smocks chewing hay and carrying pitchforks.

We found a pub in a side street after hanging around the toilets at Carlisle station as the crowd was moved, singing, towards the ground. The publican served us but he seemed a little nervous. I thought he was concerned that more of us could be following. We drank fast as time was short. Halfway through the second pint, the door burst open and we were faced by ten snarling locals waving pool cues, glasses and bottles. Now I knew why the publican was edgy: this lot had been drinking in the public bar when we had arrived. Although they crashed in through the door, they paused once they were inside.

'Come on, Chelsea lads, you want it!' shouted a long-haired youth at the front, who tapped a pool cue into the palm of his hand for effect.

Funny: if I had envisaged the situation beforehand, I would have been terrified. Trapped in a strange pub, outnumbered by locals armed to the teeth, intent on doing us damage. It was obvious that this wasn't a situation which we could talk our way out of or where rescue in the shape of the police or fellow Chelsea fans was imminent.

One of the London boys from the train grabbed a barstool by the leg and tossed it into their group, and instinctively we charged into them. We pushed them out into the road, but this turned out to be a bad move because it gave them room to swing their cues and land their bottles. Ronnie took a couple of nasty whacks on the bonce but kept focused on their main boy, the one with the cue. He eventually closed on him despite the efforts of the guy's mates to bring him down. I decided to help keep the others off Ronnie as he disarmed the greasy-haired bloke with the cue. One of them then turned round and faced me. I was concentrating on watching his fists and head when he booted me so hard in the shin I had to squeeze my eyes shut with pain. He followed this with a clean smack in the mouth and I tasted blood immediately. Fortunately, Ronnie had dealt with the bloke he was after and grasped my attacker in a bear hug from behind which enabled me to punch him with all my might in the groin. He staggered away, regurgitating whatever alcohol it was he had been drinking minutes earlier.

We left the pub and jumped in an almost separate free-for-all across the road where Peter and the other lads seemed to be all rolling around the road as one. The Carlisle lads had seen their numbers had diminished and that Ronnie had disabled their leader, who was still comatose on the ground, and they started to remove themselves from the brawl and run off. We decided to do the same before the police arrived.

In the stadium we were the centre of attention. The main Chelsea firm were disappointed they had travelled all this way and there was no resistance from Carlisle. They had strolled into the home end, which apparently had been vacated in anticipation of the Chelsea fans' expected attempt to take it. All sorts of faces came over to us and asked us to repeat the story about how we 'had a row with Carlisle's main crew'. Ronnie, with his bloodied black face and ripped T-shirt (only he would travel to the other end of the country in winter in just a T-shirt), was asked to tell the story time and time again. They listened excitedly to the already embellished version we were recounting and then shook their heads, patted us on the back and said, 'You lucky bastards.'

These were the best days for me. Soon things began to

change, though. I witnessed two beatings dealt out to completely innocent bystanders in close succession and they started
me thinking about the morality of what I was doing. It played
on my mind and acted as an antidote to the drug-like hold that
going to Chelsea had on me. At Aston Villa we ran into a
coachload of boys who were intent on seeking out and attack-
ing a mosque and at Coventry I watched as two hundred
Chelsea boys stood for the entire game with their backs to the
pitch, making Nazi salutes. Someone explained there was a
black player on the pitch. It was only then that I realised a very
racist agenda had somehow taken hold and we were all expected
to subscribe to it.

While some of these blokes were certainly political animals,
the bulk were not. I knew many of them and I could see they
were being swept along by a fashion, many mouthing racist
chants and songs but going home and living happily alongside
people from all creeds just the way they always had.

I first noticed Ronnie looking uncomfortable at a home
game when fans had brought in bananas by the lorry-load to
throw at one of the new black players. But it seemed they had
divorced in their minds the focus of their apparent hate on the
pitch, and in the Asian areas of various inner cities, from people
like Ronnie – black guys who had grown up Chelsea supporters
and fought with and like the rest of them up and down the
country. In their eyes, Black Ronnie wasn't black.

Ronnie's life had been tough. I don't know what happened
to his parents. He never said and I never asked. He was proud
of the fact that he came from Peckham and often mentioned
this but somehow I doubted that he'd ever been there. The
Peckham story was something he used when he came to our
school along with the other kids from Beechurst, to create an

air of toughness or being someone. The implication was that there was a family in Peckham who would materialise should anyone give him a hard time. But no one did because Ronnie was once of the nicest people you could ever meet. I never heard him say a bad word about anyone. He was big and muscly but he never bullied. He had little money but was generous to a fault. He was kind to smaller and younger children and he was fiercely loyal.

He took me up to Beechurst once, a huge red-bricked Victorian complex where the kids lived in manufactured 'families'. An auntie and uncle, who were not married, would run one unit of two boys and two girls, although efforts were made to keep brothers and sister together. They tried to live as family units within the larger community of the home. Ron seemed happy enough and he never spoke ill of the aunties and uncles, but some of them looked decidedly dodgy to me. He claimed that in the evenings, the kids held secret parties and they all shagged each other stupid, but I put this down to wishful thinking.

Chelsea was his passion. He loved the team and he loved the culture. There were many more black kids at Chelsea than there were in Winhurst, but I don't think that was why he felt so comfortable there. We never discussed the right-wing thing. Maybe, like me, he thought it would pass and was just sitting tight. I don't think it crossed his mind that he could be in any personal danger. It certainly didn't occur to me.

The coach to Preston was leaving from Fulham Broadway at seven-thirty in the morning. I drove up with Ronnie – we were the only two who could afford to go that day – and parked up in a Fulham back street and walked over to the Shed end where three coaches were waiting. We exchanged small talk with some people we knew and started to board the last coach which, we could see, wasn't quite full. Beer and banter were already flying about as I came up the steps. I recognised most of the faces on here but knew very few of the names. As Ronnie became visible behind me the banter stopped, the coach fell silent and all eyes were upon us. I tried to pay the guy at the front but he seemed embarrassed and kept looking down the aisle as if he was trying to get some sort of signal from someone.

'I don't know if you want to be on this one,' he finally whispered. 'Everyone on here is up for a ruck. Why don't you try the ones in front?'

'Nah, we're up for it, too,' I replied, not picking up the correct vibes at all and a bit put out that they thought of me and Ronnie as innocents or shy of having a ruck. Ronnie was tapping me on the shoulder but I was still trying to hand the guy my tenner.

'Look, we've got no problem with you, pal,' he said. 'But your mate ' – and his eyebrows signified some area over my shoulder – 'isn't welcome on this coach.'

He seemed glad he had got it out and stood up and walked down the aisle as if to say that was the end of the matter. I looked down the coach and my eyes were met with blank and a few hostile stares. Ronnie had already stepped backwards on to the pavement and I shrugged and followed him. We didn't go to Preston and Ronnie never went to Chelsea again.

CHAPTER ELEVEN

Daniel

We didn't come across Pugsley Pullinger every day but when we did something always seemed to happen. He fought everywhere he went. He and the Wheatleys and others had even taken on and maimed the bouncers at a West End nightclub one Saturday night and ended up at the Old Bailey for their pains. A year or two inside didn't seem to have calmed him down, though. He scrapped in the same way other people spoke. It was his way of communicating.

I got caught up with him one night and I got the biggest hiding of my life. There was a wedding reception at one of the mental hospitals' social clubs and we decided to gatecrash. That wasn't as outrageous as it sounds because one of the rules was that if you booked the halls for a social function, you traded off the cheap price with the fact that social-club members were still allowed into the bar and hall regardless. We weren't members but behaved like we were. All the staff were local people so they let us do as we pleased, especially if Pugsley was with us.

The wedding was between a local girl – a hospital domestic – and a lad from Liverpool. The groom had a large contingent of mates and family down from his home town and I picked up a vibe very early on that they resented our presence. Eventually, the bride came over, still in her white dress, and asked if we would mind moving into the other bar so that guests who were arriving could use our seats. It seemed a fair enough request to me and I gathered up the packets of fags and lighters in the hope that we would just move quietly.

Pugsley, however, had different ideas. He studied her intently, his brow furrowed. She wasn't the best-looking of girls.

'Who's been hitting you with the ugly stick?' he enquired.

'I'm sorry?' the girl replied, genuinely confused.

'Which one married you, then? I bet he's got a white stick and a fucking labrador. You're pig ugly, you are.' He roared with laughter at his own joke whilst we winced or smiled weakly.

She turned away in a flood of tears and ran over to her new husband and his mates, all suited and booted and drinking at a big table on the other side of the dance-floor. The groom comforted his sobbing bride, as words were spoken in numerous ears and the entire male side of the guest list headed towards us.

'Beam me up, Scottie,' laughed Pugsley.

I hoped against hope that this wasn't going to escalate into something nasty. There was me, Steve, Jacko, Vic, Pugsley and Keith, who was fresh from the navy and rejoined our small gang. There were at least twenty Liverpudlians standing menacingly in front of us.

'You've upset my wife, mate,' said the groom, fixing his stare on Pugsley. 'I want you to leave here now, all of you, but not before you, pal, go over and apologise to her.'

Maybe, just maybe, Pugsley would have left without causing a scene, but insisting on him apologising to anyone was a bridge too far.

'Mate, no offence meant,' Pugs said disingenuously as he rose to his feet.

We all got up too, but before we could head towards the exit Pugsley had cracked the groom on the jaw, floored him, and was into the next one. I remember nothing after that although there were numerous versions of what happened next. I awoke an hour later in hospital in a darkened room. An Indian doctor was shining a torch in my eyes. 'You've been hit very hard, several times, with a blunt instrument,' he informed me.

I was badly concussed and needed more than twenty stitches in my head. Steve said he'd seen one of the scousers hit me with a chair but the doctor thought it was more likely to have been a cosh of some description.

Outside the room sat Pugsley who had a broken hand and a bruised and battered face but who otherwise seemed full of beans. 'All right, Johnny boy?' he shouted as I was wheeled out of the room to a ward where I was to stay the night for observation, with a big bandage and plaster on my bonce.

'How are the others?' I sat up and asked.

'Vic has had to go to Roehampton to get his jaw rewired – they can't do it here. Steve and Jacko got carted off by the Old Bill and Keith has been up here for a few stitches and gone home.'

'Oh, that's all right then, as long as no one got hurt.'

The sound of Pugsley's chesty laugh rang loudly in my ears, as my head thumped and the porter pushed me away down the corridor.

Those mental homes haunt me. Winhurst people worked there, courted there, shagged there, married there, raised children there and some even died there. There were several of them, huge and forbidding red-brick Victorian fortresses. Prisons, masquerading as hospitals, pretending to be communities. Some even had their own churches, as if those confused souls wandering aimlessly around the grounds and up and down ceramic-tiled corridors had a choice in the matter of worship.

As children we would sneak into the grounds and watch the patients from a safe distance. Yet these people were more harmless than we could ever have imagined. 'Binners' or 'looneys', we called them. At a young age we had a perception of strong men, with manic staring eyes, rocking back and forth as they were restrained by manacles or straitjackets. But most of the time these people were incapable of harming anyone but themselves. They shuffled along their well-worn paths and circles as only people who have been nowhere and have nowhere to go can. Full of largactyl ('lead-boots', the male nurses called it), their bodies went through their daily pathetic routines whilst their minds waited to die. And to keep it all clean and tidy, their wards backed on to the on-site crematorium.

I wondered who they were. How did they get here? What happened to their families? I mean, no one is born with a week's worth of stubble, an ill-fitting tweed jacket with leather patches on the elbows, a non-burning dog-end attached to their bottom lip and wearing fluffy bedroom slippers, are they? Visits were few and far between for the long-term patients. My parents told us they came from London, as if that explained all. Some had been in there since they were children. Get pregnant or lose your parents in the early part of the twentieth century and you could have been packed off to Winhurst. Others had been damaged by the wars. The first acid casualties were beginning to arrive. The rest were just casualties.

We grew up with the patients and accepted them. The day-trip scenes in *One Flew over the Cuckoo's Nest* could have been based on Saturday afternoons in Winhurst town centre during the 1960s and 1970s. On Saturdays the more together 'nutters' were allowed to the shops to spend their pocket money. Mostly they were content to huddle together in front of the library with their treasured transistor radios pushed tight against their ears. One chap would walk up and down the High Street with a bedroom slipper neatly balanced on his head, and now and then a naked man or woman would make it into Timothy White's or Woolworth's before the police plucked them away and ferried them back to the hospital in the back of a panda car.

When I was working a mate came down from Deptford to play in a football match at one of the hospitals. He was distinctly nervous when taking throw-ins as a vacant-looking but powerful teenager rocked violently back and forth beside him on the touchline. As we drove away up the country lane after the game he saw a young girl riding her bike with a patient some yards behind. To our amusement he tried to stop the car to persuade us to rescue the girl.

Sometimes things went wrong and the sirens would wail. This was meant to warn us that a dangerous patient had escaped but it only encouraged us kids to conduct our own search. One hospital housed the criminally insane. Reggie and Ronnie staged their famous 'swap' escape from there. On another occasion, a poor man answered his door in Mills Road to an urgent knocking, only to be confronted by and beaten to death by one of these absconders. Events like this were rare; normally they only harmed themselves. Suicides were an occupational hazard for train-drivers passing through Winhurst station, and finding a decomposing body in the grounds or surrounding countryside of a hospital was not unusual for staff or dog-walkers.

Inevitably, we made fun of them and wound them up. One

chap used to hang around outside the school. He had no dodgy motive – he may have been forty but he thought he was fourteen. One day he swaggered up to the playground. He had acquired a leather jacket, which he couldn't wait to show us. He did a twirl and written on the back in silver studs was the proclamation: 'Hells Angles'! Another old boy used to come into the café we used at lunchtime. We'd fill his tea mug with tomato sauce, sugar and salt and he'd knock it back and then rub his tummy and say, 'Oooomh.'

When we were older the patients sometimes used our local pub which was situated bang in the middle of most of the hospitals. A long-haired and long-fingernailed geezer from the pop group Fleetwood Mac was one acid-scorched celebrity who would come in, sit in a corner and nurse his pint for hours on end. We liked to put 'Albatross' on the jukebox and watch for his reaction. But there never was any. I think some of us took some comfort from his reduced circumstances – a sort of 'There for the grace of God went he'. Other mini-celebrities drifted in and out. A fellow that played a detective in *Z Cars* was one. He had a booze problem and when he did a runner from detox, The Wheatsheaf was his destination.

The men were safe from us but the women weren't. We were predatory young males. Diane was beautiful. The first time she walked into the pub I was struck by her long black hair and flowery dress. She drank orange juice, so alcohol didn't seem to be her problem. Once I spoke to her I was convinced she was the Summer of Love personified. She only saw good in us and wore her heart on her sleeve. She had been educated at Princess Anne's school and her daddy was stinking rich, but she had got in with a hippy crowd and now she was hooked on heroin. She showed us the puncture marks on her arms to underline this.

Many of us were familiar with most drugs by this time, but not with heroin. Heroin was for hippies. We were lads, Chelsea boys – no thanks.

She spoke well, as my old English teacher would say. She was always nicely turned out and even stood her round of drinks. Older men, sensing her vulnerability, tried to buy her alcohol and take her off somewhere. But she knew the score and stuck with us. She felt safe and I think we were good therapy for her. Until one day. We were full of Holsten lager ('damage', we called it) and had been playing pool. Diane was wearing tight silk flared trousers. As she bent over the table to take difficult shots, we were scrutinising every contour of her arse. Some of us started patting her bottom and she smiled. When the pub closed we went back to one bloke's house whose mum and dad were away on holiday. Lee led Diane upstairs. Ten minutes later he was back and Steve bounded up the steps. Five boys later it was my turn. I eased into the bedroom and Diane was sitting on the bed, naked from the waist down. It was so clinical. No one had even bothered to pay any attention to the top part of her body. She looked at me and said miserably, 'I'm not a whore.' This episode became Wheatsheaf folklore. I had been blanked by a nutter in a gang-bang. Or did you hear about the bird who, after shagging six blokes, decides she's being used? But I knew what she meant. She wasn't a whore, or a loose woman for that matter. She was a child again. She needed protecting. But there was little point or will on my part to try and articulate this. When I say the hospitals haunt me, it's incidents like that which haunt me. It took a lot of liquid damage to wash that away to the recesses of my mind.

And then there was Irene. Diane brought her down to meet us. She was a self-confident, middle-aged woman who had obviously been quite a stunner in her time. She came from Twickenham and said her husband was a very senior policeman. She claimed that she had been knocked off her pushbike on Kingston Bridge and that the accident had caused her to have severe mood swings and that was what she was being treated for. I don't know. She didn't seem mad. She walked into The Wheatsheaf like she was the hostess of a Women's Rotary Club dinner who'd run out of wine and was replenishing her stocks. Glen, who was always more interested in what he could steal than what he could shag, kissed her on the back of the neck and removed her gold pendant in the process. She was none the wiser.

Unlike Diane, sex was her main interest, and she invited most of us to have relations with her in the nearby grounds of the hospitals. And most of us did. Irene was loud and hearty and would delight in telling the whole pub about our sexual underperformance. She was interested in foreplay, post-play and just about any other play that was going. We were just after a furtive fuck and back to the pub. Until Tony Bond.

Tony appeared in my life intermittently. He was the most intense person I ever knew. At school we shared a warped sense of humour and always tried to outdo one another. I gave up trying to compete when I came back from the dinner break, lifted the lid of my wooden desk and found a freshly laid brown human turd curled up across my books. Mind you, he was the one who persuaded me that by lying on my arm for a sustained period until I got pins and needles and then had a wank it was like someone else doing it. It was. But the twenty-minute wait and discomfort seemed hardly worth it after about the hundredth go. Tony laughed all the time. I never saw him not laughing, even when he was having a fight. Sex, though, was his overriding passion, his reason for existing. If a girl innocently bent over near him to pick up a tissue, for example, he would charge across the room and simulate doggie-fashion sex with her. At times, he did really remind me of a dog on heat.

Leaving behind his teenage years had not diminished Tony's obsession with female flesh. That's all he thought about. He was a career fucker. He didn't, I reckon, get that much more than the rest of us, but he worked on the principle that if you tried it on with a hundred women, ten might say yes and one might be worth it. Well, he must have been having a barren patch when I mentioned Irene. He was down at The Wheatsheaf in a shot and, after the briefest of introductions, left the pub with her. Tony never mentioned it but Irene certainly did.

'Where's Tony?' she would ask. 'He's the only one of you lot who knows how to satisfy a woman,' was her constant refrain. Tony, though, had had his fill and was undoubtedly out searching for his next conquest. Irene started to get obsessed about him. She wanted his phone number. Demanded to know where he drank. Stopped having sex with the rest of the boys in the pub. Tony kept well away. And then Irene stopped coming. Eventually, some weeks later, a subdued Diane told us in the pub that Irene had hanged herself at the hospital with the straps from her handbag. Some mood swing.

*

High summer 1976. It's hot, hotter than any of us can remember. All the windows and the doors of The Hyperion are flung open to let some air in to this Saturday-afternoon dinnertime session. Because the doors and windows are open, Joey Roper, the manager, turns the volume knob down to take the edge off Elton and Kiki on the jukebox. Simon, the youngest Duckett, is leaning against the bonnet of my bashed-up Morris 1100 in the carpark and gulping back a pint of Holsten damage. He's deep in conversation with Terry Baker, who's nearly naked save for Levi cut-downs and a gold rope chain. Terry's a bit overweight and the sweat is pissing out of him. His feet are bare and he moves from one foot to the other as the tarmac heats up and burns his soles. I'm fed up trying to get Chester the gypsy off the pool table, he's just too good; and stroll outside to join Simon and Tel.

'Two fucking barrels he took, straight through the stomach and still he came at him.'

They're still talking about the murder three weeks on. Mind you, it's the first ever on the estate, so you can understand it.

'He had it coming,' says Simon. 'I ain't gonna lose no sleep over him. Eh, John?' True. But whisper it quietly. Suddenly everyone's a bit braver about Sid Smith. The story's getting embroidered by the day so I'll tell it how I think it happened.

There had been some history between Andrew Halliday and Sid Smith. I think Sid resented the reputation that Andrew had acquired as a dangerous person. Physically, Andrew was not particularly big or strong, but he was capable of sudden and vicious violence, and people steered well clear. His behaviour had become too outrageous even for Steve Langton, who had long since stopped knocking around with Andy. Steve told me that one night after they had been to the Global Village at Charing Cross Andy had poured lighter fuel over a tramp and set him alight. Another time they got into a ruck with some younger lads and, even though they were easily on top, Andrew had bent one of the boys' arms up his back until it snapped. 'He'll kill someone one day,' Steve told us earnestly when he started to hang out with us. Most unsolved crimes of violence and arson in Winhurst were attributed, mostly wrongly I suspect, to him.

After Andrew did his first bit of bird in a men's prison, Sid took the piss out of him in the pub. 'S'pose you think you're hard now, do you, Andy, 'cos you've done a few months in Brixton?'

Andrew didn't rise to the bait on that occasion but some time later they had had a fight in The Hyperion. A 'fight', by all accounts, was the wrong word. Sid just attacked Halliday and almost killed him. Because it was Andrew, this didn't arouse much sympathy, although it was a clear case of Sid, who was a huge man, playing the bully. No one really liked Sid, if they were honest, and no one really liked Andrew. But for some reason, people were more scared of Sid and they pretended they liked him. I found both of them equally terrifying.

After his hiding from Sid, Andrew lay low for some months – although to be fair he was now a loner and rarely used The Hyperion or the other local pubs. But he did turn up again, this time with two mates – people, it was said later, whom he had met in prison. They played pool whilst Sid and Barry Duckett sat on stools at the bar. It was lunchtime and the pub was almost empty. This time Andrew kicked it off, smashing Sid across the head with his cue when he had his back to him. He should have known better because apparently Sid reacted as if a lolly stick had fallen on his nut. Barry took out one of the blokes and Sid dealt with both Andrew and the other one. Again, Andrew was hospitalised and the story was that he had lost a testicle through being kicked so hard.

Things went quiet again for a while. I was in The Hyperion one day and Mr and Mrs Halliday, Andrew's inoffensive parents, were in the saloon bar when Sid spotted them as he walked out of the toilets. I was in the saloon bar because Sid and his cronies never went in there and this night I was, unusually, with a girl. Sid pushed open the door and approached the Hallidays' table where they had been sitting in silence, two halves of Guinness placed neatly in front of them.

'Where is he, then? One bollock. Your son.'

Mr Halliday, who knew he was the one in the most danger here, said nothing and looked straight ahead.

'Go away, Smith,' spat Mrs Halliday. 'You and your family are nothing but trouble.'

Sid laughed and gently, almost, lifted up their table with his huge hand and let their full glasses slide down into their laps. When he had safely returned to the public bar, Mr Halliday pretended he wanted to go in and remonstrate with him and I went through the motions of telling him Sid was not worth it and allowed the poor old bloke to rescue some credibility.

Early the following evening Andrew Halliday borrowed his older brother's bike and rode up to the home of an acquaintance who lived up on the Heath. This bloke owned a shotgun for shooting rabbits and foxes. We don't know what Andrew told him but he lent Andrew the gun and loaded two barrels for him. With the shotgun over his shoulder and wrapped in a blanket, Andy rode through Winhurst and back down on to Common Way, where he leant the bike against the wall of number 13. The back door to the lounge was open. He would have known the exact layout of the house, as it was identical to his own.

Sid's stretched out on the settee, a nearly full ashtray on the arm, watching *The Six Million Dollar Man*. The kids are lying across the floor, chins cupped in hands, enjoying the adventures of Steve Austin. Linda, Sid's wife, is upstairs. Not taking any chances this time, Andrew empties both barrels into Sid's body before he has time to react. The kids stand screaming in the room. Linda comes hurtling down the stairs, and as she passes Andrew in the hall he calmly hands her the gun and leaves by the front door. He walks back down the garden path and rides the bike the few yards back to his house.

The others are still blathering on about Sid, about how his family and mates will get Andrew when he comes out of prison. I can't see Andrew ever coming back to the estate when he does one day come out but I am worried about his mum and dad. The council have said they will move them but nothing has happened yet.

Even old Joey Roper thinks he can get cocky now that Sid's dead. Linda, Sid's wife, walked into The Hyperion the other Sunday clutching a brown urn to her breast.

'What's in there, Linda?' enquired Joey.

'My Sid,' she replied.

There were only about ten people in the pub at the time but apparently you could have heard a pin drop. What made him say it, I'll never know, but Joey suddenly came out with: 'I'm sorry, Linda, but your Sid, he's barred. He can't come in here. He's always causing trouble.' At that he disintegrated into fits of laughter and everyone else in the pub did likewise.

Linda unscrewed the lid of the urn and began to shake the contents about. Ashes flew all over. She even shook the urn over the customers' drinks like sprinkling pepper on to a Sunday roast. 'There you are, you bastards. Get rid of Sid now. He's in your pub forever.' She launched the now empty urn into the optics and turned and left. That's how Sid Smith got laid to rest in The Hyperion.

*

Steve Langton screeches his big brown Rover into the carpark. Everyone's pleased to see him because if Steve's down for the day from Brixton you're going to have a laugh one way or another. He'd had to get out the Watermead area in the end. He burnt down the glass-making factory where he had been working. The foreman sacked him for being late or sick or something and Steve went back that night and set it alight. The firm had to relocate elsewhere in town. Amazingly, Steve got bail pending his Old Bailey trial. On his brief's advice he used the period to get married to the long-suffering Mel, leave the area and get a job. Even more amazingly, the judge did not pass a custodial sentence, believing that Steve really was trying to straighten himself out.

Living in Brixton just added to his allure. The accepted wisdom was that the further into London you lived the harder you were. Sutton boys were tougher than Winhurst; Tooting boys were harder than Sutton; Stockwell nastier than Tooting, and so on. Bollocks, really, but that's how it worked.

Steve has just been to visit Andrew Halliday on remand in Brixton, although he would prefer it if we kept quiet about that down here.

It's 2.30 and Joey is shooing us all away. Steve, Jacko, Simon Duckett and I decide to head down to the football club where we'll be able to carry on drinking. We park the Rover outside the grand wooden gates that say 'Founded 1919' and march through the turnstile.

'Press,' announces Steve authoritatively, flashing the man a playing card that happens to be in his pocket, and he clicks the four of us through. We don't watch the game – we don't even know which league this shower of shit play in – we just sit in the clubhouse and carry on drinking. This place holds only bad memories for me.

The silly old wanker behind the bar won't serve me when it's my round. He wants us to finish our drinks and leave. He won't say why. One of the sad tossers in here has obviously complained. What sort of person comes down here on a Saturday afternoon, anyway? Homosexuals, child molesters and weirdos in anoraks, flared trousers and clasping transistor radios. There is not one woman in the whole ground.

'Well, we're not going,' I tell him.

'I'll call the police,' he counters.

'Call the fucking police.'

Finally, two uniforms do appear, have a word with the barman, who points over to us.

'Come on, lads. Drink up and make tracks. You're not welcome here, it seems.' The policeman pulls a face and motions over to the barman. The copper can see that we're reasonably sober and not causing trouble.

Steve squeaks his chair back and rises from the table with an exasperated look on his face. He calls the two coppers away from the table. They start to talk. Lots of nodding of heads and serious looks. The coppers go back to the bar and say something to the barman, have a last look over at us, and leave the club.

Steve sits back down.

'What did you say?' I ask.

'Told 'em I was Lavender Hill CID and I was working on a drugs enquiry and they'd probably just fucked everything up,' he laughs.

They were all right, really, those two coppers – not like the bastards I'd met again in court the previous week. I was out in the Morris 1100 a couple of months before and saw I was being flashed from behind. In the mirror I could make out two men, possibly three, older than myself, in an ordinary car. I didn't know them from Adam so I put my foot down a bit. But so did they and they were right up my arse. I suppose I panicked and I went flat out through Wandsworth, breaking the speed limit and jumping red lights as they did the same. By the time I got to Vauxhall I was horrified to see that their car had grown a flashing blue light. On closer inspection I could make out that one of the men was holding it out of the window on to the roof. This was a plain-clothes police car up my arse. A real police car suddenly drove across my path, forcing me to swerve and slam on the anchors. The uniformed officers pounced on me as I climbed out of the driver's seat and threw me across the bonnet of my car,pinioning my arms behind me and handcuffing me. I told them that a gang of blokes had been chasing me in a car and I was frightened for my life. They believed me and unhandcuffed me straight away. My pursuers pulled up alongside and two young men got out the front and a uniformed policeman got out the back. They said I had been speeding on the A3 and when they tried to flag me down I had sped off. I protested that I hadn't known who they were and I hadn't seen the uniformed officer in the back – I really hadn't. No matter, I was taken to the station and charged with dangerous driving, speeding and jumping numerous red lights.

I appeared at Lavender Hill Magistrates Court to answer the charges. I had decided not to retain a solicitor, figuring that right was on my side and that if I put over my story any honest magistrate would acquit me. I was so naïve it hadn't occurred to me that the police would tell a different story.

I gave my evidence and thought I put it over quite well. This was an unfortunate misunderstanding between a new driver and off-duty policemen. I was horrified when the three officers gave their testimony and claimed that my defence that I didn't know they were policemen was a pack of lies. They stood in the witness box and swore on the bible and claimed that the one in uniform was in fact driving and not sitting invisible to me in the back seat. Despite my telling the magistrate this was a complete lie, he preferred to believe the policeman, understandably, I suppose, asking himself why policemen would lie under oath to secure a fairly minor driving conviction. And why would they? I was not known to them. There were no scores to settle. It was malice pure and simple. I was fined two hundred pounds and had my licence taken away for a year.

In the foyer of the court the policemen stood in their uniforms, which they had worn to paint an impressive picture, smoking fags and chatting. I strode over to them. I wanted to hit them so badly I was nearly crying.

'What was all that about? Why did you make up those lies?'

They laughed at me. 'Look, son, you'll have to learn this: our lies count – yours don't. That's how it works.'

*

Five thirty and we're back in The Hyperion. Within a few hours it's full up and it is rocking. 'The Boys Are Back in Town' and the distinctive voice of Phil Lynott resounds around the bar and the lager is getting chucked back at a rate of knots. A burly man dressed in leathers comes into the pub. He's got his crash helmet under his arm and I notice him thread his way through the crowd to the quietest corner of the bar. I spot him again later playing pool with little Stevie Rose and Paul Marsh. He's caught my eye because he doesn't fit. One, I don't know him, and two, he just doesn't look right. Sticks out like an off-duty or undercover policeman. They're always so obvious – you just move out of earshot, normally. At chucking-out time Rose and Marsh come over to us lot. We've been drinking for twelve hours now and really are the worse for wear.

'That geezer over there is a brown-hatter. He's invited us to his house for a party and he says bring your mates if you like.'

Doesn't look like a poof to me. Queers look and act like John Inman out of *Are You Being Served?*, don't they?

'Where does he live?'

'21 Common Crescent.'

Common Crescent on the estate. Can't be. Never clapped eyes on him before.

'Tell him we'll be along shortly,' grins Steve with a twinkle in his eye.

Terry Baker's old man and one of the eldest Ducketts, Roy, want a Chinese but the rest of us decide to take a stroll back on to the estate.

Number 21 turns out to be the house with the big hedge. The burly man in leathers must be Daniel, the young man who talked me out of rat-bashing all those years ago. We knock on the door and Daniel answers and welcomes us in. He's holding that front door open a bit longer than he thought he would be, as about twenty of us walk through into his lounge. Stevie and Paul are sitting on the sofa, all polite, with a whisky each. Daniel tells us his name and pours us all a drink. He has no beer but is well stocked up on spirits.

'Right, what music do you lads like?' he asks as he starts to fan through his album collection. I notice he is quite muscular and very hairy – not at all like your typical uphill gardener. 'T Rex?' he asks, holding up *Electric Warrior* to little or no reaction. It is taxing him trying to guess our likely musical taste – he's already flicked past The Incredible String Band, Deep Purple, The Byrds, Crosby, Stills and Nash and Neil Young.

'Got any Frampton, Daniel?' asks Tony Bond, which surprises me. I remember at school when the Music master, desperately trying to appeal to our baser instincts, asked us all to bring in our favourite record from our own collections and then discuss its qualities in front of the class. Tony turned up with 'Monster Mash' by Boris Pickett and the Cryptkickers. And he was serious.

Of course Daniel doesn't have any Frampton. He's got nothing post-1973. But he has got *Motown Chartbusters Vol. 5* and we tell him to put that on. At his urging we help ourselves to drinks. There is a photo on the mantelpiece of his mum and dad. They look quite elderly and I assume they must be dead and Daniel's now living alone.

'Are you local?' he enquires of no one in particular, which shows what a sheltered life he's led, considering at least half of us here live within yards of where we're sitting.

'Not too far.'

Some of us spread out into the kitchen. Daniel is tapping his foot in time to Marvin Gaye and gently shaking his head to the beat, trying to make it feel like a party rather than twenty strangers sitting and standing in his living-room and kitchen. But soon the scotch and the vodka stop resting on the top of the pool of lager sitting in most people's stomachs and start to course around the bloodstream. Daniel too starts to loosen up.

'You know, I've lived here nearly twenty years and tonight is the first time I've been in The Hyperion,' he's telling John Craven, who is the eldest among us and closest to Daniel's age. In the background drunken shouting and banter is increasing faster than Daniel's Christmas drink is being consumed.

'I don't really get out much. It's been difficult, really, what with looking after my parents. But now they've passed on I must get out and about.'

JC is nodding intently but not listening and is swigging now from Daniel's bottle of cooking sherry.

'You seem a nice crowd – I don't know what all the fuss is about.'

'What fuss is that, Daniel?'

'You know, the reputation of The Hyperion,' he replies. 'Supposed to be a bit of a roughhouse.'

Three or four of the boys are mucking around doing the conga from the kitchen back into the lounge, whilst simulating anal intercourse. We're all looking over at our host for a reaction. Daniel tags on to Simon Duckett and then everyone joins in.

'Hands off my arse, Daniel!' jokes Simon and Daniel takes it in good part. 'Shut that door!' someone else shouts, mimicking the catchphrase of Larry Grayson, another celebrity poof. Steve Langton loves it. The wind-up is off and Steve's going to take it to the next level. He whips his T-shirt off, throws it to the ground and starts doing a weird sort of hippie dance. We all copy. Even Daniel, who is throwing his head back in laughter and loving every minute of it.

'What a lovely tattoo,' he gasps, looking at Simon Duckett's chest-piece. It's meant to be an eagle but looks more like a seagull. Meanwhile, Steve has shed his jeans and, again, we all follow suit. Daniel holds back.

'Come on, Daniel, we're all boys together,' urges Steve.

Daniel agrees and flings his strides across the room with a flourish, like a women's-libber burning her bra. We calm down a bit but continue to drink, smoke and chat, wandering around the house, every one of us just in our Jockey Y-fronts. The householder thinks all his Christmases have come at once.

I'm piecing together Daniel's life. His elderly parents have protected him from the 'rough' boys on the estate, not allowed him out and sent him away to boarding-school. He became an adult without anyone noticing and spent the next ten years nursing one parent, then the other, over his and her final years. Maybe that's when he started questioning it all, their values and their teachings. Or maybe he just got lonely. Anyway, he's finally plucked up the courage to walk into the local pub and make a conscious effort to mix with the people who live around him. Tonight is a revelation. The enemy is not the enemy at all. These boys are rough and ready, but they're not bad people. Look what fun we're having. Look how they accept me. Those silly old parents. God rest their souls.

Terry Baker bursts in to the lounge. 'The queer cunt. He's just touched me up in the toilet.'

He sweeps all the ornaments off the mantelpiece with one violent stroke of his arm. That's the spark that ignites it all. I doubt if Daniel has done any such thing. In fact, I know he wouldn't have. Above the mantelpiece hangs a print of an oil painting, an elephant coming out of the bush. I recognise it from the upstairs floor in Boots. Steve Langton takes it off the wall puts his foot straight through the canvas and re-hangs it. We all hurriedly dress and then charge around the house smashing whatever we can. The music stops suddenly as Terry Baker rips the arm off the record-player. JC has smeared his face with Marmite from the kitchen and is writing 'Man United' in tomato sauce on the wall. Some Ducketts have disappeared upstairs – to see what they can filch, I expect.

'Boys, boys, stop, for God's sake, stop! What's happened? What's the matter?' Daniel cries as I busy myself ripping the stuffing out of the sofa with a bread knife.

'The Black Panther. Donald Neilson. I am Donald Neilson!'

JC growls in Daniel's uncomprehending face. JC has an unhealthy interest in the recent Donald Neilson murder case and the victim Lesley Whittle. And when he's really drunk he claims he has written to the notorious Peter Samuel Cook, as he likes to call him, the so-called Cambridge Rapist, in prison.

Daniel is careful not to physically restrain anyone as we clinically destroy his house.

A knock at the door. We all stop and all eyes are on Daniel. He moves to the hall and opens the door.

'Winhurst CID. We have had reports of a disturbance. We were at another party locally and thought we'd just check on things.'

'Thank God. Thank God. No, no, the boys have just got a bit boisterous,' jabbers Daniel, relief whooshing out of him. 'If you could just get them to leave. I don't want to make any complaint.'

'Can we come in, please?'

There, standing in the hall, are Terry Baker's dad, Terry senior, and Roy Duckett, who had read the situation cleverly as they walked up the garden path to join the party after their Chinese meal in The Oriental Rendezvous. We keep silent and all sit around looking at Daniel trembling in his underpants, standing in the middle of the room with our two senior drinking pals.

'What's been going on here, then?' quizzes Roy, throwing a knowing look at Daniel's near naked state.

'Nothing, nothing. They're good boys. They've had too much to drink. If you can ask them to leave, I'll clear up.' He's looking around for his trousers but I saw Tony Bond stuffing them down the toilet earlier.

'Not as easy as that, sir.' Old man Baker has decided to give us some entertainment. 'We have reason to believe drugs are being used on the premises.'

A look of horror drops down Daniel's face. 'No officer, no, no, no. It's nothing like that.'

'Well, sir, we will have to search you.'

He is incredulous, standing there in just his underpants.

'Remove your pants, please, sir.'

Daniel hangs his head and slowly pulls his pants down and steps out of them. His shoulders rise up and down uncontrollably as he sobs out loud. We can't help noticing that Daniel almost does not have a penis. A tiny flap of skin is just about visible among a mass of pubic hair. Everyone is silent. A pattering noise causes Daniel to raise his head, only to see the older of the two policemen, Terry Baker senior to you and me, pissing into his plastic waste-paper bin next to the fireplace.

CHAPTER TWELVE

The Drugs Don't Work

In those first few years after leaving school Vic and I got into drinking and Jacko started nicking cars. He began with his brother's yellow Escort – borrowing it and then putting it back – and then, as his confidence grew, getting quite choosy and going for sports cars and other powerful models. I wasn't really into it. I couldn't see the fun in driving around in a car all night, but that didn't stop Jacko sounding his horn outside my bedroom window long after I had collapsed into bed in the early hours of a Sunday morning. I tried to ignore him but sometimes I was forced, through fear of him waking Mum and Dad, to get up and join him in the Jaguar purring outside on these pointless night-time jaunts. Places like Brighton and Hastings, full of happy childhood memories, were suddenly within our routine reach; but in the dead of night, with not a soul around, they seemed strangely unattractive.

He got nicked and he got nicked and he got nicked. Finally, after what seemed like a hundred TDA (Taking and Driving Away) convictions, he got borstal and was banished to East Anglia. Back in Winhurst we'd all been watching with interest a high-profile campaign by the family and friends of an East End man to free him from prison. George Davis had allegedly been fitted up by police and was serving a prison sentence as a result. His loved ones started to daub the slogan 'George Davis is Innocent OK' all over London and then in desperation pulled off some other stunts, like digging up a cricket pitch before a big match, to attract attention to the case. We decided that Jacko deserved similar support.

It was my idea but Steve Langton's eyes lit up. It appealed to his sense of excitement, rebelliousness and the ridiculous. He loved it and took immediate command. After The Hyperion shut we jumped in Steve's Rover and drove to the local park where a well-manicured bowling green was the central feature. In those glorious days before security lights and CCTV we were able to take our time loading paint tins and spades out of the boot. Big Bob got busy with the spade and within half an hour he had carved out 'R. WELLS IS INNOCENT' in six-foot-high letters in the middle of the green. Steve and I followed him as he dug, pouring white paint into the trenches.

We didn't expect the front page of the local paper the following week. 'WHO IS THE INNOCENT R. WELLS?' the headline screamed. Everyone in The Hyperion knew we were behind it and we revelled in the admiration and the notoriety.

The following weekend we headed out to another park in the borough and did the same thing again. There were about ten of us and we trashed the green altogether in our drunken excitement. This time it made the county paper: 'R. WELLS DAUBERS STRIKE AGAIN!'

The following weekend the police were waiting outside The Hyperion. A uniformed officer leant out the passenger window and called me over to speak to him. 'Okay, John, we know it's you. You've had your fun. Enough is enough.'

'Don't know what you're talking about.'

'Okay, son, have it your way. We'll catch you and you'll be well nicked. You'll be in there with your guilty little mate, like a shot.'

Steve wanted to up the ante. He reckoned that the Old Bill would be patrolling all the nearby bowling greens so we had to change tack. There was a big meeting coming up at a nearby racecourse and his idea was to dig a trench across the winning line, fill it with paint and daub the slogan. 'This will make *The Sun*,' he assured us.

We were to strike on a Tuesday night. This had the combined attraction of confusing the police (the other attacks had been at the weekend) and being the night before the big race. Steve insisted we all wore gloves and balaclavas and warned us that if we got caught it would definitely mean bird. We arrived at the dead of night and managed to park the car where it was not visible from the main road. As we started unloading our DIY equipment, I spotted a Jeep driving along the course towards us. We jumped back in the car and he passed us. It was an all-night private patrol and we decided, thankfully, to give it a miss.

The campaign continued, though. Other friends of Jacko got in on the act and started spraying up poster sites and fences. Finally, Jacko wrote to me from borstal, which was a bit of a giveaway if his letters were being monitored, and asked us to stop. He said his mum was almost suicidal over it all and the screws were giving him a hard time.

There was one final article in the local paper which explained who R. Wells was. It finished: 'When asked if she believed in her son's innocence, Richard Wells's mother said, "Hardly. He pleaded guilty to thirty-seven offences at the trial."'

With Jacko away, Vic and I threw ourselves into our drinking with renewed gusto. We went out every night and drank ourselves stupid. We were not wrestling with any inner demons nor were we emotionally lost in any way. We just liked getting pissed. That's all there was to it. We got into one another's minds almost to the exclusion of all others. We refused to take anything or anyone seriously and developed a sense of humour that *we* didn't understand, let alone anyone else. If some acquaintance happened upon us in a pub, for example, and came over to make polite conversation, one of us would tell him to fuck off or we'd both collapse into giggling laughter. And this was before we got on the drugs.

Vic was particularly rude to girls. He was a good-looking bloke and plenty showed an interest, but he was more likely to shower them with lager than compliments. Sometimes he did just that. Janice made the mistake of inviting the two of us back to her bedsit near the pub. We were mullered and incapable of responding sensibly to her sexual advances. She was a funny girl, Janice – didn't really put it about but had a thing about Vic and me. I was sober enough to get her tits out as Vic foraged in her drinks cabinet for vodka. I was sort of absent-mindedly slapping them as she lay on the bed when Vic roared at me to get out of the way. He came charging across the room and started butting them like a bull and then poured vodka from the bottle over her naked torso.

'What did you do that for?' I asked as we scampered away from the flat. Vic pondered this and shook his head and said as if he were talking about some third person we had no control over: 'What next?'

Our behaviour when we'd been drinking, which was most of the time, became more and more explosive. We got banned from more and more pubs and were forced to go further afield just to get served. We thought nothing of throwing drink over the publican or launching our glasses into the optics. We soon established a reputation as a pair of loose cannons – fun to be around but unpredictable. Inevitably, we got into fights, and simply by going berserk managed to survive intact.

A few years before, the Winhurst residents had been successful in getting the Methodist Hall shut down on public order fears, and the local disco was now held at weekends at the Bowling Alley, a few miles away. Because we formed the largest network of friends at the Alley it became our territory, the Winhurst boys', and whenever youths from other areas turned up we fought them. We usually won – of course, the numbers were normally in our favour. Most of the scraps were over almost before they started. Some screams from the girls and an opening up on the dance-floor would reveal two people rolling around on the floor. The DJ would interrupt The Village People and a couple of bouncers would come running in, break it up and eject the two opponents. Occasionally people got hurt. A few years before, an older boy we all knew died after a brawl when a bottle was jabbed into his neck and severed his jugular. The guy was well liked and there was a great deal of shock locally. But his death didn't modify anyone's behaviour. Fighting was part of the whole package: a drink, a dance and, if you were lucky, a punch-up and a shag.

It was a very dangerous age, the biggest danger being yourself. The problem was that you'd wake up one day and think you were invincible. In fact, you didn't think it, you *knew* it! Nothing too bad would happen to you. You didn't even think about it. The bloke you were fighting wasn't going to be the guy with a long knife which would pierce your heart. And even if he was, you'd knock the blade out of his hand. The guy whose head you were kicking around like a football wasn't going to die or suffer brain damage. You had this invisible armour and a sense of utter destiny. Come what may, you'd be okay. It never registered that just about every other bloke on the scene was wearing that same armour.

The rituals at the Bowling Alley were clearly mapped out. Girls arrived before boys. They turned up in chattering and giggling groups of six or seven. They bought rounds of drinks and put them on a table. After maybe an hour of more shrieking and laughing, an anthem like 'I Will Survive' by Gloria Gaynor would spur them on to the dance-floor where they would stay until the end of the night. The boys turned up in twos and threes well into the evening, having been drinking early in the local pubs. Positioning themselves around the edge of the floor or along the bar, they would chat to other boys, drink more and every now and then visit the toilets to drop a few pills. As the night started drawing to a close, the DJ would put on 'Three Times A Lady', signalling the beginning of the smooch records. If you felt like it, or felt confident, you'd step on to the floor and ask a girl to dance. Normally you'd know them, know they were going to say yes. They'd be waiting for you to ask. Or that's what you'd hope. If she did say no, you'd hope no one noticed and head for the bar fast with that 'I've got a raging thirst' walk. And the girls wouldn't stay out there too long alone when the slow ones came on, not wanting anyone to see they hadn't been asked.

If there was something there with the girl you were smooching with, you'd carry on in the clinch into the next record and you might end up snogging. And if you're snogging you might end up shagging. If there was nothing there, you'd separate your bodies, smile at one another, and wait for the next partner.

Smooching with a bird was another set of rituals and signals in itself. Some girls managed to just about keep their body from touching yours, even though they were holding your waist. They were not too sure, or they were saying 'I'm only dancing with you because I know you, I don't fancy you'. Others pressed their tits up against you and let your lower body touch theirs. When you moved your hand down from the small of their back and pressed a buttock, they grabbed the hand from behind and pushed it back above the waist lest anyone think they might be a floozy. Some rested their head on your shoulder throughout the dance. This could be good news or bad news: normally the head sideways nestling on the shoulders signified that a sustained relationship was wanted.

Steve Langton taught me to Just Say Yes to drugs. One night after the Bowling Alley, still high on alcohol, we went back to his flat in Brixton. His wife was away on a course and he decided to have a party. No females could be persuaded to come. So he purchased some blow for us to smoke. At the flat he laid out the paraphernalia on a coffee-table in the centre of the room.

'You gotta listen to this,' he enthused as he put a Tom Robinson record on his stack-system stereo, 'this bloke is going to be bigger than The Beatles.'

Where had I heard that before? I watched intently as he took what looked like a brown school rubber out of some cellophane and began to burn the side of it with a lighter. He then deftly stuck some Rizla papers together with a flick of his tongue and gutted a tipped cigarette, dropping the tobacco on to the Rizla. Rubbing the dope between his finger and thumb, Steve sprinkled it on to the tobacco. Then, with a flourish of fingers and tongue, a long bendy cigarette was made. The final touch was ripping off part of the Rothmans packet, rolling it up and inserting it into the end of the home-made joint. This was the filter – the 'roach', he called it.

I didn't know what to expect. This was the 'drugs' I'd heard so much about. Was I about to be spaced out? Was this the first step on to the rocky road to a drug-induced death in the gutter? Steve passed the joint to me and I copied him by inhaling deeply and then exhaling loudly, sending the smoke in an air current towards the ceiling. Steve signalled for me to have another draw and I repeated the exercise before passing the joint on. I felt a bit dizzy but then I reckoned I'd feel the same if I inhaled so deeply on a Benson's. By the time it came round to me again, I started to laugh as Steve started to laugh at my 'why are we wasting our time?' expression as I took the joint from his fingers. This time I did feel a little different. Even Tom Robinson singing about his mate Martin was connecting slightly. I felt a bit floaty and I was suppressing the urge to giggle. Eventually I reclined on a large cushion and stared vacantly at the ceiling and listened to the records in a way I had never listened to records before. I noticed I could identify the different instruments as they came crashing in, something that had never occurred to me before, and the lyrics began to take on a significance: I knew, or thought I knew, what the writer was on about. I was still very much in control, though, and when we did finally get to our feet and negotiate the car home in the early hours of the morning, none of us felt that we had had any sort of life-changing experience.

When Jacko finished his nine months, he, Vic and I indulged some more but all three of us remained underwhelmed by the effects of smoking dope. Some of the others seemed to get into it more than we did, electing to stay at home instead of going out on the piss, constructing elaborate 'bongs' from Fairy Liquid bottles and smoking little pipes. I for one had no truck with all the preparation – all the *effort* – necessary to get stoned. When there was a danger of getting left out I'd simply pop an eighth of Red Leb in my mouth, chew it and swallow. Within minutes I was as bleary-eyed and giggly as the rest but I had short-circuited the process.

Most of the time was spent at Andy Rothman's, whose parents didn't seem to mind six or seven boys sitting in his bedroom, smoking marijuana with Steel Pulse blaring out the open window. Andy's mum put her head around the door once to tell us to keep the noise and laughing down. 'Excuse me while I light my spliff,' sang Andy, using a line from a Bob Marley track, with what looked like a foot-long joint hanging from his lips. To us it seemed like the funniest thing ever. To her, and anyone else, we would have come across as a bunch of fucking idiots. A person from the real world walking into our partitioned smoke-filled world and trying to communicate did not normally work. Half an hour later we were still clutching our sides, crying with manic laughter. But I didn't like the drug, really. I noticed that after several months of blowing, some of the crowd stopped going to work. The dope seemed to induce a lethargy that entailed not getting up in the morning. Not getting up in the afternoon or the evening either. I wasn't ready or inclined to lead this sort of existence, and more or less left the dope-fiends to their own devices.

*

'I've got a little prezzy for you two.'

Steve Langton reminded me of Fagin as he rubbed his hands

together and then pulled two little red tablets from his Levi jacket pocket. Jacko and I looked unimpressed as he said, 'One for you . . . one for you,' in a mock old-lady voice and placed a pill each in our outstretched palms. 'These are tabs of acid, gentlemen. Take them and you'll be tripping all over the place.'

'Microdots', he said they were called. I remember being nervous as we swallowed them together. I even thought about pretending to take it and keeping it under my tongue but it was too late.

Steve said with acid it was best to 'do' something. It would be exciting, he told us. So we drove down to the cinema where they were showing a new version of *King Kong*. We settled down in our seats, eagerly waiting for the trip to begin. It didn't take long. First I felt a warmth in my skull and a tingling in my fingertips. The saliva in my mouth dried up. I looked sideways at Jacko and could see he was feeling something too. He shot me an 'Oh-oh, what have we done now' look.

Steve leant forward in his seat and said aloud, 'Coming up!' and made a whooshing noise.

We all started to giggle. Within minutes the three of us were crying, tears streaming down our cheeks, not daring to look at one another. The trip had begun. I looked down at my hands incredulously. They seemed to be glowing. My stomach had butterflies that were so severe they were almost painful. I needed to go to toilet. I told the others. Anyone would have thought I had suggested negotiating the South Pole in our swimming-trunks. What, now? Can't you wait? No. The manoeuvre to the toilets had to be planned like a military exercise. Which way? Less people that way? Who goes first? Now? In a minute? Shit or piss? Just piss. The walk to the toilet past people who had to sit up in their seats to let us through was a nightmare. I felt everyone was looking at us. Maybe they were. I felt they knew what we had done. Closing the door of the toilet we were safe again. Phew! We pressed up against the walls and composed ourselves. The walls were ceramic. I'd never realised before how beautiful ceramic tiles were. Then I felt the urine leaving my bladder and charging down my penis like a cool mountain stream and then clattering out into the urinal. Jacko and Steve were on either side of me, shaking their penises in slow motion, but no pee was forthcoming. The door opened, sending in a shaft of light and dialogue from the film. A man and his young son came towards us. Jacko and I panicked as Steve made for the door. The thought of being left there with someone else terrified us and we all ran out of the toilets and straight out of the cinema.

All sorts of things happened before, some eight hours later, the effects of the drug wore off. We all agreed it had been such great fun, first in the cinema and then walking the streets, that we resolved to buy some more and repeat the experience. Naturally we talked Vic, Simon Duckett and the others into trying it out and within a few weeks the whole lot of us became complete acid-heads. On those early trips we all laughed so much that the following day our cheeks actually ached; the facial muscles had been used more in a few hours than they would normally be in many months.

There was no point staying at home on the stuff and we always endeavoured to try and do something – go up to Soho or even a Chelsea away game. We all went to Charlton one time for an evening kick-off, every one of us out of our box on the drug. The Chelsea fans made a big bonfire on the terrace and afterwards rampaged through a caravan site as the travellers who lived there set their dogs on them. It could only happen if you were on acid.

That was the thing about acid: things happened. Articulate in your mind the worst thing that could happen to you whilst under the influence – like your Uncle Charlie coming in the pub and telling you your parents had been injured in a car crash – and it would happen. Things happened that I cannot explain but they definitely happened. Jacko and I were sitting in my front room one night examining and discussing the patterns on my mum's curtains as only people on LSD would do. The floral patterns were beginning to move and merge into one another when suddenly I saw a face form and it was the face of a little girl who used to live on the estate. She had left many years before and I doubt if I had ever given her another thought until then. I said nothing.

'Did you see that?' said Jacko casually.

'See what?'

'That face on the curtain.'

'Yeah, I did.'

'It was that skinny little girl who used to live next door to the Mileses,' he stated.

'I know.'

It was the strangest thing. Maybe Jacko thought I was just going along with him, but I knew I wasn't. We had both hallucinated the same thing: a face from long ago of a girl whose name neither of us could remember.

You knew what other people were thinking and it frightened me when someone verbalised what you knew they were thinking minutes earlier. I didn't fancy people knowing what I was thinking, especially as you couldn't control what came into your head like you could what came out of your mouth. Then I started turning these 'new powers' on myself when on acid. I know this sounds like hippy talk, man, but I started to discover myself, examine my inner fears and thoughts on life in general. I didn't like it at all. The acid was still causing the others to giggle non-stop for five hours whilst I was wrestling with all sorts of bad thoughts and insecurities. And, of course, everyone else picked up on it.

'What's up, John?'

'Come on, John, we're having a right crack here.'

Often I would have to go home alone where I could deal with all the shit flying around my head. I suppose these were my first 'bummers' or 'bad trips', and it became a lottery which way my trip would go. The more I worried about having a bummer the more likely I was to have one. There was no one bad trip in particular that made me stop, although I can remember getting under my bed one day, closing my eyes and fighting a head battle of epic proportions to hang on to my sanity. When I finally succumbed to the desire to go to the toilet I was astounded to find I had been under the bed for twelve hours.

What made me stop taking acid was no personal willpower victory, it was simply me finding a drug more to my taste. The DJ at the Bowling Alley gave me three French blues. Speed. He said I'd be 'up' all night and I was. The buzz hit me like a bolt about twenty minutes after I had knocked back the pills. I felt good. The music was right, the company was right and the moment was right. My hair felt right, my trousers felt right. Everything felt right. Unlike the acid there was nothing hallucinatory or introspective. I strode out on to the floor and, uncharacteristically, danced alone to a song. For once the steps worked. They were in synch. The drink flew down and I skimmed around the room, chatting to girls and generally being very charismatic. Vic and I started telling one another how much we loved each other. This was me. My drug.

Steve and I pooled resources and we headed over to a drug pub in Kingston called The Three Fishes and arranged a deal to buy a thousand blues for two hundred pounds, the idea being to sell these on at three for a pound, thereby making a profit and having supplies for ourselves. We soon found that drugs (or at least drugs that produce such feelings of well-being) and business did not mix. We'd turn up at the Bowling Alley with plastic bags full of pills in our underpants and once we had the amphetamine down our necks and became full of goodwill to fellow drug-abusers we were handing them out free of charge.

Just as the acid had, though, the speed soon started to display its down side. Worst of all was the ever-increasing dose required to attain the buzz and recapture the euphoria of the first few times. Almost as bad was 'coming down' – the period when the euphoric effects of the drug had worn off and you just wanted to go to sleep but couldn't because of all the amphetamine swimming around your bloodstream. Last but not least was the paranoia it induced as the stocks built up in your body. Until we started taking these drugs, 'paranoia' was as foreign a word to us as 'pension' or 'mortgage'. But soon we started doubting one another and the people around us, not all the time but now and then. Before the women, the drugs were the first thing ever to come between any of us.

Jacko and I got very bad on it. Vic, Steve and the others limited their indulgence to the weekends but Jacko and I even took time off work so we could stay on speed after the weekends. At one point we found ourselves doing twenty-five pills a day and not sleeping from Saturday night to Tuesday. I dreaded his knock on the door, as I knew another marathon session would be starting. When it came to this stuff, even though by now I knew it was bad for me, I had no willpower. Jacko was always more enthusiastic for the drugs than I was. Only just. I couldn't blame him for that. Because he couldn't drink, drugs were a revelation for him. Now he could be outrageous and abuse a substance without spending a week in bed afterwards. Vic was the leader as far as alcohol excess went, but Jacko soon led the way in the world of drugs. When the others pulled back a little he was all the more determined to keep me on the journey with him.

Months of taking all this gear had left my bodily defences low and I fell to a bout of flu that I couldn't shake off. After a week or two I went down to the family doctor to see if he could give me anything. Dr Philpott hadn't changed from the days he came out to visit me for my earaches imagined or real, and tell Mum to keep me off school. Seeing him again churned me up. Memories of my innocent childhood flooded my mind. He asked after Mum and Dad and all my brothers and sisters. For once I felt ashamed, felt I had betrayed the nice family Dr Philpott thought we were, felt sorry for myself. This was one of those times when I had no idea of what was coming next. I just started crying as Philpott regarded me with astonishment but sympathy. The more I tried to stop, the more it came out. I hadn't seen the bloke for ten years but I told him about the acid and the speed and how I thought I was now a drug addict.

Philpott was great. He expressed no real disapproval or shock, except when I told him that some days I took thirty pills, and he explained in detail the medical effects of each drug. He said speed was not addictive (he could have fooled me) and suggested I took a holiday, away from my friends, and got the amphetamine out of my system.

'Take it from there,' he said. He didn't even tell me to stop. He said to come back in a month's time. I never did.

Coincidentally, I did have a fortnight's break arranged – a holiday in Benidorm with the boys from work, none of whom shared the chemical interests of my crowd. It was the first time I had been abroad and I loved it. Getting pissed and sleeping relatively normal hours. Not worrying about taking or not taking little blue pills.

When I got back I felt refreshed and cleansed but Jacko was still bang on it. A load of us went to see a band up at The Half Moon pub in Fulham and Jacko suggested he and I go out and sit in the car. 'The Logical Song' by Supertramp pounded out the radio. A chap he had met in borstal was with us and the two of them rolled up their sleeves and produced syringes.

'Leave it out, Jacko!' I exclaimed.

'No, no, don't worry,' he reassured me, 'this isn't smack.' He had pre-mixed some white concoction. 'It's sulphate. The same as speed. Just crushed up, that's all. If you knock it up your arm you get a hit much quicker.'

In a matter of two weeks he had become an injector. I couldn't believe it. I declined their invitation to put any up my arm but compromised by snorting a long line of the white powder. Jacko and his new pal rolled their sleeves down and lolled back in their seats.

'John, you gotta feel this rush, mate,' Jacko sighed as his eyeballs rolled upwards.

CHAPTER THIRTEEN

Money for Nothing

Knocking the speed on the head left a bit of a void, I suppose. On Friday night I'd get off work as soon as I could. Fight the hordes in Waterloo Station and squeeze into a Winhurst-bound train. Once home, Mum would warm up a dinner and I'd wolf it down. I'd be in The Hyperion by seven at the latest. Everyone would be there. Normally we'd then get into Winhurst town by nine and crawl around a few pubs before descending on one of the mental homes for a 'staff' disco that enabled us to continue drinking until one in the morning. Next day I'd rise from my bed at about ten thirty when Vic or Steve would be at the door and we'd go off for the Saturday dinnertime session. Drinking would be more relaxed than at night and the pub would be filled by a different crowd.

*

Wobbler sits in his usual chair over in the corner. He wears a black overcoat and a flat cap in all weathers. He sits quietly, occasionally rolling a cigarette from his Old Holborn tin and sipping from his half-pint of bitter. Rolling the fag and sipping the beer is quite an effort for poor old Wobbler, who is all too visibly suffering from Parkinson's or some other such affliction – hence the unkind nickname. The sad thing is that almost everyone who drinks in The Hyperion assumes that because he shakes uncontrollably and he prefers his own company he is a divvy. 'All right, Wobbler!' they shout. 'Go easy with that glass, Wobbler, you're spilling it.' He just looks ahead and never rises to the bait. Two or three times during the four-hour session he'll muster all his strength and, in a superhuman effort of muscular cohesion, lift himself out of his chair and walk painfully slowly over to the bar to recharge his glass. He always has the right money and the bar staff know what he's drinking. No words are exchanged. Lads playing pool pretend he has jogged them or the table is jigging to raise a cheap laugh as he passes on the difficult journey back to his chair.

They all forget that Wobbler was a lad once. He had money in his pocket, he had his health and all his faculties. Lose one of those attributes, it seems, and you're no one in this young man's world. Lose two and you're not worth a wank. Lose all three and you'll be in one of the institutions that, ironically, supply a living to half of the people drinking here. The likelihood is that Wobbler was the same as us. He drank, he fought and he shagged. He had mates, confidence and front. He was wild and pushed back the social barriers of the day. His parents fretted over him. The occasional enthusiastic girlfriend rubbed his cock in his trousers. He eventually married one of these girls, had kids and got a house off the council. Stopped going to the pub and used the social club instead because it was cheaper – what with the kids, money was tight. Kids grew up and left home. Wife gets cancer. Mates start dropping dead. Wife dies. Develops Parkinson's disease. Uses pub next to his house because his body won't take him all the way to the Working Men's Club any more. Drinks even less because he has no money. Spends money on drink that he should have spent on food. Sits and looks at the lads in the pub. Doesn't feel aggrieved when they take the piss out of him. Feels sorry for them. He's glad, for their sakes, that they don't know what's coming.

*

A lot of older men came in at lunchtime. It was about the only time some boys drank with their dads and uncles. The coalmen came in when they'd knocked off and opened up a card school, tossing coins and notes into the ashtray, which was used as a kitty. Some of the racing lads were in, gathered in a corner, holding their pints of lager, some barely taller than the counter itself. They would have arrived in Winhurst some years before, full of hopes and dreams, having signed on with one of the trainers as an apprentice jockey. But for ninety-nine boys out of a hundred, the furthest they progressed in the sport was notching up a handful of rides as teenagers and then they were destined to be fodder for the cheap labour racket that was the racing industry until they could bear no more. Not having to worry too much any more about their weight, they knocked back the drink and exchanged 'inside' information about the day's racing.

'Ours at Lingfield will not get beat Monday.'

'Keep it under your hat, but I know the Guvnor's had a right few quid on ours in the 3.30 today.'

'The way my horse is working out it'll piss up next time out.'

The older men especially liked to eavesdrop these conversations, hoping they would hear some good tips. Some even plied the jockey boys with drink in exchange for information. But the reality was that for every dead cert these boys were training, lads in Newmarket or any other racing town were gathered in pubs equally convinced and equally tipping their own charges. The myth (which I am sure was perpetuated by trainers and owners) that stable lads supplemented their meagre incomes by benefiting from backing winning horses was, of course, totally false.

Local people sometimes called them 'stable rats' for some reason but there was really very little animosity. Over the years many of them married and raised families in Winhurst and they were part of the fabric of the town. Roy Barry was one who knocked around with us a bit. He was a bit taller than the average apprentice and a smart dresser. He'd have a drink with us and tag along on our expeditions out of town but his objective was to pull women and that's what he was good at. He was older than us – a young-looking early-thirties – and unlike most of his contemporaries he still got rides on a regular basis. The other racing lads looked up to him and respected him. He was a bridge between their community and our community. But Roy rarely won a race. In my naïvety I once broached the subject with him: 'Roy, how come you keep getting rides, year in year out, when you never win?'

He smiled as he lit another Benson's. 'Do you really not know?'

I didn't.

'I get rides, John, because I'm good at losing. I'm good at stopping horses.'

I was only a little wiser.

'Look, when a trainer wants to pull a horse, he books me. I can make it look like it's trying.'

'But why would a trainer want his horse to lose?'

Roy looked around the table at the others, his face saying 'is this bloke taking the piss?' I decided to leave it there.

Keith's dad came over and plonked his glass on the table where Steve, his son and I were sitting.

'See you're all brimming with energy,' he chided as he surveyed us slumped back in our chairs, legs outstretched, beer glasses held below our chins and resting on our chests. For some reason he suggested we go out and earn some dough rather than sitting around getting pissed – even though, on this day, he was sitting around getting pissed with us.

'Doing what?' we asked.

That stumped him, for a while at least, and then he came out with: 'Spyholes. Every flat needs one and most don't have one. All you need is a brace and bit and a few spyholes and you're away.'

Sounded good enough to us. We drained our glasses and climbed into Keith's MGB and headed off to a hardware shop. For twenty quid we bought a brace and bit and five spyholes and drove off, half drunk, to find some flats. Private flats, we decided. Council tenants aren't going to be screwing each other's places.

We alighted on Hogsmill Villas and Steve strode to the first door. We had divided up the company's assets so we looked vaguely like workmen. Steve held the door-viewers (as the spyholes were called on the packet), I clasped the brace and Keith had the bit protruding threateningly from his fist. The first lady politely told us to get lost but the second door we tried, to our amazement, said yes – what a good idea.

'How much?' asked the owner.

'Five pounds to supply and fit,' replied Steve authoritatively although he had in reality just plucked the price from the air.

He motioned to me to start drilling and, adrenaline rising, started pounding on the next door. Within an hour we had earned twenty-five pounds and had already paid for the brace and bit, our opening investment.

Back in the pub we laughed and joked at the easiest money we'd ever made. We swore each other to secrecy and Hyperion Security was born, our first board meeting being held over a table of lager glasses and overflowing ashtrays. Keith quickly identified a wholesaler in Neasden and, having added £25 each to the £25 we had just made, we purchased over two hundred spyholes at 45p each. Naturally, the quality of these was inferior to the solid Chubb ones we started out with – indeed, some customers would later claim that you could not see out of them. When I tested them, it reminded me of trying to see through the bottom of a beer glass, but they looked the part anyway.

The following Saturday we drove over to Kingston where there was a large estate of privately owned flats which we later christened The Gold-Mine. Steve started knocking and we worked flat out, fitting thirty viewers and earning ourselves £150. We were so excited we forgot to go to the pub at lunch-time. Steve was like a man possessed, his confidence rising with every job and his already provocative sales patter beginning to take shape.

'Good morning, Madam. I'm from Safeguard Security. I expect you had notification that we would be in the block today?' Madam shakes her head. Steve feigns mild surprise. 'Anyway, as you can see, we are here today and we are fitting our all-purpose door-viewers at a special discount of five pounds per door.'

'No, thank you. I've got a chain.'

'But that's not a lot of good, is it, Madam? You've heard about this spate of barging entries, I'm sure.'

'Barging entries?'

Keith and I look at each other, puzzled, too. Barging entries? All-purpose? The shit was really spilling out of Steve's mouth.

'Yes, Madam, barging entries. A caller knocks on your door, you open it, with your chain on, and *bang* he's in.' As he said this Steve had pushed his shoulder up against the door and acted out the famous barging entry. Madam stood back, slightly shocked, as Steve smiled at her sweetly but with a tinge of I-told-you-so.

'A fiver?'

'Yes, Madam, that's all. Hard to believe, isn't it? Now, what height would you like it?'

That Saturday we earned more in one day (albeit split three ways) than we did in a week. We were managing to combine a thoroughly good laugh with making money. I got some leaflets knocked up and we found that our success rate doubled if we leafleted a block in advance. Unfortunately, I allowed Steve to influence the design of the leaflet and we ended up with a montage of newspaper headlines sufficient to scare the life out of the Yorkshire Ripper. I remember 'Old lady axed to death in her home' and 'Intruder murders sisters' among others screaming out from the top of the flyer. We opened a bank account and before we knew it over a thousand pounds had been deposited. It all seemed too good to be true.

We went out every evening in the summer for two or three hours and all day Saturday. For some reason people objected to us calling on a Sunday. Soon we were all pulling in what we earned in our normal jobs. I started to have visions of packing in the day job and expanding the business across the country, but was scared to tell anyone lest the idea got nicked. Riches and stockmarket flotations beckoned. But problems began to emerge.

Firstly, they were down to our sheer inexperience. We were doing a middle-aged woman's door in Surbiton. As usual, Steve had moved on in search of the next sale and Keith and I worked on the door. The practice was for Keith to drill from the outside whilst I stood just inside in the customer's hallway. When I saw the tip of the bit appear on my side of the door I would thump it and he would come round to my side and drill through from the inside, making a nice clean hole to simply screw the spyhole in to. This lady was very nice and she engaged me in conversation about the inexorable rise of crime in Surbiton. I missed the tip as it came through the door and before we knew it the sickening sound of wood splitting filled the hallway. The owner and I looked horrified as the door splintered down the middle. I shouted at Keith to stop but when I peered around the door he already had. The tool was hanging in the door and Keith was bent double, wiping tears from his eyes. I quickly shut the door and turned to face the woman, desperately trying to get the vision of the helpless Keith out of my mind. My facial muscles couldn't understand if they were fighting back tears or laughter. I tried to apologise as the lady stood staring in shock at the door when Steve came striding in. I noticed through the crack in the door that Keith was now on his knees, gasping for breath.

'Madam, this door is rotten! You really should have warned us!'

Speechless.

'I'll tell you what we'll do. I'll send my fitter here to the DIY store and he'll get some Polyfilla and a touch of yellow paint and your door will be as good as new. But I'm sorry, there is no way we'll get a spyhole in there. That door is rotten through and through. I'm surprised it has not fallen off the hinges. We won't charge you but you really do need to get the door seen to.'

The poor woman ended up believing that we were doing her a favour and I quickly bodged her door with Polyfilla and paint that was such a different shade of yellow it might as well as have been red.

Other times the drilling of Keith, me or Vic (who by now was on the firm more for the laughs than any financial rewards) was so poor that the viewer pointed down to the floor or badly to the left or right. When this happened Steve would shout: 'We're finished, sir, would you like to come and try it?' The homeowner would then come to the door, screw his eye up and see me, Keith or Vic prominently in full view. Little did they know that we would be lifting one another up or even kneeling so that we accommodated the viewer's awry line of vision.

One flat was answered by a plump woman of about fifty. She was wearing a dressing-gown and fluffy pink slippers. She loved the idea of a spyhole and made us all tea. She introduced herself as Muriel. Her husband, she said, was in the other room. We could hear a telly but the door was firmly shut.

'He's not up to much.'

We didn't quite know what she meant by that. Was he infirm? Simple? Sexually impotent? Muriel's hormones, though, were still up to a lot – that soon became obvious. As she bent down to find sugar in a kitchen cupboard she gave us all a lingering eyeful of her large breasts hanging in the nightie she wore under the dressing-gown. Her cleavage was wrinkled and reminded me a bit of orange peel but there was no doubt about the eroticism of the situation. We all looked at one another, trying to remain calm both in our facial expressions and in our trousers. As we sipped our tea with her, she sat on a kitchen stool, her legs tantalisingly apart, inviting us to drop to our knees and do up a shoelace to get a good view – something that none of us had the bottle to do. I noticed varicose veins and bumps on her shins but her thighs and upper legs were fleshy and smooth.

'I bet good-looking lads like you have all got girlfriends.'

We couldn't believe this – she was turning the conversation around to sex within seconds. I was alarmed at the way none of us was moving the situation on. Here we were, four sexually experienced and active young men faced with a scenario straight out of the Readers' Letters page of *Knave*. A nymphomaniac, large-breasted, middle-aged woman was coming on to us in her kitchen whilst her unknowing husband sat in the next room.

As she moved around the kitchen I took a deep breath and patted her bum. 'You've got a lovely arse, Muriel,' I said.

Steve, Vic and Keith spat their tea out and two of them scurried out into the hall to fit the spyhole.

'You boys wouldn't be interested in an old girl like me,' she laughed, but didn't chastise me for getting too familiar.

Vic stood looking at the floor, trying to control his giggles. I went up behind her and put my hands underneath her arms and fondled her breasts whilst pulling a face at Vic from behind her. This time she did move my hands off her – but slowly.

'Don't do that. If you get me going you'll wonder what's hit you. You might be young but I'd wear the four of you out and that's the truth.'

That was an invitation to a gang-bang if ever I heard one but her directness cracked Vic up too and he joined the others giggling and fumbling in the hallway. Left on my own with this woman, older than my mother, suddenly I was bereft of all my cockiness and confidence. She stepped towards me and grabbed at my crotch in an almost violent way. She had hold of me like a vice but I neatly lifted myself off her grip and walked out in to the hallway.

Steve told Muriel her spyhole was ready to test.

'Is it in the hole?' leered Muriel. 'Do you boys do anything else?'

We'd really and truly entered *Carry On* land now. We took her fiver and Muriel took our leaflet. Back in the car we could do little more work.

'That was on a plate, that was.'

'She was a raving nympho.'

'We could have had a fours up there.'

'Did you see them tits? Like two fucking great melons.'

'She was well up for it.'

'She was game, all right.'

And so on. But no one could explain why, when every young boy's fantasy actually materialised in front of us, for all our mouth and bravado, we ran away like little kids.

Vic and I even went back. Some days later Muriel called my house because my number was on the leaflet. Said she was interested in having some kitchen cupboards built. I said we'd come round and have a look. I rang Vic and told him. We decided, because when it comes to matters of sex, true friendship often flies out the window, that we wouldn't tell the other two and would go round on our own. Once again, although she knew we were coming, she answered the door in her dressing-gown. She had obviously applied a bit of perfume and a touch of lipstick. It was a strange episode altogether. Muriel pointed up at where she pretended she'd like the cabinets and I fondled her breasts. Not a word was said. We started talking about prices and Vic had his hand inside her nightie feeling her fanny. Our knobs were almost bursting the zips of our Levi's.

I went to lift her nightie right up so we could get a good look at her body and she pushed me away. 'My husband is in there,' she whispered.

We stopped and continued the conversation about the cabinets. I said we'd call her with a date when we could get round to put them up. I never did.

Steve's selling prowess was a pleasure to watch, even if it did sometimes make us wince. He managed to combine earnestness, threat and cheeky-chappie, most of the time perfectly. He became bored quickly and constantly pushed back the barriers of what he thought he could get away with.

One day, he declared: 'I can sell these any way I want. People are so fucking thick. Watch this,' and he rapped on the next door. A man who certainly looked like he had his wits about him answered.

'Good evening, sir. Please let me introduce myself: John Reynolds, Safety Director, Safeguard Security. I expect you've heard about the influx of otters?'

'Otters?'

'Yes, sir, otters. They've been coming up from the Thames, making their way up here to the surrounding flats and have then been gnawing away at people's doors. Unfortunately, some people have opened their doors and have taken a nasty bite from the animal for their pains. Kingston Council have given us permission to approach flat-owners and see if they would like one of these installed.' Steve brandished a spyhole under the man's nose.

'What does that do?'

'This is a door-viewer, sir. It enables you to look out your door without opening it. If you hear a noise, look through this and, if no one is visible, you can be sure you have an otter problem.'

'Then what?'

'You shout at it through your letter box and they run off.'

The man shook his head with a what-is-the-world-coming-to look of resignation but, to our amazement, he agreed. When he handed over his fiver he muttered something about being under the impression that otters had not been in the Thames for centuries let alone prowling around the hallways of lease-hold properties.

Steve's boldness grew and grew, as did the money in our coffers. We expanded our range to include chains, mickey-mouse alarms and mortice locks. The locks were fitted by a carpenter who couldn't believe the price Steve was getting for the job. But I was becoming more and more alarmed by our sales representative's tactics. By now he was the crime prevention officer ('I didn't say I was from the police, did I?'), house-holders could claim back the cost of the viewer on their rates and had they heard about what happened to the poor lady in number 6? Soon we were attracting the attention of the real police. We were summoned by phone to visit the genuine crime prevention officer at Kingston police station. I went along and a very nice man told us there had been a few complaints. He advised us to tone down our act and asked if we would let him or his regional equivalent know which areas we were about to work. He was very good about it, considering. Of course, we did no such thing.

One afternoon a young man with a serious speech impediment answered a door. It was obvious from his body language and extremely cross face that he didn't want a spyhole but he couldn't get the words out. Steve pretended that he had inter-preted his stammering as a yes and proceeded to tell us to start drilling. Fortunately, the man was able to slam the door on us and obviously managed to make himself understood on the phone when he rang the police. Outside the flats a lone policeman was waiting for us to emerge. He called us over to his squad car and explained that he had had a complaint that we had used threatening behaviour. He took our names and addresses and fed them into the police computer via a radio. After a few minutes of waiting around the limited information on Keith and me crackled back through his receiver. Steve objected to this interruption and, to emphasise that he thought we were in the right, strode off to knock on some more doors. We obediently followed. After a couple of knockbacks we walked back over to the policeman who was becoming quite animated. The radio was still spewing out Steve's record: '1973 arson; 1973 burglary; 1974 arson; 1975 theft; 1975 TDA . . .'

When it finally finished the copper looked at Steve, his eyes open wide and blinking pointedly. 'You're a mobile crime wave, you are.'

'That's nice. Here I am, trying to go straight, and you lot just won't give me a break. I might as well give up and go back to nicking.' Steve threw his clipboard to the ground to emphasise his tantrum. He'd taken to carrying a clipboard around but all it held were diagrams of old women with axes embedded in their skulls used when illustrating to customers what might happen to them if they did not buy our product.

The policeman fell for it. 'Look, son, just go easy. Your sales patter needs moderating, that's all. If people don't want to know – leave them be. There's plenty of other customers.'

Not all the police were as pragmatic as this guy. Another time someone must have complained because as we sat in Keith's MGB counting up our fivers in the quadrant gardens of some flats in Carshalton, the Special Patrol Group came screeching in. The SPG were nutters. Imagine the worst Mill-wall football mob dressed in police uniforms and you're halfway there. The Met had set up this 'crack' group to fight crime on the streets. They cruised around in carriers hoping for the call that enabled them to jump out the van mob-handed and give it to street-brawlers, drunks, hooligans and sometimes totally innocent people. Testosterone and truncheons. Not a good blend. Their pride in their mob was as high as that of any football firm and they certainly went the extra mile. Problem was, few really could or did take them on because the SPG had the law on their side, a fact they seemed to overlook as they rapidly constructed their own macho self-image. Finally, after their over-exuberance resulted in a few too many high-profile beatings, the Met disbanded the group or called it something else.

This day we reacted just right. We didn't jump out the car and run or adopt aggressive poses as they surrounded the car.

'Out the fucking motor!' screamed the first.

As we got out, other policemen were already opening the boot and nosing about inside. We explained what we were doing.

'Oh yeah, and what's this, then?' said another, flourishing the brace and bit that was lying on the back seat as if he had discovered gelignite.

'It's a brace and bit. You drill with it in the door and then you screw the spyhole in.' I acted out a drilling motion with my hands and a couple of the policemen smirked.

But the one who had challenged us didn't like being made to look stupid. He stepped forward, trod on my foot and kept it there while he glared at me. The biggest one, meanwhile, was making the wankers sign to Steve in an attempt to bait him. All of them stood with their legs apart and they were clearly adopting what we called the 'hoolistance': the pose of a man inviting another to hit him but meanwhile looking like a dog straining on the leash – a stance much favoured by football hooligan groups when they came face to face with one another. Their highly polished truncheons gleamed on their hips. They were keyed up for a row and their disappointment in the fact they were not going to get one was tangible.

'We could nick you for threatening behaviour,' said the one with his foot on mine.

'We haven't threatened anyone,' I responded and the man breathing on me looked behind at his mates. His face was asking them: 'Is that enough to give this little bastard a clout?'

'If I say you've threatened someone, you've threatened someone. Okay?'

I shrugged and a dangerous moment passed.

'Fuck off home. If we get another call about you scaring old ladies we'll be back and we'll batter the fuck out of you.'

Steve was fairly expert at handling the police. He had long experience of them and their ways. I remember once when he was walking through the estate. I was about fifteen and he was eighteen, already a veteran of approved schools and borstals. A squad car pulled up next to him and two plain-clothes officers got out the back seat and approached him. I was sitting on a garden wall and watched with interest as the scene was played out.

'Langton, a quick word, please,' said one of the detectives.

'We'd like to search you, Langton,' said the other.

Steve stepped back from them and looked over at me but obviously decided I was no good. Behind me digging his garden was Old Man Doyle.

'Mr Doyle,' shouted Steve, 'do you mind coming over here and witnessing these police officers search me, please. Thanks very much, Mr Doyle.'

The detectives stared over at Old Man Doyle, urging him with their eyes to ignore Steve. But, although Steve may not have been his favourite person, I imagine, like most people on the estate, Doyle had even less time for the police. He wandered over. The detectives gave Steve a half-hearted search, said, 'Thank you – we'll see you again,' and got back in the car to be driven off.

'Thanks, Mr Doyle,' I heard Steve say.

'You want to be careful, Steve. They'll have you soon whether you've done anything or not.'

Years later when I asked him about it, Steve explained that because he had got off at the Old Bailey with burning down the glass factory the police were determined to set him up. That day he was convinced they were going to plant drugs on him. It was the difficulties with the local police that had forced Steve to move to the genteel London suburb of Brixton.

Incidents like the pull from the SPG began to freak me and Keith a bit but Steve regarded them as a restraint on his trade and an invasion of his civil liberties and he wasn't going to be hounded off the most lucrative, legal venture he had yet become involved in. For Keith and me it was a fun sideline, but for Steve it was becoming more and more his focus.

We'd got a job in this ground-floor flat and Keith and Steve pressed on up the stairs for more work whilst I stayed and leisurely drilled this old man's door.

'Good idea, these,' muttered the old man. 'It's just not safe any more, even in your own home.'

We'd made the sale so I'd thought I'd temper whatever bollocks Steve had spun him. 'It's not as bad as all that. I think the papers blow it all up.'

The man agreed and offered me a cup of tea. 'I'd have

bought one and fitted it myself,' he went on. 'I used to be a chippie but I don't get out now. My wife's upstairs with cancer.'

It was a strange turn of phrase, like his wife was in her room with a person called cancer.

'I'm sorry to hear that.'

'Thanks. It is a terrible disease, you know. My poor old girl – she's just wasting away, you know. There's nothing of her now. I have to lift her in and out the bed and she don't weigh more than a feather.'

I was overcome with pity for this old man. His partner of a lifetime was dying before his very eyes and he was telling a boy he'd never met before and would never meet again all about it.

'Have you got any children?' I asked, hoping that there was someone about sharing their burden.

'My boy David. He's out in Australia.' His smoker's pigeon chest swelled with pride. 'Done good for himself, he has. He's in the building trade like me. But he's got a firm. Employs hundreds of men. He's very clever, our David. He rings every other Saturday to see how his mum is.'

That's fucking big of him, I thought. When I finished he passed over a blue note.

'No, that's okay. Forget it.'

He protested but I said goodbye and shot off before he could take offence.

Back in the car it was time for the count-up, our favourite ritual. 'One hundred pounds exactly,' announced Steve and then he started rummaging through the briefcase that contained our stock. 'But we've used twenty-one spyholes today. We're a fiver short.'

'Well, I haven't had it,' said Keith.

The few seconds' silence was embarrassing.

'I did the old man for nothing. His wife has cancer. I just couldn't charge him.'

Steve snapped the briefcase shut. 'Oh, that's all right then. We don't charge any old people, or ill people, or poor people and then we go skint.'

'It's only a fiver, Steve, take it out of my cut.'

Soon after, Steve announced to us he was giving up his day job. He had decided to stop being an electrician and to become a full-time spyhole fitter. It was at that point that Keith and I realised we had to amicably dissolve the business. Steve was hard enough to keep on the leash when we were doing it for pin money. Fuck knows what strokes he'd pull if he were actually relying on the money for his total income.

We divvied out the kitty of several thousand pounds and drank to a successful venture and a hilarious year or two. Steve moved his area of operation to Fulham, Chelsea and Kensington where he reasoned people had more money and were more likely to accept his doubling of the price. He was raking it in and this time keeping most of the money. Normally he would select the most desperate drunk from the pub to do his fitting and pay him a straight twenty or so for a day's work. He bought a new car and rented a big house in Hammersmith. It looked like Steve Langton was finally going places.

The place he actually ended up was Wandsworth Prison. Fulham police were far less understanding than our local filth. It seems almost from the day he started operating on their patch they were building up a dossier and when they finally arrested Steve they threw the book at him. He was charged with a catalogue of offences: criminal damage – it seems, in some cases, he was telling the fitter to start drilling the doors before he'd even rung the bell; impersonating a police officer – the 'crime prevention officer' ruse; fraud – telling tenants the money could be reclaimed from the local authority; demanding money with menaces – threatening home-owners who were reluctant to pay for something they didn't want, and so on. Steve served four months on remand whilst waiting for his case to be heard at Knightsbridge Crown Court. Fortunately he had earned so much money he was able to afford a top barrister who defended him well. He was found guilty on some charges and not on others and the judge decided he'd served long enough on remand, commenting: 'Mr Langton, I believe that you are a resourceful young man and when you leave this court today there are a number of avenues available to you. I advise you strongly not to reclaim the tools of your trade, namely your brace and bit, from the police. I hope you will channel your energies into something that does not throw up the temptation to indulge in illegal practices and bring you back before this court.'

CHAPTER FOURTEEN

Imagine

Although Jacko veered off in a different direction from the rest of us, Steve, Vic, Keith and I closed ranks and made our own fun. Jacko had started to knock around with a younger crowd, a crowd into drugs as a way of life, not a pastime. We saw him less and less. Keith, however, seemed determined to make up for his lost years in the navy. Now that he was back, he couldn't get enough of the daily adventure that was our life then.

Our base became Highmead Grove social club. This was the subsidised bar for the employees of this mental home. Steve's brother Gary worked and lived there in the employees' quarters. When Steve finally got booted out by Mel, Gary found him an empty room and Steve moved in at the hospital. This was a highly irregular arrangement but no one, even the managers, said a word.

In fact Steve and the rest of us had become the focal point of social life at the hospital. From the bar Keith operated a pirated-video rental service and when the club held discos in the adjacent hall we stood at the door and took an entrance fee from partygoers. People came to us for all sorts of things.

A black doctor approached us in the bar one day. 'I understand you chaps might be able to do me a small favour.' He explained that his car would be worth more written-off than it was on the second-hand market. Could we help him? There was fifty quid in it for us. I phoned Jacko, who was all for writing off a car with the owner's blessing. We took the vehicle from the hospital carpark with the intention of driving it up on to Winhurst Heath and rolling it into the large fishing pond. Jacko was at the wheel but when we got there we found bars that none of us realised were there prevented us getting out of the carpark and on to the green.

'Don't worry,' said Jacko. 'You lot get out and I'll write it off.' He then proceeded to slam the car into reverse and put his foot down and repeatedly smash into an oak tree that stood a few yards in front. Eventually we abandoned the car but not before noticing a courting couple parked up across the road watching us with total bewilderment.

The next night the good doctor was back, saying the job wasn't good enough and that the police had contacted him and demanded he retrieve the vehicle.

Steve looked up to the heavens. 'If you want a job done properly, do it yourself,' he huffed more for the doctor's benefit and signalled for Keith to join him.

Half an hour later they were back, Steve minus eyebrows and with heavily singed hair. Keith said Steve had just walked up to the car in broad daylight, emptied a can of petrol over it and then threw a match at it. The blast blew him backward almost on to Keith's car.

Another time a Jewish landlord contacted us offering five hundred pounds if we would remove some squatters from one of his local properties. An off-duty policeman who sometimes drank in the club put him on to us. A monkey was a lot of money and Steve wanted to make sure we did it right. The difficulty for us was that we knew many of the squatters. They were local junkies, some whom we had gone to school with or who were well connected in the area. We didn't fancy a war with anyone for five hundred quid. We drove around Winhurst until we found a similar empty house. On breaking in, we found that it had running water and was in a reasonable state. Then we went to see the squatters and Steve negotiated with them. He got them to move without any hint of threat, even transporting their gear (such as it was) in Keith's van. Two hundred pounds obviously assisted their co-operation but we still pocketed one hundred each for an afternoon's work.

When Steve was finally asked to leave Highmead Grove the money he had earned from the spyholes helped him secure a lease on a large Victorian house in Clapham. Very rapidly he got us all in to share the cost and so began another surreal period of our lives. Steve, Vic, Keith and I all had a room each, as did two Scottish guys Steve had met in a pub. For the sake of ease we called both of them Jock. Against our better judgement a final room was rented out to Pugsley Pullinger. To be fair to Steve, Pugsley just sort of told us he was moving in and even then none of us had the balls to tell him no.

Almost straight away Steve and Pugsley hit on a plan to reduce our rent. The house boasted a large cellar and we all gave it a clean of sorts and ran some wiring down so it had an electric light. We got hold of a mattress and a chair but there was still no heating, no natural light and it was damp and musty. We put an ad in the local paper: 'Small room in large Clapham Common house, suit student.'

A stream of prospective tenants turned up and politely and not so politely told us we had to be joking. Then Timmy arrived. I guess he was just the person Steve and Pugs had in mind. He was the son of a vicar from a village in Dorset. He was studying at a London poly. We reassured him the cellar was just somewhere to put his head down but he was welcome to share all the other facilities with us. Amazingly, he agreed.

'Three months' rent in advance,' demanded Pugsley, who had a strong antennae for mugs.

Timmy, and that is how he introduced himself, was perhaps the most stupid person we ever came across. If he ever deposited any food in the fridge we ate it. If he dared eat any of ours we screamed at him. We made him run to the pub for our fags and ride to the video shop for our videos. Pugsley, particularly, soon exercised a cruel hold over him. I say he was stupid because he could have gathered his belongings and left at any time. Instead, he fought the unwinnable battle to please us. If he was 'naughty', Pugsley would pull him out of the armchair by his ear and throw him down the stairs of the cellar and lock the door. Whilst we all abused Timmy to varying degrees we were paranoid about leaving him alone in the house with Pugsley. When he arrived he was a non-smoking, mildly spoken nice young country boy. Within a few months he was effing and blinding, smoking forty fags a day, had experimented (under duress) with soft and hard drugs and had been forced to watch us having sex with various girls who from time to time were persuaded to come back to our regular 'parties'.

One of these girls was June. She was a beautiful Geordie girl with large breasts and a tiny waist. Steve rescued her from an uncertain fate at one of our get-togethers and she soon became his live-in girlfriend. She was a kind-hearted girl who managed to moderate everyone's behaviour towards Timmy a little and injected a small dose of humanity into our everyday life. June had been working in a Kensington Girl fashion shop in her home town when the managing director, Cliff Whyte, had spotted her and asked her to come down and work in one of the London flagship stores. One day she was telling us about her boss. 'He comes into the shop sometimes and takes me to lunch. We go to the Hilton Hotel and we sit at his special table which is on the top floor and it's all glass and it overlooks all of London.'

'What's his name again?' I interjected.

'Cliff Whyte.'

'Cliff Whyte! You're joking. He's in the papers all the time. He's one of the country's top businessmen.'

'Is he?' she asked.

'Fucking right he is.'

'What happens after these meals, June?' asked Steve. 'Does he take you to a room and pump you up?'

June reddened. Steve assured her he wasn't being jealous, he just needed to know. 'We did a few times, but not since I met you, Steve.'

'Did he give you money?'

June reddened again with anger. No he did not. What did he take her for? I could see where Steve was going. How rich was this bloke, he asked me. When was the last time she shagged him, he asked her. Unfortunately for June she was completely under Steve's spell and agreed to the plan that was formulated over the next hour.

June was to go to Cliff Whyte and say she was pregnant and needed two thousand pounds for an abortion in a private hospital. Why wouldn't Cliff go for that? Of course he would. June wouldn't lose her job. Cliff could afford two grand and everyone would be happy.

It almost worked. Cliff was sympathetic, apparently even worried. He told her he would sort it out and we sat at home eagerly awaiting the imminent pay day. June came home from work and said Cliff had been in the shop to see her. He had arranged for her to have an 'operation' at a luxury private hospital. We hadn't thought of that. June rang him some days later and told him the good news that she had lost her baby. The Jocks had a new idea and suggested that she start black-mailing him over their sex sessions. June decamped to Newcastle the following week.

Timmy finally followed the road back to the safety of his parents when Pugsley came in from the pub and wired him up to the electric light and began to electrocute him for fun. They were the only two at home that night although Timmy had been with the Jocks during the day. From the safety of Dorset he rang Steve and apologised for doing a bunk. He was sobbing and crying and was terrified that Pugsley would follow him down to his parents' house for telling. He explained about the electric shocks and said he that he really believed that Pugsley was going to kill him. When Jock and Jock returned home the next day from wherever they had been, they asked where Timmy was. We told them he'd left and what Pugsley was supposed to have done – although Pugs denied this happened at all.

The Jocks looked at each other guiltily. 'Shit, poor cunt, we spiked Timmy's drinks yesterday lunchtime with some blinding acid!'

It came as a relief when the landlord finally got rid of us all and I returned to my parents' home in Common Way. It was a bit like entering detox, I imagine. I was surrounded by mementoes of my childhood. Same chairs, same ornaments, same parents. Sanity and simplicity washed over me. The drink, the drugs and the debauchery seemed a million miles away. But of course, they weren't – they were just around the corner.

The Hammersmith Palais not long after I was back at home was a bad day. Keith, Vic and I had scored some speed off a black geezer at the bar and we took it into the toilet to snort. Keith unfolded his piece of paper and it was obvious from the painfully thin line of powder that we'd been sold short. Keith wanted to sort it out there and then but Vic and I thought it was a bad idea. Blacks were plentiful in here and the way the guy was openly dealing suggested to me he was either connected to the bouncers or they were scared of him.

There was no telling Keith, though. He was a thoroughly decent person and never picked on anyone in his life. His whole being was ruled by a strong sense of right and wrong, and if he thought he was right, anything went. And he could row. In some ways he was worse than Pugsley Pullinger when he started. He didn't have the same bulk as Pugs but he made up for it with sheer viciousness. What could Vic and I do? Walk? Not really.

'There's a lot of them,' cautioned Vic hopefully.

'I've only got a problem with one,' replied Keith.

We strode out the toilets and Keith confronted the man. He was conciliatory and asked us to follow him back into the toilet where he would sort it out. Vic and I sighed with relief. In the toilet, by the basin, Keith unfolded his paper again. I saw in the mirror that two other men with dreadlocks had followed us in.

The black man studied the powder, shook his head and his dreadlocks swung from side to side. 'You having a laff, man. You've had some outta that okay. Don't take me for a mug, man.'

Keith grabbed his head by the ears and whacked it against the mirror. The mirror smashed. Before we knew it, Keith was standing up on the basins kicking the man to the ground holding the taps behind him for support.

'Leave off, Keith,' cried Vic and I as the man slumped to the floor and Keith jumped all over his head. We were afraid he might kill him. Vic and I were in shock at the demolition, as were the dealer's two mates, who let us pass as we walked out of the toilet.

We decided we should go although it took some persuading Keith who wanted to have another drink. Outside we walked up the road to the car. Vic was driving and he pulled out the side road where we had parked and turned right back towards the Palais. It was early and there were still queues of people waiting to be admitted and we had to slow right down due to groups of girls milling around in the road.

It all happened so quickly. A car was level with us going up towards Shepherd's Bush. I didn't even look in it until it happened. The driver was a black guy but not one of the blokes in the toilet. He said something to Vic and Vic rolled down his window. The black man's arm flashed out and Vic said, 'Ouch.' I always remember that. 'Ouch.' The car sped off and I glimpsed the dreadlocks through their back window. Vic had been cut badly. Blood in quantities I had never fathomed leaked from the side of his head. We moved him over to the passenger seat and in our panic drove to a hospital in Winhurst rather than one in Hammersmith or Fulham. At the hospital, we realised that the top half of Vic's ear had been sliced away. The doctors even asked us to search the car for the part of his ear that was missing, but to no avail.

*

We'd been at the races. At lunchtime I had drunkenly entertained the others by pulling my trousers and pants down to my ankles and conversing with the pub manager across the bar. He had no idea he was chatting with a man who was naked from the waist down. With everyone in the pub chuckling and look-ing over at us he did eventually click that the piss was being taken. Another member of staff whispered something in his ear and he charged around to my side. I had just about got my jeans up when he knocked me clean out.

Later I did some coke and some acid on top of all the drink. By the evening the acid was wearing off but the coke was still running the show. I met up with Jacko who was looking notice-ably thinner than the last time I'd seen him and we decided to visit a pub a few miles outside of Winhurst. I have no idea why we picked it. Neither of us had been there more than once before. I'm sure there was some drug-induced logic behind it but I've forgotten now.

It was almost a village pub and we ordered our drinks and rested our tired bodies on stools by the bar. From the lounge we could hear a piano and some singing. We moved next door and saw a middle-aged man was playing the piano and two young girls were standing on either side of him singing 'Ave Maria'. One of them smiled over at me as we leant up against the wall. She couldn't have been much more than sixteen. She had long curly hair, the sweetest smile I'd ever seen, long eyelashes and a petite figure. I noticed there was absolutely no trace of make-up on her face.

'I'm going to marry that bird,' I said, nudging Jacko.

'What bird?'

She came to the bar with her mate and I made some stupid remark as she passed. She stopped and made conversation. I fought the drink and the drugs rampaging around my body and tried to come across as half-normal. Her name was Laura. She was sixteen. Just left school and had started work at a bank. No, she didn't have a boyfriend. She lived in a big house between here and Winhurst. Daddy was buying her a car for her seventeenth. Yes, she would meet me in here the following Friday.

Friday was nearly a week away but I could hardly wait. I couldn't sleep or eat. I borrowed four hundred pounds from Dad and went out and bought a second-hand Triumph Spitfire. I got my hair cut. Bought some new clothes. I felt like I did all those years ago when I used to ride up and down past Paula Harris's house but this was a million times stronger.

I had my doubts but Laura turned up on Friday and she looked better than ever. She wore a cotton poloneck with a thin discreet gold chain on the outside underneath a black leather overcoat. Her dress came down over her knees where a pair of leather boots ended. I thought conversation might be difficult but there were no problems there. She didn't stop. She came from Kent originally and had lived up here for about five years. She had a brother and two sisters. Her father was a big-knob at the Royal Mint and did I want to go back and meet them? No, I didn't. But I went. Her mum was very welcoming and totally at ease with her daughter's judgement. Her dad, though, was altogether more suspicious and made the comment that I was old enough to be Laura's father. A slight exaggeration. I found out later that he had forbidden her to go to the pub and meet 'this man' unless she brought him home.

There was no profession of love on either side. It was strange. We both just knew that this was different. On our second date we agreed to open a joint building society account to start saving. For what? I sold the Spitfire and got a car that I could actually get in and out of and the relationship built. Laura's dad became no more comfortable and was at best silent when I was at their house, at worst plain rude. I couldn't blame him. He wanted the best for his beautiful, sweet and innocent little girl and he wasn't stupid. He knew I wasn't it. He knew very little about me but saw enough not to like what he saw.

Inevitably my alcohol and drug intake reduced. I was out with Laura or at her house most nights, so it wasn't possible. Slowly but surely my perspective was changing. I started to take an interest at work. Recently I had rarely been there. The unions had managed to get us seven weeks' holiday per year and I added on at least another three in sick leave. Then I would get days in lieu for doing overtime. Some people thought I had left. I know one year I went right through the entire calendar without doing a Monday.

I was elated. It was like being set free even though until I met Laura I had no idea that I wasn't happy with my lifestyle. Starting each day without taking drink or drugs or the prospect of doing either was more of a buzz and a novelty than taking drugs themselves. Near abstinence was becoming addictive.

After six months Laura and I became engaged and she finally allowed us to embark on a sexual relationship. This was unreal as most of the girls we knocked around with were stuffing their knickers into their handbags after the second vodka and orange.

Relations with Charlie, Laura's dad, didn't really improve. I was his daughter's boyfriend; he was my girlfriend's dad. We just tolerated each other. When we fixed a date for getting married he went along with it. He said he'd give Laura the same big wedding her sisters had had. But it was implicit he disapproved. He said he thought Laura was too young. I'm sure he did think that, but the real problem was me. I think he believed I was unstable. He knew I mixed with the 'wrong' crowd. He wasn't sure where I was going in life. He wasn't a bad judge. He was baffled by the fact that I had, in his eyes, a good job. He couldn't understand how I had ever got in at the *City Telegraph* let alone survived and even progressed there. He thought that sooner or later they would suss me and boot me out on to the street.

'Have you thought about a career in the Civil Service?' he enquired over one Sunday lunch.

Had I thought about a career in the Civil Service? No, I was planning to become presenter of *Songs of Praise*, actually.

'Good pension, good prospects for the right people, early retirement.'

'Doing what?'

'I might be able to get you in on the clerical side of the Royal Mint.'

'I'd rather be on the dole,' I retorted, to which his face drew taut.

'Sooner or later, my boy, you are going to have to decide where you're heading. You're sailing far too close to the wind.'

He booked the Elmwood Castle, where Laura's sisters had been wed. It was costing him thousands. He told me. Time and time again. He dragged me with him to choose the menu and sort out the seating arrangements. I couldn't understand the urgency or get into the planning: it was only December and the wedding wasn't until Valentine's Day. He became more and more silently angry that I wasn't getting into the spirit of it all and showing gratitude for his generosity and effort.

Then John Lennon got murdered in New York and I was devastated. Dad woke me up that morning. He rarely woke me up so I knew something was wrong. The last time had been when I was a kid, to tell me that the bookie's clerk had been murdered. We all sat around the kitchen listening to the bulletins on Capital Radio. Links were provided by non-stop

Beatles and Lennon songs. All the lyrics seemed especially poignant. On the train on the way up to work no one was reading their papers. No one spoke. Everyone sat there rocking to the movements of the train, staring vacantly ahead or out of the window. It was a nation in shock. A nation pondering over how Beatle John figured in their lives. At work Audie, who was even more of a Beatles fan than me, had decorated my desk. He had arranged a bunch of flowers he had bought from Buster Edwards, the Great Train Robber-turned-florist at Waterloo, in a circle with a copy of John's new album, *Double Fantasy*, propped up in the middle.

It sounds like a lot of sentimental claptrap but Lennon's death did affect a lot of people deeply, although it is hard to comprehend with the passage of time. I don't look back on it now and feel an empty sadness like one might for a dead relative or a friend even years later. But at the time it was personal. For people born after 1950 and before 1965 The Beatles provided the backdrop to their growing-up. They personified being young. They represented them in the world. And John was so real. He said the things you like to think you would have said if fame had been sprung on you. Like all of us, he was a cocktail of opposites. He was wise and stupid. Kind and nasty. Spiritual and ordinary. And now he was dead and a part of that generation's life was dead. It served as a stark reminder of everyone's mortality.

'I want to have "Imagine" played at the wedding,' I announced.

'That's nice,' said Laura sweetly.

The vicar spoke to the organist and she said it would be no problem as long as we could provide the sheet music. Laura found a music shop in Winhurst which sold it and that was that.

Charlie got to hear about it and did his nut. 'What on earth do you think you're up to? Demeaning the most important day in my little girl's life by having a pop song played on the organ at her ceremony?'

'It's a tribute to John Lennon.'

'It's a bloody piss-take.'

I'd never heard him swear. He was livid and I couldn't really understand why. I'd been to a wedding recently where they'd played 'A Whiter Shade of Pale'; how would he have coped with that? The upshot was that he wasn't coming. That was it. We'd reduced the ceremony to the level of a stag do, he claimed. Laura, bless her, stuck with it even though she worshipped her father. I stuck to my guns, yet by February the shock of John Lennon dying had worn off and I was thinking perhaps I should abandon the idea. But it had gone beyond John Lennon and 'Imagine'. This was now a battle between Charlie and me. Seeing the guy was paying for everything and he felt so strongly about it, I should have quietly dropped it. But I didn't. Two days before the big day, though, Charlie picked up his suit. He was coming.

After the wedding relations improved although there was always an undercurrent of mutual distaste between us. Charlie liked to call family meetings – occasions I did my best not to attend. His position as head of the family – the organiser general – was being eroded as his kids began to fly the nest and I think he resented my small part in that. He retired from his job soon after our marriage and his feeling of dispossession, I think, increased. Suddenly scores of people no longer depended on him. He came around to our little flat and decorated it. Picked up Laura for work in the mornings. Found good second-hand furniture for us. At worst I resented it, at best I showed no appreciation.

Then Charlie got ill. I reckon he knew it was something serious because he took a golfing holiday alone whilst we all awaited the results of his tests. When they came back, basically they showed he had cancer of the this and cancer of the that. There was talk that he could recover and he underwent some seriously debilitating stomach surgery. He could barely eat afterwards but the doctors claimed they'd got the cancer out. Some months later, and following extensive tests, Charlie got an envelope through the post saying that tests had shown that there was now no evidence of cancer. He was clear.

'It's wrong,' Charlie shook his head.

And he was right; a phonecall followed soon after and Charlie was summoned to the specialist. His results had been mixed up with those of another patient.

'I hope the other chap didn't commit suicide when they told him the cancer was back,' Charlie laughed wryly.

It was all downhill from then on. From leading an almost normal life to living in his armchair, to lying in his bed. Finally he went into the hospital. By this time he was down to seven stone and we knew Charlie wasn't coming home.

But even from his death-bed he was still organising: ensuring his pension was in order for Eve, doling out advice and even arranging his own funeral, right down to what hymns would be sung and what music would be played. In the final days the whole family were permanently gathered around his bed as the centre of their universe crumbled away before them. Even through the morphine he had bouts of stunning lucidity. His daughters fussed around his pillows. Puffing them up, making them comfortable, with tears streaming down their faces. Eve sat on the hard hospital chair, her lower face permanently buried in a series of tissues. John, his only son, tried to hold it all together, doing what eldest sons are meant to do. I hung back in the corners of the room feeling like a gatecrasher at a tragic party but wanting to demonstrate my solidarity.

He sat up suddenly and it scared us. It was like he had been woken from a nightmare. A couple of wisps of grey hair fell forward on to his face. His eyes, now sunken deep into their sockets, were burning and his bony hands, all stretched brown skin over bumpy blue veins, trembled.

'Snap out of it!' he demanded.

Laura tried to ease him back on to his pillow mountain but he was having none of it. We were all jolted to attention. Had the drugs made him delirious?

'Snap out of it now. What do you think you're all doing sitting around sobbing? It's me now but it's you next!' He paused with almost theatrical effect: 'Cancer is going to get you . . . something's going to get you. It just happens to be my turn now.'

He slumped back exhausted into his pillows leaving his audience, his loved ones, stunned.

'It's the morphine,' said Laura as we drove home that night.

It wasn't the morphine. It was the ultimate act of selflessness. Even though he was ravaged with pain and sadness himself, he couldn't bear to see his babies, his wife and his friends in such a state of despair. His outburst was carefully thought out. He had successfully transferred their focus away from him to themselves. By getting them to think about their own mortality, their own future trials, it would obscure their pain at his own death. It was not only a caring, generous and courageous thing to do, it was also very clever. It summed the man up.

Cancer's gonna get you/Something's gonna get you.

I couldn't get it out of my mind. Over and over again, like a Johnny Rotten mantra.

The next night I sat beside his bed and clasped his hand. I didn't plan to do this. I just did. I doubt if my hand had folded into his since the day we met, in fact I'm sure it hadn't. He turned his head to me and smiled, the warmest enveloping smile I had ever encountered.

'You're not such a bad lad after all.'

I cried. The tears poured out and I let my face fall forward on to the bed. Charlie gently stroked my head. Here was a man whose lifespan was now being measured in hours comforting his stroppy son-in-law. A peace had been made. An acceleration of the friendship and respect we would have eventually enjoyed. Finally, when I knew the time was right, I got up and leant forward and kissed his forehead. Then I left the room. The next night I didn't go up. The next night he died.

We progressed trance-like to the funeral day. It was a big turn-out. Friends, neighbours, colleagues and all manner of people whom Charlie had helped or befriended in the past filled pavements outside the little church. We, the family, filed inside and took our seats in the front pews. Everyone shuffled in behind us and the vicar stood at the altar. He nodded to a lady in a corner. The opening bars of a familiar song suddenly echoed from speakers in the four corners of the church and John Lennon's distinctive voice jolted me out of my reverie:

Imagine there's no heaven
It's easy if you try . . .

Epilogue – Changing Man

Driving home in the early hours of the morning always makes me melancholic and pensive. It's then that I think the bad things. I don't know why, because normally it is all right in the morning.

I'd left the firm at the end of my night shift and was waiting at the lights at Vauxhall Cross when I absent-mindedly watched a wino walking towards me. I always see them here. This place on the left is some sort of doss-house. He spots a can of Special Brew standing on a wall and reaches up and picks it off. He tips it from side to side and his face lights up as he feels the weight. He throws his head back and pours the contents of the can down his neck. Suddenly, though, he has cast the can into the road and is spitting the liquid out of his mouth into his beard and on to his clothes. Then I realised some other tramp had emptied that can earlier and refilled it with piss before perching it on that wall.

It started me thinking. How did this guy get to that stage? He was about my age – possibly younger, they age so fast, those men. He wasn't born with a red nose and a craving for strong alcohol. Chances are he sat in warm rooms when he was a kid, cuddled his mum, watched *Flipper* and played football down the park. If someone had told him or his family that thirty years on he'd be homeless, smelly, drunk and dying, they would have been horrified. They would not have been able to comprehend it. What were the key moments in his life that led him here? And there's a fucking army of these people as well – thousands in London alone and swelling by the minute.

I ease past a milk float, the only other vehicle I've seen for ten minutes. These days this is the nearest I get to a speed or acid comedown. How I'm feeling. The lights are red and I contemplate jumping them but now they're all camera-ed up it's not worth the risk. Sitting there I see a fox in the road. Contemplating me. Watching me watching him. I could just push the accelerator down hard, swerve towards him, and I know I could get him. But we're not really interested in one another and he just trots to the side of the road without a backward glance.

Something comes up on Radio Five about a man who goes to collect a table leg from a furniture restorer and stops in his local for a pint. Someone thinks it's a gun poking out of his plastic Sainsbury's bag and phones the police. They arrive as he's walking the last few minutes from the pub to his house. They surround him and shout at him to put his gun down. He laughs as the beer repeats on him. So they pump bullets into him. Not into his legs or arms but into his chest. The man is dead. But not to worry: the Police Complaints Authority has been informed. Some complaint, that. Hello, I'd like to make a complaint: you have shot my husband, my dad, my brother, for carrying a table leg. Now they're saying that another police force is going to investigate the matter. That's all right, then. Nothing like a good, independent enquiry. It is a tragic mistake, according to a police spokesman. A tragic fucking mistake indeed. The police make a lot of tragic mistakes.

Then I start thinking about Jacko. He's been dead ten years now. *Ten years.* I remember Dad telling me that as you get older time flies. I didn't take too much notice. But he was right. As you get older it positively whips by. Things you think happened a month ago turn out to be a year ago. Songs on the radio you think are fairly new are actually nine years old. Your friends' babies suddenly have acne. If it's flying past now, what will it be like in ten years from now? Although that ten years' time will feel like a year. Twenty years ago I was drinking down The Hyperion, dropping blues, shagging the odd girl. It seems like yesterday. Yet in twenty years' time I will be sixty. Tomorrow I will be forty years of age. All that bollocks about life begins at forty. People of thirty-nine coined that one to make themselves feel better, the same way that Christians made up all that shite about God and life after death. To make themselves feel better about dying. To make themselves feel better about being here in the first place. To make people behave while they're here. And my mum and dad probably won't be here when I'm sixty. The thought hits me like a jab in the stomach. I don't want to be an orphan. Life doesn't begin at forty. Death begins at forty.

I feel bad because I said to Mum once, without thinking, that if I had had a choice I wouldn't have come here. The injured look on her face springs into my mind. I didn't mean it like that. It's a fact, though. Who would? Everyone you know dies. Everyone you love dies. Many die horribly. Your parents are going to die before you. I wasn't depressed when I said it. It was a rational comment not intended to hurt. I'm here. I'll make the best of it. I'll enjoy lots of it. Have enjoyed lots of it. But, had I had a say in the matter, I wouldn't have come. Simple as that.

But I've done it too! I suddenly feel despair. The lights blink amber and I pull away. I've brought kids into the world who didn't ask to come. I brought them in for me, not for them. Maybe I should sit all three of them down and say: by the way, kids, statistically, one of you is going to die of cancer. One of you will suffer from mental illness and me and your mum are going to die before you. Didn't know that, did you?

In a way I'm glad I'm not with them, facing them every day. I'm sure they're happy with Laura and Roger.

Listen to me, I'm calling the cunt Roger now. Roger who lives with my wife. The man my wife prefers to me. The man who is probably this minute now lying naked next to my Laura. Even now I feel sick at the thought of it. Sometimes I torture myself by imagining them having sex. It used to be all the time. Whether she does it with him like she did with it me. And it was me that left her – that's the galling thing. I left her and the kids for a bird at work. A bird that wanted to have sex. Couldn't get enough of it and wanted to do everything under the sun. She once caught me wanking and teased me for doing it – 'Save it all for me,' she said. After a bad row once Laura had said, 'I'm fed up with being a receptacle for your semen.' That did it for me. It was such a clinical way of saying that she didn't love me anymore. It summed it up, I thought, and I went. Moved over to Ealing, into a flat with Heather. I should have thought ahead a bit. Heather loved sex. She loved the buzz of a new relationship. Within a year she was shagging someone else as well as me. And I went back to Laura. But the damage had been done. And she'd met Roger by then, a traffic policeman, who'd come to her aid after she had broken down on the motorway.

I switch back to thinking about Jacko because his death is slightly more palatable to me than thinking about the terrible thing I've done to the kids, to Laura, to myself. He didn't make forty. He didn't make thirty. Maybe he's better off. So his life ended upside down in a wheely bin, a long way from home and his family and friends, after a hit went wrong and his junkie 'mates' panicked and dumped his body unceremoniously into the green box on wheels. But he hasn't had to watch us all get old and fat, start developing illnesses and dying, losing family. He lived his life in the fast lane and he crashed. I think about the last time I saw him. It was about three months before he died. He'd come up from Brighton for Big Bob's thirtieth birth-day drink and we all went to a pub in Waterloo. We had drifted apart long before. When he got on smack he operated under a different regime. He eventually moved down to Brighton with his new smackhead bird. That night at Bob's do we got drunk like the old times. All of us, the ones that were left even then, Vic, Steve, Keith, Bob, Tony Bond. The girls. And we'd had a bit of speed too like the old times and there was a general love-in. Then I remember me and Jacko hugging and both crying over in a corner away from the rest. It was the strangest thing. We were talking about nothing. Normally people cry about things that have happened, not things that are going to happen.

I wonder if Wendy knows he's dead. I doubt it. I've never seen her since she told me that day in her house to leave. I heard she married and moved to Kent. I heard that after the abortion she got a job and got a flat and lived alone in Maidstone of all places. For the first time the guilt of what we did to her hits me. She was a kid in love. With Jacko, not me. I was merely the next best thing to Jacko in her eyes. She was a kid forced to grow up in the most brutal way. I get the urge to find her. Twenty years on. Not in the hope of rekindling anything or finding a partner but to say sorry to her. To tell her about Jacko. To try and make things right.

I turn left off the A3 and glance over at the Bowling Alley. It only makes me more depressed. I think of Laura and me dancing cheek to cheek to 'Reunited' by Peaches and Herb. I think of all of us up there. The top kiddies for a while. Selling the drugs. Younger boys buying our drinks because they wanted to be seen with us. The fights. The laughs. The girls. The cars. And now there is no one left. In five minutes I'll be in bed – on my own. Get up in the afternoon. Watch Jerry Springer or some other American cack. Get some chips or Chinese in the evening and watch *Coronation Street.* Then back to work to earn more of the money that I have nothing to spend on.

Never dreamt that I would be doing nights for this printing company. They're busy at the moment producing all the offer documents and company brochures to accompany the boom in City merger activity and Internet floats. Overtime is rife. I never dreamt that the *City Telegraph* would get rid of me at thirty-nine years of age either. No one told me I was in the departure lounge. The unions had been broken for some time and I was moving upwards. Been running my own department for ten years now. Had absolutely no idea that the new ruthless managing director was looking at me and saw only dead wood. I had admired the way he came in and starting chucking out the freeloaders at last. I could see my department moving ahead. I was still young and dynamic. I was deluded. I've got sixty-six grand in the bank and I can't believe it. Never had so much cash. I love opening my bedside drawer and looking at the figure in my building society book. I look forward more these days to the time when the clerk puts my six months' interest on than to my birthday or Christmas. That's all I've got, though. My flat is rented. My wife and kids live at my old house where I am now a visitor, welcomed politely like an uncle

they are all indifferent about. My job is transitory. It won't last.
The worst thing is, who did I turn to to get me this job? The
fucking union. They fixed me up. Years of me fighting them
and then when my own side fuck me off I go cap in hand to
them. There is nothing to look forward to either. I've been to
headhunters and recruitment agencies; I've applied for jobs in
the papers. Fuck all.

I've thought about going to see Steve and see if we can go
into business together. Langton's Skip Hire is the biggest hire
company in the south of England now. He's made an absolute
fortune and lives down Purley way in a big house. Last time I
saw him he was talking about retiring and moving to Spain.
What can I offer him, though? Sixty-six grand? The one thing
he doesn't need is cash.

I still see Vic but he depresses me even more. His second
marriage has just gone down the tubes over his drinking.
Getting pissed used to be fun. Funny how young men getting
pissed was almost admired. 'You should have seen John, he was
out of it, you'll never guess what he did . . .' to roars of laughter
and shaking of heads. When you get past thirty-five it's not
funny any more – it's pathetic, sad, annoying. Your nose goes
red. There's no one drinking with you. Vic is a postman now,
but that won't last long. All he wants to do is drink and
complain about the cards he's been dealt. What about me? I
made the mistake of going to Corfu with him last year. We tried
to kid ourselves we were enthused about being single again, on
the loose, on the Med. But we both knew we were two sad old
cunts. Rejected and dejected. Vic drank a bottle of Smirnoff
blue before we got on the plane and had to be straitjacketed
when he started abusing everyone in mid-air. His scarred and
reconstructed ear doesn't help. They thought they were dealing

with a violent psychopath, not a depressed, middle-aged man who wouldn't harm a fly.

Keith is in the nick still although he's coming out soon and I'm looking forward to seeing him again. But he mixes with a different crowd and I don't know him like I used to. I think he's on the verges of organised crime but he never says and we never ask. He's done the whole body-building thing and then door-work and then bodyguarding. His latest stretch was for beating up a businessman over a debt. He maintains a flat in Maida Vale and drives a nice car but no one knows really what he does. Even when he's not inside we see him less and less. It's strange because out of all of us Keith was the one who never got into trouble with the law and he was the one with the principles.

And what about Pugsley Pullinger? If anyone has lost the plot he has. I saw him only the other day walking his dog. I hoped he hadn't spotted me but he had.

'All right, John?'

'All right, Pugs. Nice dog.'

I looked down at the ugly and vicious pit-bull terrier he was just about preventing from taking a lump out of my leg. Couldn't think of what to say to him. What have we in common now?

'What's the dog called?'

'Colin.'

'Colin?'

'Yeah, Colin, what's wrong with that?' Pugsley's eyes narrowed. I knew the look.

'Nothing, Colin's a nice name.'

Haven't seen Ronnie Matthews for years. He moved to Peckham, believe it or not. So, perhaps, he did have family there after all. Vic bumped into him somewhere about five years back. He was dreadlocked and spoke in an unintelligible West Indian dialect. Vic, never one to mince his words, said: 'For fuck's sake, Ronnie, you was raised near Kingston, Surrey, not Kingston, Jamaica. Talk properly, will you?'

Vic said he seemed happy though and he hugged him and generally made a fuss. Promised to come down to Winhurst to see us all but we're still waiting.

Big Bob seems happy, too. He married Pam. He's still brick-laying although I don't envy him there, out in all weathers bending over the trowel at our age. I think he did himself the best favour when we were all starting on the drugs – he dabbled a bit, but never over-indulged. Pam was strong as well. She did him a big favour too by keeping me and Steve and the others at arm's length without falling out. I think about Bob, Jacko and me as six-year-olds standing on the drains at infant school. Thirty-five years on and Jacko's been dead ten years, I'm fucked up and only Bob seems to be happy.

I popped into Winhurst the other day to get a birthday card for my eldest. Standing outside the Winhurst Centre selling the Big Issue was this old, scruffy bloke with long lank brown hair and a beard. I had to look two or three times before I could be sure, but it was Keir Hubbard. I popped into the pub because I knew Vic would be in there, on the same stall, in his postman's uniform. Vic peeked out the window and agreed it was him. Three lagers later we strolled across the road to speak to him. Neither of us had seen or spoken to Keir in twenty-five years.

After a few seconds he recognised us, a huge smile breaking out somewhere between the beard and the hair hanging down his face. We prepared to show him the pity we thought he needed.

"How is Colin?"

He didn't seem to know the whereabouts of his twin, and it emerged he didn't really want to. His parents had died and Keir had inherited the big house on Winhurst Heath. He wasn't even selling the Big Issue, he was mucking in for a pal who had an appointment down at the social. Sure enough, the pal duly turned up and resumed the selling. It seems he had a few bob, too, and spent his life travelling between Amsterdam and London with the Reading and Glastonbury pop festivals thrown in. He came into the pub with us and we got drunk together. Vic and I updated him on us and ours and when he finally left I knew we'd depressed him and it was him feeling sorry for us.

Up ahead I just about see the figure of a person step out of the trees, just past the next set of lights, stretch out his arms and point at the car that is a hundred yards in front of me. I've seen them before. The Old Bill. Four o'clock in the morning. They park in the slip road next to the lights and one of them jumps out from behind the tree and points this speed gun at you and then jumps back. They adopt the stance of Charles Bronson in *Death Wish* holding the instrument in both hands, arms fully extended. I guess, if you are speeding, they radio ahead to another car that then pulls you up. It makes me mad. What difference does it make if someone is breaking the speed limit on a deserted B road, in a London suburb, at four o'clock in the morning? If you're black you can get murdered on a London street but they can't do anything about it. If you're white your house gets screwed and they can't even come around to investigate – you get a mass-produced letter of sympathy instead and the phone number of Victim Support. But if you're driving home from work at night, God forbid, the Met deploys the full gamut of its resources against you.

I think of the poor bastard they pumped full of bullets for possession of an antique table leg. That bastard policeman who scared the wits out of Jacko and me in the Cycling Prohibited alley. I remember when that detective smacked me repeatedly around the head with his newspaper, when those laughing cunts lied in court just to ensure I lost my licence. I think of Jacko, his body all stiff and stuffed into the wheely bin. I think of Laura going down on Roger. I think of everything and nothing. Then I decide to do it. All this in milliseconds. No angst. In a few seconds' time I will be a murderer. Or am I already a murderer? Are murderers murderers before they murder? Or only after?

I just know that if I want, I can get away with it. I saw a figure jump out in front of my car, your honour, and point a gun at me – I panicked and drove into him before he could fire, your honour. I know it will work. I might hold my hands up. I might die doing it. I'm going a bit faster now and he jumps out into the road thinking he's got a nick. He's only young. But I make sure he knows what I'm doing. I catch his eye, like the fox, and smile as I whack the accelerator to the floor. A tragic mistake.